The Amateur Historian

The Amateur Historian

JULIAN COLE

MINOTAUR BOOKS

A Thomas Dunne Book
New York

This is a work of fiction. All of the characters, organizations, and events portrayed in this novel are either products of the author's imagination or are used fictitiously.

A THOMAS DUNNE BOOK FOR MINOTAUR BOOKS.
An imprint of St. Martin's Publishing Group.

www.thomasdunnebooks.com
www.minotaurbooks.com

Library of Congress Cataloging-in-Publication Data

Cole, Julian.
    The amateur historian / Julian Cole. — 1st U.S. ed.
        p. cm.
    "A Thomas Dunne book."
    ISBN 978-0-312-58659-1
    1. Brothers—Fiction. 2. Private investigators—England—Fiction. 3. Police—England—Fiction. 4. Missing persons—Investigation—England—Fiction.
5. Murder—England—History—Fiction. I. Title.
    PR6103.O4415A8 2010
    823'.92—dc22

                                                                2010010465

First published in Great Britain by Quick Brown Fox Publications
First U.S. Edition: July 2010

10 9 8 7 6 5 4 3 2 1

For Gina

"...the wages paid for unskilled labour in York are insufficient to provide food, shelter, and clothing adequate to maintain a family of moderate size in a state of bare physical efficiency."

Poverty: A Study of Town Life, B. Seebohm Rowntree

The Amateur Historian

PROLOGUE

In a moment, Rick Rounder knew two things. The first was hard, cold and resting on his trapped fingers; and the second was a smell. Petrol, oh Christ no, not petrol. He knew the blade, knew it before the searing pain caused him to slump against the door and vomit in shock and agony. Freeing his bloodied hand, he rolled away. Sam moved to help and Rick shouted a warning – "Petrol!" – before collapsing at his brother's feet.

For a few seconds nothing happened. Time steadied itself, waiting. The sun still shone out of a blue sky, the Minster still stood a safe distance away. Rick banished his pain and tried to think. Before thought could turn to action, the door trembled in its frame, then jolted for an instant, before splintering apart. Fire and smoke came out in a giant, incendiary burp. Needles of wood filled the air. As for Arthur Smitten – Smitty, school bully, failed father – whatever he had been, he was no longer any of these. Now he was a burning ball, rolling through the blackened doorframe and then, with final, unlikely grace, unfurling into a dive that took him over the balcony. Half consumed by flames, he flailed through the air and fell to earth.

"The Human Torch" was how the headlines in that night's paper put it. There was no mention of the girl. That piece of news was kept back for a day.

CHAPTER ONE

THE Percy family gaze in puzzlement at the concertina lens emerging from the box. No-one is sure what is going on or why it is necessary to stand still for so long.

This is the only time the family has had their photograph taken, and the experience is a new and troubling one. All the family are present, Martha, Thomas and their eight children. Such a burden of procreation has reduced Martha in stature and robustness. She is not the woman she once was, but she is proud of her brood. Thomas has a contrary view, believing his offspring to be an encumbrance without which he would have progressed further in life. The evidence for such a proposition is unlikely to be found in one of the dingy back-street beer houses Thomas haunts, and where he would rather be at this very moment.

Eventually, the photographer is done and the Percy family members scatter, freed from unnatural stillness to follow different paths that lead to chores, play or the foaming solace of a pint of beer.

It is 1901 when the image is captured in a dingy brick backyard in Hungate, York. A century later, a magnifying glass held over the photograph turns the faces into a grainy puzzle of dots, conveying little about their inner selves. But the photograph does contain clues. The clothes are ragged and there is litter on the ground on which they stand. No image can do justice to the smell emanating from the ashpits or midden-privies shared by all the families nearby. As is the custom, these noisome lavatories are left full for as long as possible in order to save the one shilling the Corporation charges for emptying.

The name of the photographer employed by Mr. Rowntree has been lost to time, but his handiwork remains. The print acquired by the amateur historian is cracked and curled. His stubby fingers pay particular attention to the young girl in the photograph. She looks so lovely and innocent. Her hair is long, and probably blonde, and she is wearing a white smock over her dress, with her hands clasped over what would have become her womanhood, had she lived that long. She appears serious, but it is easy to imagine a smile playing just out of sight, waiting to captivate her features.

The historian smiles himself, despite the fact that he is upset by what he knows about the lost girl. Sometimes, he thought, life has a strange way of balancing out, and he felt that someone from this careless generation should learn that lesson.

CHAPTER TWO

RICK Rounder brought the old Holden to a halt on the dusty road in Queensland. The dissolving sun sat on the end of the bonnet, a huge orange globe that made further driving impossible. He wound down the dirty window and stuck his elbow out. It had been a long drive and he still had a way to go. He could sleep in the car but he didn't fancy another night like that, waking dry and desiccated, his mouth like the inside of an old shoe. No, he wasn't having a car for a bed tonight. He needed his bed and Naomi beside him.

He had slept in so many places, seen so much of the world, and always he had kept moving as if motion itself were a reason to live.

As he had told his brother ten years ago, "Stand still and you might as well be a fossil."

Sam had scowled in that way he had.

"Stay here and you could do well, what with your charm, good looks and youth."

Rick tried to raise a laugh.

"Two years, Sam. That's all there is in it."

"It wasn't your fault, you know. The mad bastard had killed her before you got there."

Rick said he knew that, but he was going just the same. That afternoon he went into York to buy a rucksack.

The sun was going. The huge disc swallowed the road, drenching the landscape in molten fury. Rick let his eyes recover by taking in the dusty scrub and the sparse eucalyptus trees. He lit a cigarette and watched the smoke rise from his fingers. He drew hard on the cigarette, then let his hand flop out of the window and describe circles in the dusty paintwork while the cigarette smoked itself, held between his index finger and the finger with the top missing. A girl had died and he had lost a bit of his finger: it didn't seem much of an exchange.

He should give up, he thought, as he dropped the cigarette out of the car window. Almost before it hit the ground, he leapt out and scrunched the embers. He'd learned that quickly, living in a dry land where fire was always thirsty. Rick stretched his legs. His sandals were white with dust and his brown legs were chalked to the knees.

The sun, having had its grandstanding moment, sank without further fuss. It was a semi-circle of blinding orange, and then it was gone, swallowed by the horizon.

Rick got back into the car. He could see where he was going now that it was dark. As the lights bounced ahead of the car, he wondered if it was time. There had been so much motion, all the endless miles, and so many countries. Australia held him more than anywhere else, so limitless and far away. America had been everything he had imagined: the big small country or the small big country. He would have stayed but Naomi saw to that. She smiled and he followed her to this place of heat, snakes and poisonous spiders.

Rick steered the Holden along the black road and wondered what to tell Naomi. She'd go mad about this, swapping Queensland for York. "Are you off your bloody Brit head?" That's what she'd say. Something like that.

RICK Rounder was escaping from what happened on a beautiful day in November when a painterly sun had shone out of a blue canvas sky.

The flats were less than a mile from York Minster, which could be glimpsed in the distance. Incident tape fluttered in the breeze. A tethered dog barked and snarled in a lathered fury. Rick swore at the dog.

Radios crackled, blue lights flashed. Rick ducked into the stairwell and climbed the concrete steps two at a time, followed by Sam, who was panting already. He'll get fat if he's not careful, Rick thought, and to think he used to be the fit and sporty one. Rick reached the top of the stairs. He knelt at the door and lifted the letterbox.

"Smitty. Are you in there?"

Arthur Smitten, the school bully. Smitty, shitty Smitty. Ten years on, he was a petty criminal with convictions for burglary, stealing cars and aggravation. Smitten and his wife were separated and she wanted a divorce. Their daughter, Tanya, had spent the night at his flat, leaving her mother free to be with her new man. Tanya's school friend knew she was there and had called in on her way to school. They had planned to walk the short distance together, like they always did.

In the morning Tanya's father had shouted through the letterbox that Tanya wouldn't be going to school any more. She wouldn't need school; he'd be taking care of her. The friend ran to tell her mother.

"Smitty. Are you in there? It's Rick Rounder, here to talk..."

The sudden motion, the halitosis stink, and the clatter of the letter flap sent him stumbling back.

"Course I'm in here, you stupid bastard! That's why you're out there. It's a power game, isn't it? You and me; me and you – with only this door keeping us apart."

The voice was weedy but oddly triumphant.

"God, they take anyone in the police these days. To think what a pathetic pimple you were at school, and now look at you, a swanky whatever you are. What are you now, Rounder?"

"Sergeant. Detective Sergeant."

"So, Sergeant Shit-face, what are you doing here?"

"Talking to you through this letter-box."

"So what you got to say?"

"I want to check that you're all right. And to see that Tanya isn't frightened. Can I speak to Tanya, Smitty?"

"Not at the moment you can't."

"Never mind. Later, then."

"Why the fuck should I trust you, Rounder? Just because we were at school together, you and that bastard big brother of yours? That's history – who cares about history? You won't be getting any old school invitations from me, pal."

"You just have to trust me. I'm the best chance you have of sorting out this mess."

"What are you then – a marriage counsellor as well as a copper? I don't have time for this bollocks."

"You can trust me, Smitty."

"Mr Smitten to you. I'm a member of the public. I pay your taxes… or I would if I ever paid any."

"All right, Mr Smitten. Let's shake on it."

Rick would never be able to explain what he did next, when he lifted the letter-flap and inserted his hand.

"Go on, Mr Smitten, shake on it."

Rick felt foolish, crouched in front of the door. He did not feel at risk, just ridiculous. The door had once been blue. Now it was grubby and scuffed, hardly any colour. He could sense Sam behind him and knew he would be scowling.

He heard the stage whisper – "What the fuck are you doing?" – just as his hand was grasped. The embrace was warm and rough, flesh-padded sandpaper. The warmth pleased him, suggesting life.

"So, Smitty, Mr Smitten. That's good, shaking hands is good. Now I would like to shake Tanya's hand too. Do you think that would be possible?"

"No, that wouldn't be convenient at all."

"Never mind. Perhaps later."

That was when Rick felt the blade on his hand, and the sickening pain, and the smell of petrol.

"IT WASN'T your fault, you know."

Rick stared blankly at his bandaged hand.

"Looks like I'll have to resign my place at the Yehudi Menuhin school."

Sam hated the way his brother hid behind a tired joke. It was so emotionally stunted. He wanted to tell Rick to stop the wisecracks, to absorb what had happened, and to carry on, to use the tragedy to his advantage, to capitalise; but he did not say any of these things. What he said was: "You could always take up the triangle instead."

"The manicure adverts will be out," said Rick.

"Smitten was a mad bastard, you know," said Sam. "A proper

hopeless case. You weren't to know, none of us knew he would…"

"I thought I could sort everything out; instead, he did that to the girl."

SMITTEN'S final steps were traced in the hall. A trail of blackened smudges led to the empty doorframe with the blistered paint, suggesting half completed DIY. Smitten had carried most of the flames with him, so the flat was relatively unscathed. Rick comforted himself with the thought that the girl should easily have survived such a fire. Yet he knew he was kidding himself, felt certain this couldn't end well.

Rick followed Sam in a daze of agony as blood dripped from his finger. They found Tanya in a meagre bedroom. There were boy-band posters on the wall and assorted dolls on the floor, many missing at least one limb or in some cases a head. A drawing book lay open, suggesting a happily busy child; the picture she had drawn indicated something else. The words "Mummy and Daddy" were scrawled beneath a vivid illustration of two people fighting. Above their heads the girl had written: "I hate you." Either the parents were shouting at each other, or the girl had been trying to convey her own thoughts. Tanya could no longer explain what she had intended.

Rick looked at the dead girl and let out a small, desperate sob that would stay with him for most of his life.

"SHE was dead by the time you started talking, you know. Dead by the time you did that stupid thing and put your hand through the door. Dead…"

"I get your point. The girl…no, stop calling her that. She wasn't 'the girl'…she was Tanya Smitten, aged nine, only daughter of Arthur and Sonia Smitten. She should have been on her way to school but instead she was dead, killed by her own father. Stabbed by her own bastard father, lying there bloodied and lifeless and all cut about…"

They had found a note on the kitchen table.

14

"Sonia…If I cant have her, you cant eiver. She's mine forever and ever, you mad bitch." 'Her', not even a name. The omission had cut deep with Rick.

"So what will you do?" Sam said, patting his brother on the knee. Rick stared back, not saying anything but wondering why Sam was doing that business with the knee. Then he said it: "Quit, I'm quitting. That's what I'm going to do."

"What, quitting what?"

"The police, you, York, Yorkshire…the lot. I've had enough of everything. This shitty life. I need more, I need to be away from here. I've been thinking it anyway, but what happened to Tanya, well, that kinda seals it…made me see what I've got to do. I've got the money now, you see. Same as you. Mum's money. I'm going to buy a flat and rent it out. I've seen one I like, down Ogleforth."

"Must cost a bit."

Rick didn't answer. He couldn't think of anything else to say. He was too drained to go on, yet he wanted to move as soon as possible. He would spend the next ten years fighting that paradox.

RICK Rounder, ex-copper, Yorkshire through and through, brought the big old Holden to a halt in the dust at the cliff top and stepped into the warm night. The hot engine ticked as he walked towards the door. Something unseen scuttled into the undergrowth; something else slithered. As he climbed the steps, he looked beyond the house to the sea. It was hard to separate land and water at night. Different shades of darkness, that was all. Further off, down the hill and on the main beach, light escaped from the bars and got lost in the velvet dark.

Naomi was asleep and he didn't want to wake her. He drank a cold can of lager on the balcony and stared at his damaged finger. He went to bed: she didn't stir. He'd have to tell her in the morning.

CHAPTER THREE

THE amateur historian puffs as he pedals his second-hand bicycle. His purpose is not exercise, which has never interested him. He finds physical activity bothersome, especially when his chest complains. If this happens, he stops and breathes deeply. The pain usually passes: one day, it may not. On this day, though, no invisible hand clutches his heart as he rides unsteadily along a wide road leading out of York.

Like much else in this city, there is a story in the smallest detail, even something as simple as the stones used to build the garden walls facing the road. The historian in the man knows so many of the old stories that float about York like atoms from the past. He likes that bit about atoms from the past, until he remembers that it is not one of his. He wishes it were.

"It's all about interpretation, you see. History is there to be read by those with the eyes to look."

The houses here, the man thinks, are not new-smart like those expensive flats popping up all over the place, every single one unique, or so the adverts say, and every one three times too expensive for ordinary people. This is an older sort of smart, Edwardian and onwards. The large houses are set apart, with trees and long drives. The front doors are far from the road and passers-by are kept at a respectful distance. His own front door opens on to the pavement, putting him amongst the people, more's the bloody pity, people being what they are.

The history lover heard once that the stones used to build these garden walls came from the old debtors' prison at the Eye of York. The prison walls tumbled and the stones were distributed among the wealthier so they could contain their gardens and keep the world at bay. They always find a way to improve their lot, do the well off – always have, always will. So the man thinks, his mind running on familiar rails, his resentment as circular as ever.

The first houses along this road are huge, hiding behind prison stones and drooping trees, as if not wanting to be seen. Then the larger houses give way to smaller semis, probably built in the Fifties. The man inserts the 'probably' into his interior monologue "because I don't know for sure; to be honest, I don't really give a damn. If you want to know, ask an estate agent, that is if you can bear the conversation." He engages in interior conversation most of the time, preferring his own thoughts. Other people had opinions that got in the way and spoilt everything.

The man wobbles over a junction, passing a massive house at the crossroads. He had needed a cover for this task and had thought of jogging, then decided against it. He is not built for exertion, least not of that kind. His heart does not take kindly to it. So he had got a bike instead. He had bought the bike from a widow in a bungalow. It had belonged to her dead husband and she hadn't argued when he offered half the asking price. The widowed woman showed him a picture of her husband, but he didn't know why she thought he would want to look at that. Her hands were frail and wrinkled, all bird-like and unpleasant. The old woman cried when he took the bike but he felt good because a bargain's a bargain, even if it's a bike you don't really want.

So that is what the history lover has been doing, riding up and down this road, on the look out. It might even get him fit, all this exercise. That would be ironic because he has never sought to be fit. Fitness is vanity with a sweat got up, isn't it? Sweating for the sake of it is not for him. Leave that to the stupid gym people and the idiot joggers, slipping about in their own perspiration. He has a higher purpose, which is why he cycles up and down this road looking for an opportunity. It seems fitting to search in an area like this. No good seeking the streets round his way; there's no one classy or rich enough. The cheeky little bitches near where he lives take the piss. One of them called him a sad old fucker the other day and she couldn't have been more than twelve. The man had not know such words existed when he was that age. Sometimes it upsets him so see what the world is coming to.

The background has to be right if history is to be served properly. So the history lover cycles up and down, careful not to attract attention. Never wear anything bright and don't catch anyone's eyes. It takes a certain skill to prowl, especially on an old bicycle, but the man believes he has it. If you live apart, you learn how to watch and to take note.

The history lover has been weighing up the possibilities. Nine years old would be perfect, just like poor Esme, but it would take time. There is no use being slap-dash about these things. Skill and determination is what it takes, and the ability to plan. This isn't a job for the feeble or the easily defeated; it is a job for a man who knows things. That's why he is right for the job. He feels uplifted that history has chosen him for this experiment.

There are difficulties in such a task. Parents take their pampered darlings everywhere by car, in those big flash vans the middle classes love. Either that or they drive massive vehicles with fat tyres that could cope with the North York Moors, never mind the school run. All this makes his task harder.

The late autumn sun shows this area at its best. The low sun gilds everything, burnishing the turning leaves, throwing golden light through the windows and polishing the expensive cars. Children are being dropped home, a dog is barking. An ordinary day, beautiful in a way. It's like wearing those glasses for 3D films: put them on and suddenly everything looks different, exciting, more rounded, deeper, more real than real. That's how everything looks today. Anticipation is the word for it.

Then it happens. He sees a smallish girl, eight or nine, with shiny blonde hair. She unleashes the hair as she stands in the drive of her parents' big house, letting it unravel from a ponytail, making herself free. She is wearing a traditional uniform, so she probably goes to one of the private schools, which is what you would expect round here. She looks trim and neat in the uniform, although she is starting to come undone, the blouse loosened from the skirt, the socks collapsed into wrinkles. The man doesn't know for sure if Esme was blonde, but he reasons that a degree of interpretation is inevitable in such a study.

She is alone, this blonde child. She stretches, enjoying her space after the confinement of school. Then a little yappy dog runs out, a fluffy runt thing. The dog isn't good but nothing is ever perfect. Taking note of the house and its number, putting the little girl to memory, letting her image settle in his mind, the history lover heads home on the dead man's bicycle.

CHAPTER FOUR

IT WAS late in the afternoon and the sinking sun was radiating low shafts. Soon enough it would be dark, but there was glory in the departing day. Pauline Markham laughed at herself for glimpsing glory in her own back garden. But how she loved this large private space. Hawthorne hedges marked the boundaries at either side while trees sketched out the end of the garden. The holly tree kept its leaves, providing somewhere for the birds all year round, so long as they didn't mind the thorny landing. The other trees, the copper beach and the silver birch, had few leaves now, and the diminishing light picked out the capillary spread of their branches.

Pauline walked towards her house as the sun made the red bricks glow. She had never thought they would be able to afford a detached house, not down this road, but here they were, the four of them in this lovely house. Five, if you counted Ben. It hadn't been her idea because she didn't even like dogs, two children and a husband being quite enough. But she had relented, as she often had before. Graham now had his dog, only she did all the work. She took the dog for walks, gathered its shit into crinkled plastic bags left over from the supermarket, and occasionally forced him to suffer a bath. She had coerced Ben into the bubbles earlier and afterwards he had scuttled into the garden in search of cleansing mud.

Still, she had grown fond of Ben, or Benjy as the girls preferred. Sally and Polly loved that dog, even if their fondness did fall short of picking up the mess he made. You can't have everything, as her mother was always telling her. Sometimes she wondered if the phone calls to her mother were any help, but still she punched out the familiar digits, chatting about this and that, passing on the small details of her life, and listening to her mother's coded reprimands.

Stopping for a moment, Pauline glanced to the left, then to the right, taking in her neighbours' gardens. It was green and private out here in the summer. Autumn stripped away the seclusion, but she enjoyed the openness, and the chance to look into other people's gardens. 'Being bloody nosy' was how Graham described it, but it was all right for him, he was out while she looked after the girls and that blessed dog. True, his money had paid for all this, the nice detached house, two cars and the girls' education – as he had told her more than once, when they had had words. She realised with a jolt that she was thinking like her mother. "That blessed dog" and "having words" were expressions her mother used.

She supposed her world was complete, perfect in a way. Yet it could seem a dreary perfection. Perhaps there was no such thing, just striving after something that could never be got. She did have a lot: a decent husband (even if he was called Graham; how had she managed to marry someone called that?); two lovely girls; a big house. It would be fully dark by the time Graham returned, dark for hours.

Sally had gone to Jessica's for tea. She had seen her after school, but only for a moment, a whisked kiss and a goodbye. She resented this when it happened. Sally would rush out, pink with excitement, and ask if she could go round to see a friend, usually Jessica or sometimes Beatrice. For a while it had been Theresa but they no longer got on. She hadn't mourned that friendship because Theresa's mother could be difficult and smelt of wine in the afternoon. She was superior and lofty and wore too much lipstick. The other mums called her the Illuminated Mouth.

Polly liked to come home and play outside, usually with George from next door. George was really Georgina, but hardly anyone called her that, and not in her hearing. She had a sharp tongue for a girl of eight. "It's George, plain and simple," as she put it.

Walking down the side of the house, she opened the gate to the garage and went inside, pushing past the bikes, one for each of them with Graham's the newest and most expensive. A mountain bike had seemed excessive in somewhere so flat, or so she had thought. He had smiled a thin smile, and bought one anyway.

Apart from the bikes, the garage was empty because Graham

liked to put his BMW away at night. Her red Polo stayed out in the drive. It was parked there as she came out of the garage and crunched over the gravel and then stepped on to the flagstones. It had all seemed such an expense but Graham had been right, it did look good, the clean caramel-coloured stones against the greenery of the front garden. She looked beyond her red car, down the drive towards the gates, which were another Graham extravagance, all twisted black metal with flashes of gold, like the fence round a stately home. Yet there was something wrong with the gates. She couldn't tell what it was and walked closer. Then she doubted what she saw, not understanding what it was, hoping it was wrong, a mental aberration, a stray moment from a nightmare. She started to jog, then ran. Ben was hanging by his lead, swinging from the gates, his small black legs kicking furiously. His bark was soundless, stolen by the lead pulled tight round his neck. She undid the knot and Ben fell into her arms, a quivering black heap. White foam flecked his mouth and his eyes had rolled upwards, but he was still breathing. The need for action took over and Pauline stood with the dog in her arms and ran to her car. Then she stopped, stone still. Where was Polly? She must be next door with George. Putting the dog on the front passenger seat, she started the car and rang Gloria on her mobile.

"Gloria, something awful has happened with Ben. I'm off to the vets. Can you keep an eye on Polly?"

"Yes, of course."

Pauline started the car, eased through the gates and drove off, thankful that Polly was all right. The girl spent half her life round there, another hour wouldn't matter.

The traffic was heavy but she reached the surgery in five minutes. She brought the car to a screeching halt and rushed inside with the dog. He felt so heavy for a small dog.

The receptionist called one of the vets out. The young woman touched Ben's throat, put her face close to his mouth.

"I'm afraid it's too late," she said. "He has stopped breathing."

Pauline said that couldn't be right, she didn't understand.

Stumbling back, she sat in one of the reception seats. A woman on the next seat was holding a cardboard box. Scratching and scrabbling noises came from inside the box.

"But he's our family dog," she said, to no-one in particular. "They'll all be so upset and Graham is bound to blame me. He'll say it's my fault – he usually does. How can Benjy be dead? He was such a lively little thing."

Her mobile rang.

"Yes?"

"Pauline, you sound kind of strange."

"I feel kind of strange. Benjy's dead."

"What do you mean?"

"I mean what I said – he's dead. The poor dog just died."

"Oh, Pauline – I'm really sorry. But there's something I have to tell you. I went to find Polly but George said she had gone. She said that a man had come, her Uncle Pete or something, and he had taken her away."

"She hasn't got an Uncle Pete…"

Pauline rang off, said "Fuck!" more loudly than she had intended, and ran to her car, leaving the young vet holding the dead dog.

CHAPTER FIVE

NEWS of the old Queen's death reached York on January 23, 1901, and was reported by the Yorkshire Herald as follows: "The Queen passed away this evening at 6.30. In this brief sentence the news of Her Majesty's death was first conveyed to the citizens of York, little more than an hour after the occurrence of the event. The telegram containing the intelligence reached the Post Office, York, at 7.18…"

The bell of St Martin's Church in Coney Street rang out a sorrowful cadence, while Great Peter at York Minster chimed in a few minutes later. Events were cancelled as a mark of respect, although the entertainment continued at York Theatre Royal, a shocking occurrence, according to some. The funeral was held on the Saturday. Banks were closed and York Market was brought forward a day to fall on the Friday. The Lord Mayor sent a telegram in which "deepest sympathy" was expressed and he decreed a day of general mourning for the funeral.

The first Esme Percy knew of the momentous news was hearing her father say "The old Queen's dead." He stood like a statue in the parlour, concentrating with the effort. Then he prepared to leave for the public house on the corner, declaring he would head off for a respectful drink – "Before that pompous old bastard Purnell bans alcohol until the Queen is good and buried."

Esme knew about death and understood its smell. They killed the cows close to where she lived. After each act of slaughter, the blood would glint scarlet against the grey cobbles as it ran down the alley and into the common sewer. The metal grate was just outside the yard and the blood added to the rank stink, what her father called the dead person smell.

Taken in drink, to use the words Esme remembered from church, her father would sway above the grate and utter strange phrases, calling on God and the Devil or any other being within his hearing to end this stinking life.

On a sunny September afternoon, eight months after they buried the old queen, Thomas Percy stepped over the channel, his rough hand playing with his daughter's long hair. He was heading to the beer house again, and that thought put him in a good mood.

"Now then, girl," he said. "What is this with the blood? Not much of a toy for a girl, is it?"

He did not see the feathers Esme had dropped into the blood because he never noticed the details. She had watched their progress, seeing the way the red soaked up the whiteness.

"You should be doing something other than staring at blood, lass." He had stubble, blackened teeth or gaps left by missing teeth, and smelt of tobacco and beer.

The beer house stood on a corner and came to a sharp point where two alleys met. Thomas Percy wanted a drink, and having no money to hand did not stop an honest man from trying. He would walk in hope to the beer house, where he would step through the back door into the taproom. Here, if luck or finances prevailed, he would put down deep roots at the bar, joining the "perpendicular drinkers" who stood for want of a seat in a small room slippery with spilt drink and heavy with the miasma of cheap tobacco. If luck did not shine, there was always the pawnshop, so long as he could find something that was not already with the bastard broker.

As her father walked away, tattered trousers flapping above second-hand boots, Esme Percy watched him go, then watched as the blood sparkled in the sunshine. The drowning feathers span and sank. She dipped her thin finger into the liquid so the blood flowed round. Transfixed, she imagined herself the source of all this blood, peed out into this channel. Then she turned and ran. She came puffing into the bare earth of the communal yard and cleansed her finger under water from the shared tap.

Afterwards, for want of other activity, her mother having not yet spotted her idleness, she followed the blood upstream to the slaughterhouse. A cow had died, killed here amid the crowded houses. Esme looked into the small slaughterhouse. The huge dead beast hung from a rough wooden beam as blood escaped the slit in its neck. Flies bothered its dead brown eyes as it twisted in thrall to unfeeling gravity. It was black and white and shit decorated its arse.

Such meat would not end up on the Percy table. The choice cuts would go elsewhere, to the people who lived in houses at the end of long green gardens. A scrap of boiled bacon would be the best the Percys would get; or no meat at all, only potatoes with skim milk, or vegetable broth.

Esme ran back along the littered passageway. Outside the gate she felt faint and staggered against the brick wall where the ferny weeds grew. She wheezed and spat a gobbet of her own blood into that of the slaughtered beast.

Restored, Esme went into the yard, which teemed with her brothers and sisters. Soon she was lost in the scrum, playing and fighting, her grubby face hidden among the other dirty faces, her sweat mingling with theirs.

Esme Percy was nine years old and lucky in some respects, going to one of the Board Schools in York. She attended with five of her siblings, two brothers and three sisters: Henry and Peter; Rebecca, Mary and Hetty; the elder two brothers, being past the age of fourteen, had left school. Joshua and Joseph now worked at the confectionery factory, helping to sustain the impoverished Percy family.

Martha Percy laid out a meal of vegetable broth, old bread and marmalade, and tea. Esme ate with the others, crowded round the rickety table in a kitchen with cracked tiles on the floor and one window facing the dirty yard. The window admitted little light, its panes being dirty, broken or replaced with grubby cloth. The carelessness in this damp basement was not the fault of Martha, who did her best. But 'doing her best' with eight children, even if two of them were bringing in wages, was not easy, and the drunken husband did not help. But Martha trudged on, the fire having long gone from her eyes.

Holes in the walls exposed damp brickwork beneath the curdled plasterwork; and the frame round the door into the yard was misshapen, so that the door would not close with ease. Mice scurried alongside the uneven walls at night and disappeared into crannies.

The last light had leeched from the sky. Martha lit candles and oil lamps, which imparted cheeriness, hiding the defects and dereliction.

Esme was sent to bed first. There were two bedrooms, one for each sex. Esme slept with the twins, Rebecca and Mary, in one bed; Hetty and their mother slept in the other. Henry and Peter shared a bed with their father, and Joshua and Joseph slept in the adjacent bed.

Esme, thin and shivering in her nightclothes, fell asleep quickly. She did not dive deep into sleep but ducked just below the surface, waking easily.

Tonight she twitched urgently and sat up when Rebecca and Mary came to bed. Her hair fell about her bony shoulders in a tangle; her eyes burned blue from between the tendrils. She held out her thin arms, steady and straight, and said something her sisters did not catch. The girls administered a cuddle, and eased her back into the sheets.

"All skin and bone, that one," said Mary, whose own slim body was shaping into womanhood.

"Nothing to her at all," said Rebecca, laughing, as she put on her heavy nightclothes and clambered into the cold bed; Esme had imparted little warmth to the sheets.

Hetty and Martha came in later. In the other bedroom, the boys followed their own sequence, Henry and Peter first; Joshua and Joseph later.

Martha liked to be asleep by the time Thomas returned. Any good humour he acquired in the public house would dissipate on the short walk home. She was asleep and warm in threadbare sheets by the time Thomas swayed out of the beer house. The chatter and rough song remained with him for a moment until the door closed and the merriment was muffled.

He stood unsteadily, doubly intoxicated by the fresh night air. It took a while to find his bearing and then he zig-zagged towards home along the alley. The yard was deep in shadow, then the clouds drew back from the moon and silvered light flooded in.

By this happy illumination, Thomas Percy found the midden privy. He pissed out the spent beer, his waters releasing a hellish stink from what was foully contained below. Once relieved, he bumped into the yard, now dark again. He staggered about until he found what he sought and, clumsily shoving the door, using his shoulder and then his feet, he tumbled into the kitchen. He managed to light a candle, which he placed on the mantelpiece above the dwindling fire in the range. Finding his bearings in the guttering light, he heard a creaking which he did not understand. He turned towards the door, putting up his fists in a pantomime show of defiance and bravery. The creak grew more insistent and the door crashed on to the tiled floor. Thomas Percy dropped his fists and put the stubby broken-nailed fingers of one hand to his mouth, shushing the unhinged door; then he looked over his shoulder towards the room where his wife slept.

Satisfied that he was the only one awake, and unconcerned by the hole where the door should be, Thomas Percy sought nourishment. He found the remnants of a meal, lukewarm vegetable broth, old bread and marmalade, and he sat on a chair in front of the embers, scooping up the soup with a stale corner of bread. He introduced marmalade into the thin broth.

Having dined, Thomas Percy settled to let his meal digest. After a subsiding fusillade of farts, each one quieter than the last, he fell asleep in a fog of his own making.

Morning found him still in the chair as weak rays of sunshine slanted through the unguarded doorway to pick out the stubble on his chin. Neighbours glanced as they crossed the yard, laughing as Thomas Percy slept.

On waking, Martha felt something was wrong. Coming into the kitchen, she saw Thomas, feet pointing towards the range, head slumped forward, a slug of saliva escaping his mouth. It was a moment before she noticed the door. She had no immediate reaction, years of dull acceptance having eroded her capacity for surprise. She put more coal in the belly of the range and went outside with a pitcher to ferry water from the tap in the yard. With the vessel half filled, Martha came back into the kitchen, trailed thin fingers in the water and dribbled droplets on his face. He awoke with a growl and saw the wet fingers and the jug of water. He made as if to stand in anger, but slumped back, troubled by the weight of his head.

"There seems to be a door missing," said Martha. "I could have sworn it were there yesterday."

Thomas hid his head in dirty upturned palms. He stayed like that until Martha poured tea into an enamel cup, which she left by his chair. He reached down an arm, wrists thick and hairy, and cradled the hot cup in his hands.

It had been some minutes since she had last spoken, but Martha carried on, as if in conversation. "Lying across the floor, it is. The door that should be upright and protecting us but instead it is lying across the floor."

"You will thank the Lord you are not lying across the floor in a minute, woman."

Thomas scowled and Martha kept her distance, able to do her chores while calculating her own safety. The children came in for breakfast, one by one, in a dribble then a rush. The family flowed around Thomas, like water negotiating an obstinate rock. The children all asked about the door.

"Mam, why is that...?"

"Where has the door gone...?"

"Why is the door on the floor, mam...?

She held her peace and Thomas scowled in silence.

Martha put out enamel plates containing scraps of bacon, bread and dripping, and poured tea for her and another cup for Thomas. She gave the younger children thin cocoa; the elder children had tea. Esme ate half of her breakfast and sipped at her cocoa.

"You will fade to nowt," her mother said, her thin lips shaping into a worried smile. "There will not be anything left of you soon, girl."

"Nothing much wrong with me," Esme said. And this was true as far as she understood it, for a girl of nine should not have to entertain too many dark thoughts, whatever fate may have arranged for her.

CHAPTER SIX

RICK Rounder was thrilled. Ogleforth was a stream down which history had flowed, depositing bits of the past, and now he was living there. Naomi was untouched by such romanticism.

"God, but this a gloomy old street," she said, standing on the doorstep. She looked at the sky, still expecting blue. "Does the sun ever get this far down or is it banned by some Yorkshire edict? The sun shalt not shine for else the people might find something to smile about."

Her voice went up at the end of her sentences, giving her speech a sprung rhythm.

"Hey," he replied, "that's my heritage you're mocking."

He turned the key in the door. Inside, there were three floors. The place was a dump after years of being rented to students. All those parties and pizzas, drugs and sex, or whatever students got up to. Rick's notion was hazy because he had never been a student. School and then the police had been his lot, until his travels.

The ground floor had a garage with a small utility room at the end. The next floor up had a large lounge and a kitchen. The sofa was marked with cigarette burns and wasted liquids of indeterminate origin; the kitchen was layered with grime. Two bedrooms occupied the top floor, the biggest having a view of the Minster.

"So, Rick Rounder, this is it, this is my home, this is where I'm to live," said Naomi in the larger bedroom. She smiled in that teasing way Rick had almost forgotten to notice. She put her arms round his neck. Rick bent slightly to kiss her. She was tall, five ten to his six two. "This is it – a gloomy old flat near the big church?"

"That big church is the oldest Gothic building in northern Europe."

"So, I've got myself a regular tourist guide then, have I? You could get yourself a horse and cart and do one of those tours round the centre of York, picking up Americans."

"I'd rather pick up Australians instead."

"I'm half American, remember?"

"I know – which half was it again?"

He ran his tongue round her neck, above the collar of her blouse.

"Have you got something on your mind?"

"Maybe."

He kissed lower again, undoing a button and nudging his tongue over the swell of her breast. He undid other buttons. The blouse came away and his hand lay white against her stomach. He had picked up a tan on his travels but he would never be that dark. Her bra glowed white and her nipples rose. This would be the first time in their new home. He ran a finger down her taut stomach, ready for more unleashing.

"Hello, anyone there? Only the door was open. Very unwise that, you know. Might have been all right in the outback but not here in York. There are some right scum-bags in this city and I should know, I've nicked most of them!"

The voice boomed up the stairs, heralding the arrival of Sam Rounder, older brother, career copper, and married – but only by a thread.

Rick pulled away and shouted down the stairwell. "It wasn't the outback, it was Queensland, you big old tosser. By the ocean and very lovely too." Rick looked at Naomi, and muttered quietly, "As he would have discovered if he'd bothered to visit."

"Where the hell are you?"

"Up another floor."

Naomi did up the buttons and leant against the window. Sam was panting when he emerged into the bedroom.

"Nice view," he said. "The Minster, I mean."

Sam arranged his fattening cheeks into a smile. His face laughed but his eyes did not as he surveyed Naomi. Then he turned to Rick. "Little brother!" The brothers embraced lightly, as if shy of intimacy, making contact for as long as it took to pat each other on the back.

"So, you're back here in York. Back to where it all started."

"Where what all started?"

"You, me, life – all of that."

Rick steered Sam towards Naomi.

"This is Naomi."

"I guessed. Only you didn't say…"

Sam shook Naomi's hand, holding longer than necessary as his eyes flicked up and down in casual admiration.

"Good to have you back," Sam said, turning to his brother. They were almost the same height, but Rick carried it off more impressively. Sam was blurring with middle age. His chin had bulged and slipped, his cheeks were touched with red, as if warmed by a blush that wouldn't go away. His once-black hair was mostly grey and needed cutting. Rick's hair was short and neat, shaved almost, with flecks of grey above the ears. He was a couple of stones leaner and looked relaxed, whereas Sam seemed haunted by something or other.

"So what's the plan, little brother?"

"Moving in here with Naomi, sorting the place out, getting a job."

"Have you thought what yet?"

"I'll tell you in a minute, over a pint."

"I suppose you drink that Australian rubbish now."

"I'll drink whatever you put on the bar."

Naomi said she would start the big tidy up. Rick arched his eyebrows, knowing that tidying up wasn't like her. He was impressed; he hadn't known Naomi could do tact.

"Go on then, Sam. A quick pint and then I'll come back to help Naomi."

They walked along Goodramgate to where two pubs stood side by side, apparently in neighbourly harmony, although ancient grudges were said to exist. Rick and Sam showed no favouritism, going into the first pub they came to. Pints were bought and they sat in the main bar, which had the air of pleasant detachment pubs have in the afternoon.

"Cheers, little brother."

Sam drank deeply and quickly. Rick sipped the straw-coloured bitter. The condescension irritated him; all this 'little brother' shit was galling; he was pushing forty and Sam was two years older, not that you'd think so to look at him. Ten years, Rick reckoned. It felt good to be wearing better than his brother. The years away had kept him fit and let him shake off York, but Sam looked as though the city had settled on him, heavy and suspicious.

"God, you wouldn't believe how busy it's got since you left," said Sam, putting down an almost-empty glass. "Targets to be hit, money to be saved, political correctness to be allowed for – all that shit and still trying to do the job."

"But look at you, chief inspector – that must count for something."

"Yeah, long hours away from home, a marriage that's full of holes and two teenager daughters who barely acknowledge me."

"Sounds gloomy," said Rick. "Can I get you another?"

"Are you keeping me company?"

"I'll have them slip a half in this."

Sam listed further woes as he drank. There was little love between him and Michelle, just a tired, snappy familiarity. He'd been seeing someone else, a younger woman in the force, but she had left him for someone her own age. "Fit looking bloke," he said, absently. Michelle had found out, just at the same time he discovered she'd been straying with another teacher at school.

"It's a fuck up," said Sam. "A sad old mess. Anyway, you seem set up all right. Naomi seems a nice sort of woman. You didn't tell me about her...York being York. It might take her a while to fit in."

"Naomi is Naomi, that's all that matters," said Rick. "If people in this city cast their eyes above the walls and had a look at the wider world, they might see that there are all sorts out there."

Sam raised his eyebrows, shrugged his heavy shoulders.

"So what you going to do, then?"

"Going private, that's the plan."

"What do you mean?"

"Go on, big brother – catch up. Your line of work, only in the private sector."

"What, you're getting a big hairy-arsed dog and going to guard a factory?"

"You know what I mean. Private investigator."

Sam looked suspicious. "What, all that sitting about in cars and pissing in bottles while spying on people just to prove they're shagging where they shouldn't be shagging, or working when they're claiming for a bad back?"

"Yeah, that's the idea."

"You're my brother. How's it going to look for me? Once the other coppers know, they'll take the piss something rotten."

"Let them. Most of them need something to laugh about. Besides, you're the boss. They probably take the piss mercilessly already."

An inhospitable silence settled between them. Sam looked at his empty glass, the bar and his watch, then stood reluctantly.

"Better get back, there's a girl gone missing. Her mother thinks she's been kidnapped. I'd say it's a bit soon to tell, but you never know."

"I could help you, you know, in my new role."

"What the hell would I need a private eye for? I've got plenty of public ones."

"Are you driving back?"

"Yeah, I'll be all right. I'm used to it. Anyway, if a senior policeman can't take a few liberties, who can?"

Sam laughed without much mirth and was gone. Rick took a small card out of his wallet and walked to the bar.

"Mind if I put this up somewhere?"

The landlord stopped scratching his stomach and looked at the card.

"I'll leave it there a week or two. And make sure you drink in here, to pay the rent for your advertisement."

Soon the cards were distributed throughout the city, in pubs, post offices, restaurants, coffee shops, anywhere that would take them. Rick now felt that he was indeed a private investigator. All he needed now was something to investigate.

CHAPTER SEVEN

THE historian parked his old van outside the Dean Court hotel, opposite the Minster. He was returning from an errand and wanted a quiet moment alone with the past. He was more content with the past, happiest with history because history did not answer back, and remained pure of the pollutants of modern life. He sat in the van and looked up at the Minster, absorbing calmness from its order and Gothic proportions. Tourists and shoppers interrupted the view, causing a rash of irritation, and resurrecting the thought that people always got in the way. He saw no irony in the fact that history too was filled with people, because the people of the past were tidier and more contained, undamaged by modern life. If only more people could think as he did, then the world would not be such a harsh place; if only other people recognised that they should pay more attention to the past rather than the present.

A traffic warden was walking towards the van. The history lover glowered through his newly cleaned windscreen, then turned the ignition key, letting the engine shudder into life with a diesel fart. He edged the old van out from among the shiny carapaces of the BMWs and Volvos outside the hotel, executed a U-turn and drove off in a fumy haze. He parked the van, freshly cleaned inside and out, at the supermarket and went in for provisions. His notion of what such a girl might eat was hazy, but he supposed that chocolate and biscuits might do. He put these into his basket, along with crisps and cola, making sure that he bought the basic lines if possible, and paid in cash, fearing that a card might incriminate. Back home, he packed the provisions into a rucksack, made a flask of tea, then headed off for his hiding place.

She had been alone for a couple of hours and would need reassurance. She would be happy to see him after such a time. He walked a little faster, keen to be at his destination and anticipating the company. He would have made a good father, he was sure of that, if only all those bitches hadn't been so unreasonable in their tastes. He was pleased with his hiding place, feeling that it fitted perfectly, so long as he had done his homework. It was, as he had calculated, dusk by the time he arrived. He looked around furtively to make sure no one was watching, and then he disappeared from sight.

THE Minster was more enormous than anything she could imagine. Its peak scraped heaven. To be that high and to pierce the sky was a miracle.

Esme Percy had set out on a daring adventure. She had slipped from the rumpus and was walking along the Shambles, the street of butchers, where animals awaiting slaughter were herded. She passed the butchers and looked up at the houses that nodded their foreheads towards each other and almost blocked out the sky.

She saw the Minster, then lost it. When the cathedral disappeared from view, she knew it was there. It was an act of faith with her: if you shut your eyes, the Minster was still there, even though you could not see it. She walked by public houses with their loud adult noises and the waft of beer and tobacco; she dodged the horseshit littering the road; and then, turning away from Stonegate, she saw the Minster and gazed at its vast stone creaminess. If she leaned back, she could see the blue early winter sky high above the round window. This window was named after a flower and she thought it might be a rose.

Esme decided to walk all the way round the Minster. She knew this would take time, as something so big could not be got round in a minute. When she reached what she took to be the front, she shivered in the wind and she knew this was the coldest place on earth. The wind pierced her thin clothes and made her think of needles.

She hurried into the gardens at the side of the Minster, almost skipping, but slowing as she passed the people in fine clothes. She gazed for a moment at one family. The father was stout and had cheeks like rosy apples, except for the sideburns that grew down his face like two hairy caterpillars. He wore a coat of material so thick it was a wonder he could walk with the weight of it; and a hat that rose from his head like a chimney, but without the smoke, which instead came from a cigar that smouldered in his gloved hand. The woman had a long and heavy velvet dress that trailed on the ground and was the colour of the blood in the alley. Her fine coat was long but not long enough to hide the dress, and her hair rose in a way that did not seem possible, shaping itself into a bun, or one of those loaves of bread with a smaller bulge on top of a bigger bulge. The prosperous couple had four children, two boys and two girls, whose clothes had never been worn before by anyone else. The scrubbed and tailored boys punched and pinched each other when their parents were not looking. Esme watched as if in a trance, and the family passed without giving her a second glance, and she returned home, dejected.

No-one had missed Esme because they all thought someone else was looking out for her. When she slipped back into the mossy, foetid yard with its privy stink, she saw her father panting and wheezing, contorting his pale, veined face as he heaved the door back into place with the help of big Sam Smith. Mr. Smith was a carpenter and strong, as well as knowing about wood and doors and how to mend what had been broken. Eventually, her father and Mr. Smith righted the door and secured it once more in the splintered frame. Esme observed the resurrection, craning her neck to see the top of the door. Above that was the wall and above that a tiny patch of blue. The sky was smaller where she lived. The Minster stole the biggest prize of sky and there was not so much left for anywhere else. Esme Percy spat pink against the wall, and went inside, wondering what was for tea.

POLLY Markham shuddered as the metal hatch swung open. The nasty man's feet came in first, stumbling as he sought his footing. Then he reached the floor and closed the hatch above his head.

"Here you are girl. I expect you've been wondering where I've been, haven't you? I've got us some treats, so we can have a nice tea together."

The man moved about awkwardly, trying to find a comfortable

arrangement, until ample flesh and hidden bones were sorted to his satisfaction.

"There, that's better. Now, we've got chocolate and biscuits, crisps and cola. All naughty food, but I don't hold with all that healthy stuff you are supposed to eat nowadays. You can't switch on the television without some bossy woman telling what to eat. Think of it as a picnic if you like, a picnic with your grandad, maybe. Have you got a grandad? Not saying much, are you?"

"You're not at all like my grandad. He's a nice man, he doesn't go around stealing girls. Why have you done this to me? What do you want? You're not one of those horrible men who like to have sex with girls?"

The history lover was hurt to be so misunderstood, and anger made his face burn. How could this ungrateful child not sense the scale and scope of his experiment?

His words came out in a hot rush. "I am not one of those perverts. I go for proper women and plenty of them find me attractive."

He thought of his young, sad Polish friend, who undressed so nicely for him, once the arrangements had been made, and the words she spoke while he satisfied himself. What she said held no meaning to him, but the words sounded warm and encouraging. She dressed quickly afterwards, pulling cheap clothes over her thin, pale body.

"See you next time," he would say. She would echo the phrase, saying "Next time" in a flat, unresponsive voice.

"No, I am not a pervert. Just a man with a keen interest in history."

"You're weird, that's what you are. Weird and nasty."

"Eat some chocolate and shut the fuck up, little girl."

CHAPTER EIGHT

RICK Rounder had an office with a computer. Some might describe it as a utility room, alerted by the washing machine, but it did for Rick and made him feel good. Except for one thing: he was an investigator with nothing to investigate, which was a perfect description of uselessness, had he been looking for one.

His mobile chirruped some damn fool tune Naomi had chosen. He silenced the electronic twittering and started his new spiel, feeling foolish, certain it would be his brother ready to mock his lack of progress.

"Rick Rounder, private investigator, how may I help you?"

How may I help you…? God, had he really just said that? Naomi said that was the proper form of words, what they said when she had worked in advertising in Sydney.

"Mr Rounder, I've got something for you and I'd like to meet."

Rounder said he would have to look in his diary. He rocked back in his chair and checked the ceiling, on which nothing at all was written, and punched the air in triumph.

"Yes, that should be fine. When and where?"

The caller said ten minutes, on the Bar Walls, at the corner above Lord Mayor's Walk, then rang off. He had an educated voice, without much trace of an accent, or so it seemed to Rick. It lacked the hard, flat cadences of York.

Leaving the flat, Rick wove between the tourists until he came to the old stone steps. He glanced at the model shop, its window full of old-fashioned toys of the sort bought by nostalgic fathers for children who weren't interested because they were too entranced by computers. The begging spot on the corner was empty and so passers-by escaped with their conscience unpricked. Rick entered the darkness and ascended the steep, uneven steps, running his hand on the time-smoothed rail, emerging into the light by the entrance to the tiny museum at the top.

This was the finest section of the walls, best for showing off the Minster, yet his mind wasn't on Gothic splendour or the sunshine caressing the honeyed stone. After years of travelling, he felt the stirring of his old self, the tug of forgotten fibres. He was about to investigate something again.

He squeezed past a group of American tourists, wormed through a clutch of Japanese visitors, and then he was there, up the steps and on to the stone platform. Benches rimmed what was a small arena-like platform that offered one of the best views of the Minster.

On the outside of the wall, traffic was snarled along Lord Mayor's Walk. Sam had asked him what had changed since he'd been away. There didn't used to be so much traffic, he said, or so many coffee bars. The proud old city now ran on exhaust fumes and caffeine.

He sat on one of the benches, worn shiny by a thousand tourist bums, and glanced at his watch. Perhaps it was a hoax. He stood, walked round, sat again, got up once more and shuffled his feet. When he sat again, he was no longer alone.

"Mr Rounder, I presume."

"That's me, mate."

"Well, Mr Rounder, nice to meet you. I would like a divorce."

"Didn't even know we were married, mate," said Rick, his words quicker than thought, and he grimaced inwardly.

"I see you consider this to be some kind of a joke. Well, a sense of humour can be a help in life, so I'll let that pass for now. But please don't annoy me because this is a matter of some delicacy."

"Look, I'm sorry. It was a stupid remark." He extended his hand, adding: "Rick Rounder. And who might you be?"

"I will tell you that when I want you to know. Can I have your e-mail address?"

"My what?"

"After this meeting, I would like to communicate at a distance to acquaint you with the details. So your e-mail, please."

Rounder gave one of his cards to the man.

"When I get home, I shall send you an e-mail with some of my details contained therein. From certain information I shall give you, you will be able to make the observations of which I am desirous."

Christ, thought Rick, this guy's wife could get a divorce on grounds of unreasonable behaviour with the English language.

"Sure thing," he said. And then the man was gone, bobbing impatiently between the tourists towards Bootham Bar.

THE first in a series of e-mails arrived an hour later. Rick sat in his small office and, as the washing machine flung out its noisy last, he read the words on the screen, starting with 'Subject: my cheating wife.' Sounds almost like a country song, he thought, as he began to absorb the details.

"Wendy Wistow is 33 years of age, dark haired, slim but not too slim, with a flat, muscular stomach from all those hours she spends at the gym, and a habit of crying 'oh fuck' at the point of orgasm. You may well feel that this last is one detail too many, but so be it. Everything should help if she is to be in your head as she is forever in mine. Married for ten, cheated on for two – that is my fate. It's funny how happiness can be there, so strong, and then turn into its opposite. I couldn't pinpoint the day when one became the other, as the shift happened gradually. Mostly she was with me and then I was without her. Everything that was right became wrong, and now I want the proof. In a sense this job I am offering you has no point, because I have my own evidence, garnered from a thousand small lies, from small suspicions grown large, from a cheated heart that knows what it knows. But I don't have the proof you could acquire for me, the photographs, the indiscretion made flesh, as it were.

"We met at university and I knew, as soon as I saw her, knew from the glint of her eyes, the shine of her hair. And the way she looked at me, her mouth slightly open, showing off the slightest gap in the front teeth, an imperfection that to me always was just perfect. She didn't notice me at all, until I made sure she did.

"We spent our honeymoon in America, driving from coast to coast, from east to west. We drove hundreds of dusty miles each day and at night we made love in cheap motel rooms. Once out

West, we stayed in an apartment on a beach some distance from Los Angeles, where the sea ran away into the shining distance and the sun came back each day.

"Perhaps you need to know more, perhaps you don't. I shall decide. Here for now are two photographs, one taken on our honeymoon, the other of more recent vintage. And here too is my wife's car registration, her place of work, her mobile phone number and a list of her friends, as well as the details of a night class she started attending some months ago...

"Yours in quiet desperation, Will Wistow."

Rick scrolled down to the photographs. His computer made internal clicks, groaning, while waiting to display the pictures. The first showed a woman who was slim and dark, as described. She smiled at the camera and leant forward a little, showing off bare breasts brushed with sand. Stray hairs flicked across her face. She looked happy and freshly graduated from innocence, a girl who had just discovered how to be a woman.

The other photograph showed the same woman some years on, ten possibly; she was still attractive, still smiling; little about her had changed, apart from the few lines etched round her eyes.

Rick read the e-mail again and wondered what to make of it. Mostly he was struck by the difference between Wistow's speech and his written words. Where his spoken words had seemed oddly structured, the written word had pace and urgency. He pondered the difference between the two, and then put the thought away. Perhaps some people were just better at writing things down.

His mobile rang. He was half expecting Wistow, but it was Sam.

"You've not forgotten tonight?"

"Tonight? No, of course I haven't. Looking forward to it."

Rick's mind had gone blank. Naomi would have to fill in the details. He changed the subject, chatted for a minute or so. Talking had never been their strong point, but perhaps that would change.

When he found Naomi upstairs, she told him. They were going for dinner with Sam. They showered together and Rick filled in the details as Naomi soaped his back. Sam was married to Michelle, who was an English teacher, two or three years younger than Sam. She'd had an affair, they both had; hers was with another teacher at the school where she taught, his with a younger policewoman. They had two teenage daughters, Samantha, known in the family as Sam Too, and Charlotte, who was known as Lotte, pronounced 'lot' and not with the final 'e.'

"So they're a happy English family then, are they?" said Naomi, as she dried herself.

"To quote my big brother, 'It's a proper fuck up'."

"Always been the eloquent one, has he?"

"The police don't encourage eloquence, it's a long word and no-one knows what it means."

He watched her fresh nakedness, her skin glowing dark.

"Stop looking at me like that, you'll make me blush. I can blush, you know."

Rick dried and powdered his manhood, then went to get dressed, leaving a settling cloud of talcum.

SAM and Michelle had moved three times in twenty years, each move a step up. Their present house was part of a Georgian terrace off Huntington Road. From the pavement the house was only just visible at night, sitting at the end of a long garden, and it looked welcoming from this distance, the windows smudged red by drawn curtains. Lights were mounted on either side of the front door, guiding the way along the dark garden. It looked prosperous, a home for solid and happy lives; which only goes to show.

They ate in the dining room, which ran into the large, airy kitchen which, in turn, led to a conservatory. Outside the back garden retreated into darkness. There was one floor below, another two above. Rick was impressed and his heart sank an inch or two.

"Some house, this," he said, raising his glass.

"Certainly is." There was an automatic quality about Sam's reply, and about the affection he directed towards Michelle. "And we like it, don't we, love?"

Michelle smiled and said: "It takes a hell of a lot of cleaning."

"Not by you, it doesn't," said Sam. "We pay someone to do it."

"You could pay me to do it," said Sam Too.

"We did, Samantha, but it was hard to tell where the clean bits stopped and the dirty bits started," said Michelle, smiling again. Rick wondered how much these smiles were costing.

"You could pay me to mess it up," said Lotte, "and then pay Sam Too to tidy it up again."

"That's all right, Lotte," said Sam. "You mess it up for free. And then I pay a fortune for someone to come and pick up all your mess."

"Let's eat," said Michelle. She could sense that the conversation was about to roll in a certain direction, the way most of their conversations did, as if weighted for disagreement. They ate the food Michelle had cooked when she got back from school, and drank the wine Sam picked up from Oddbins, although not Sam, who stuck to beer, as always. There were two bottles open on the table for the vegetable soup, and another two for the main course, a chicken stew Michelle had spotted in one of the weekend supplements.

Naomi drank one glass before she ate anything, had another with the soup. She hoped the wine would make it easier to settle. She was sitting between the girls. Lotte, younger by two years, was wearing a black hooded sweatshirt sporting the name of a band Naomi had never heard of, and had a chain looping from her baggy jeans. Sam Too was dressed all in black: tights, short skirt, skinny, tummy-flashing T-shirt, and her hair was dark and arranged into fat spikes. Rick sat opposite, between Sam and Michelle. Naomi raised her glass and watched the brothers, Rick slim and muscular, Sam strong in a bullish, too-weighty manner. Rick still had a chin where Sam was losing his beneath too much food and alcohol.

"So how are you finding York?" said Michelle.

"Good," said Naomi, putting down her glass. "Well, you know, small and damp and full of old buildings, but good. I miss the sun and the blue skies, but we'll be happy here, won't we, Rick?"

"Sure will, love."

Rick went to reach across the table but Naomi was too far away, Sam and Michelle not being the sorts to buy a small table when a huge one would do.

Lotte put her fingers into her mouth, mock vomiting at the sugary behaviour from such crusty adults, and Sam Too sniggered. Michelle cleared away the plates and said she thought it was nice, people being affectionate.

"Was that a reference to you, Dad?" said Lotte, as Michelle moved things around in the kitchen.

"What's that?" said Sam, over the rim of his beer glass. Rick wondered if the girls would always remember their father like that, obscured by a glass.

"Just, you know, we don't see you two cuddling much or anything. I think I remember it from the past, but not so much now."

"I don't know what you mean," said Michelle, who had returned from being noisy in the kitchen, bearing a lemon tart approximately like the one Delia Smith had made on television the previous week. She put this on the table and lay her hand briefly on Sam's shoulder. Sam put down his glass so he could pat her fingers, but by the time his hand rose, hers had gone.

"I'll just do a spot of tidying up, and…"

Rick was half way through Delia's tart, and very good it was too, creamy, sweet and sharp all at once, the perfect indulgence, when that tune he didn't recognise started up again. It was a moment before he realised.

"My mobile," he said. "That'll be my mobile."

"Answer the wretched thing, then," said Sam. "It'll only go on ringing if you don't. What is that tune anyway?"

Rick shrugged as he took the call and then stood up.

"Work calling," he said. "Have you still got a bike, Sam?"

"Yeah, out back in the garage."

"Can I borrow it?"

THINGS they don't tell you about York: the smells. There are three to sample, at least. Chocolate and mint from the factory still known as Rowntree's, even though it had long been sucked into a conglomerate. Then there is the lingering burnt smell that rises from the sugar factory when the beet is being cooked. Finally, there is what has sometimes been referred to as "the pong." This last stench rises from somewhere unexplained and can be experienced in various parts of the city, usually during hot spells, and suggests to the nose that the drains have turned vengeful.

Tonight, as Rick rode along the dark alley at the back of his brother's house, bumping through the puddled ruts, he caught the burnt sugar. This insidious sweetness got everywhere at this time of year.

He cut along an alley, passing between tall-sided houses. Soon, he was whizzing round the Minster. A couple of minutes later, he rode above the river Ouse then dismounted to lock his brother's bike outside the pub. He pushed through the throng of beards, bellies and pints. At the bar, he chose a pint from the bafflingly long list. The beer was properly bitter and Rick sipped appreciatively while he scanned the drinkers. Some people looked as though they had popped in on the way home from work and hadn't managed to leave. Ties were askew, suits crumpled. A party of young women, not much more than girls, laughed raucously.

Then Rick spotted Wendy Wistow. She looked close enough to the picture which had been e-mailed to him – not the topless one, the memory of which caused him a certain guilty erotic agitation. Rick found an empty spot a few feet away and hid behind his glass. Glancing over the rim, he watched Wendy, who was darkly attractive, with shoulder-touching hair and a lively face. Her companion, who wore a black leather jacket, looked older, ten years perhaps. They were animated and seemed oblivious to those around, wrapped in a conversation that Rick imagined was heading somewhere warm and illicit.

He wondered if becoming a private eye would turn him into some sort of a moralist, a hired hand in the ethics game, called on to calibrate the graduations of right and wrong, dealing with greys and uncertainties. He decided not to enter into that particular moral maze and instead went to the gents. He propped himself up at the urinal, reading the front and back pages of the Evening Press, kindly displayed by eager bar staff: someone had died in a car crash and York City had lost again.

By the time he came out, Wendy and her man had gone. Cursing his treacherous bladder, Rick pushed round the tables and the bellies, squeezed by two men with beards who were ticking beers off on a list in a notebook, and went outside. He couldn't see them anywhere.

"Has someone just come out, an attractive, dark-haired woman with a man in a leather jacket?" he asked the bouncer.

"Not my job to help nosy buggers."

The bouncer was tall, wide and immovable. The stubble on his head joined seamlessly with that on his chin. His mouth, when not grunting, was untroubled by laughter.

"No, you don't understand, I'm a private detective, and…"

"Not my job to help professional nosy buggers."

Rick had no choice but to unlock his brother's bike as the door-blocker stood a few feet away, casting a menacing shadow. He cycled around in the gloom, but Wendy Wistow and her man were nowhere to be seen.

CHAPTER NINE

RICK began to know Wendy from an intimate distance. He was her shadow, paid to follow her, yet insubstantial, a two-dimensional creature, a thing of corners and the dark side of trees where dogs had pissed. He felt a connection to the woman he followed as if he were beginning to know her. He waited outside pubs, scuffed around near restaurants, drank too much fizzy bottled beer in the bar at the Theatre Royal, and trailed her to the terraced house overlooking Knavesmire. It was a house like all the others, except that it contained a man unhappy enough to hire a private detective to monitor his straying wife. Often there was still a light on when Wendy returned late, while a cruel wind whipped across the racecourse and flung itself at the house. Rick would hear the windows rattle as he scurried in the shadows or flitted between parked cars. At such moments he felt cold and alone, but he kept going. It was his only job and the money came, along with the e-mails.

"It is my belief," ran the latest electronic instruction, "that she and the man are going to see that Harry Potter film this evening. Wendy had expressed an interest in this entertainment but I said I had no desire to see a film for children. When I said that, I knew she would go with the man instead."

Wistow always referred to his wife's lover as "the man." Rick had supplied a name, Malcolm Hunt, and a profession, teacher of history, yet Wistow stuck to "the man." Perhaps he preferred the anonymity or simply could not face using the name. This job was not doing Rick's social life any favours. He had promised Naomi a night in, a bottle of wine, a video and then early to bed. Rick played his own inner video, seeing Naomi undressing, exposing her slim, strong sexuality. Then came another image: Naomi all sour and pissed off when he left her alone with the wine and the video. She hadn't answered his farewell, hadn't looked up.

Rick had gone without words and, five minutes later, arrived outside the City Screen cinema. It was cold, a busker was committing crimes against music with a guitar, and gangs of loud young people stole all the available space. He stood in the queue, a little back so he wouldn't be noticed. He let a family of five go in front, Mum, Dad and three excited children. A warm glow of magnanimity suffused Rick's cynical bones, but it soon went cold again.

"We're sold out."

The woman on the counter was young, a few inches short of beautiful and perfectly bored with the exquisite blankness of one without too many years on her face.

"We're sold out," she said again, looking over Rick's shoulder as if in search of a more illuminating sight. He wondered if something more interesting was happening behind his back.

"They've just got in," he said, pointing to the family of five.

"Got the last tickets, didn't they."

Outside the busker was playing an approximate version of 'While My Guitar Gently Weeps.' Rick said: "I'm surprised it's not weeping bloody buckets, mate." He went over the road for an over-priced bucket of cappuccino in one of the ubiquitous coffee shops. He sat in a window seat, staring across at the cinema. He drank his coffee, sullenly ordered another. People streamed along the street, heading for the loud modern bars. He was awash with coffee. If he drank any more, the staff with the fixed tired smiles would have to pull him off the ceiling.

As he left, Rick remembered that the coffee bar used to be a bank that became a trendy clothes shop. And the cinema over the road used to be a newspaper printers. Many things in York used to be something else.

"Hell," he muttered to himself, "I used to be a policeman, now I'm hanging about in York at night following a woman who's shagging a history teacher."

Back home, he let himself in and ran upstairs, hoping to salvage something from the evening. In the lounge a solitary lamp cast a small pool of light on the floor. The curtains were open and the Minster was lit against the sky, history illuminated for all around to see. The video, the latest Coen Brothers' film, was in its box; the cork was in the wine; and a sleeping bag lay on the sofa. Rick looked at his watch: it was nine o'clock. He went up to the bedroom. Naomi was asleep, shrouded in resentment, or so he imagined. He left her to it and went downstairs. He opened the wine, a decent red, took a sip and let his tongue absorb the dark flavour. A good bottle, but it didn't taste right tonight so he shoved the cork back and sat in the puddle of light, resenting the silence. He yawned and considered the penitent's sleeping bag, but he still had a job to do.

The cinema was emptying. The busker had gone and taken his weeping guitar with him. The loud young men flowed by, while young women shrieked in gangs, exposing legs, stomachs and cleavages. The current of excitement wasn't electrifying Rick. He lurked as the cinema flushed out its audience. Eventually he saw them, holding hands amid the parents and children. It was ten thirty and most of the children looked pale.

Wendy and Malcolm Hunt walked along Coney Street, and turned over Ouse Bridge. Music from the two bars by the bridge filled the night air and young drinkers swerved across the street. The Ouse flowed by dark and unseen, swelling and rising, as forgotten as the past.

Rick hung back, keeping the couple in sight. He shivered as he crossed the Ouse, reminded how a river wind can cut. Soon he was following the couple up Micklegate, a fine and steep Georgian street by day, a place of alcoholic cacophony at night. Rick puffed a little as he encountered one York's few hills.

He trailed in the dark, stepping into doorways when they stopped. As they stopped to look in the window of a shop selling second-hand CDs, Rick ducked into a side street by a sandwich shop. He found he had company of the sort you didn't want on a dark night halfway up Micklegate, a young man wearing a tight white T-shirt over a gym-honed body was swaying in the gloom pissing against a venerable wall. The muscle-clad youth turned round, saying:

"Want to look at my dick, you pervy wanker?"

Rick declined and left quickly. He heard the man zip up his jeans, saw almost too late the gaggle of pastel-shirted mates. His heart beat faster as walked away. The young man came after him, fists dangling. Then fate, in the shape of too much beer consumed too quickly, intervened. The man vomited over the ancient cobblestones. His friends laughed and left him to it.

Rick nearly ran into Wendy, but swerved at the last minute, muttered an apology and carried on through Micklegate Bar. He crossed over and hid in the shadows of the Odeon, waiting for his prey. The traffic flowed and an ambulance went by, sirens blaring, lights flashing. Someone was having a bad night; someone usually was.

Away from the busy road, it was dark and quiet. For a few hundred yards houses or flats lined one side of the road, a high old wall the other. The houses petered out, giving way to allotments and the open spaces of Knavesmire.

On race days this place rippled with excitement. On a cold winter night, it was bleak and barren. The wind whipped direct from Siberia, or so it seemed to Rick as he crouched behind a car while invisible needles pierced his clothes. As the couple neared the house, he scuttled into steps that led to Knavesmire. They were outside the house, still holding hands. A light on inside indicated Wistow was waiting up. Rick wondered at the man's mentality, at the way he could play along with his wife's infidelity, letting her go out while knowing exactly where she went and what she got up to. Why would a man do that? If it were Rick, he would want to hit someone, and probably would.

They were kissing now, in full sight of the window. They were not hiding anything and this puzzled Rick. He was even more perplexed a moment later when Hunt followed her into the house.

Rick stood as straight as he could manage after crouching on the cold steps. The wind threw another bucket of cold nails at him as he began the long trudge home. He was cold, tired and pissed off. It was time to buy a bike. There was no way he was going to spend another night walking. Such was his last thought as he wriggled into the sleeping bag in the lounge. On the floor above him, Naomi slept alone. In the morning she would wake and wonder why Rick wasn't there, and then she would remember. She would recall this separation again all too soon, and she would reverently wish they had never had that argument.

CHAPTER TEN

The Smell of Poverty, An Essay

The annotations are those of the teacher.

YORK in 1901 was a city in which so much poverty existed. York at the beginning of the 20th Century was not the city we see today, but a place in which people lived in grinding poverty, their lives as grim as grim can be. Such grimness is hard for us to imagine.

Don't overdo the grimness, or else you will risk falling into a "grim up North" parody...

Many people in the city's slums shared the most basic of amenities. Indeed it is possible to say poverty had a smell. Today the lavatory is a private place, perhaps somewhere for quiet contemplation while doing what has to be done.

We all know what goes in a lavatory, then and now.

Many of the poorer sort of house had to share water closets or midden-privies. As many as nine or ten houses, and all the probably unwashed people therein, could be forced to share the one privy. As you can imagine, the general stink of rotten humanity from such a shared amenity must have been quite horrendous.

Do not overdo it, and the 'probably unwashed' is your own comment: stick to the known facts without adding your own emotional baggage.

Anyone wishing to discover some idea of how basic life was need look no further than the extracts from an investigator working for Seebohm B. Rowntree...

It's B. Seebohm Rowntree, as in Benjamin...

...in his famous field study, 'Poverty, A Study Of Town Life.' One place of mass dwelling in particular deserves mention. This is described plainly in the notes as "courtyard"..."Entered by passage four feet and nine inches wide. Yard partially cobbled. Six houses join at one tap and one water-closet. Five of these are back-to-back houses, and the sixth is built back-to-back with a slaughter-house. This slaughter-house (which has a stable connected with it) has a block of houses adjoining another of its sides and the front of the building is separated from a row of houses by a street only sixteen feet wide..."

As you can see from such descriptions, life in York in 1901 was both compressed and cheap...

You are preaching your own sermon here again...this is an academic essay, not a ranting newspaper column.

...and people were forced to live on top of each other, with no space to turn, no openness anywhere at all. It might seem unhealthy to dwell on the literally lavatorial, but there is much to learn from the privations our ancestors suffered in their privy...

Yuck!...

Much can be learned from this most elementary branch of history. The shared toilets, or midden-privies, were of the most basic kind, relying on containing the sewage in a brick-lined pit. Even when these privies were cleaned, they were unsatisfactory in terms of public health and sanitation. However, an un-cleansed midden privy was obviously an even greater threat to the general well being. Until January 1901, the corporation charged one shilling, or thereabouts, to clear an ashpit or midden-privy, giving, as Seebohm Rowntree put it in admirably under-stated style, "the householder a strong inducement to allow refuse to accumulate for as long a time as possible."

Good use of quotation...but do try to be as admirably under-stated as Mr Rowntree...

These communal facilities were, to borrow again from Mr Rowntree, "particularly offensive in these over-populated and under-ventilated districts." Very many of these privies were "more or less foul or leaking, with uncemented walls and floors, in not a few instances with dilapidated walls, most of them permitting of the pollution of the adjacent soil. The cementing of the walls and floors with many of the privies is insufficient to prevent pollution of the soil, as it is often cracked and so permits soakage; a large number of them are found inches deep in liquid filth, or so full of refuse as to reach above the cemented portions of the walls."

For us today, with even the most basic of accommodation offering a flushed lavatory connected to the main sewers, it is almost impossible to imagine the stench that must have arisen when these too-full pits were emptied of their foulness. Even the unperturbed midden…

Do you mean undisturbed…?

…must have stank to high heaven every hour of the day.

It is worth noting that many of these stinking privies were only separated from the pantry by the thickness of one brick. It is possibly because of such insanitary arrangements that planning controls today stipulate that a lavatory cannot be built next to a kitchen, without a separating corridor…

Possibly is a dangerous word…why not find out if this is indeed the case and then weave this information into the fabric of your historical narrative?

Not all houses dwelt in by the poor were as bad as those described here, but life was grim for many of the populace. From the safety of a century away, it can be seen that our lives are in many ways much improved, certainly in respect to sanitation and the general cleanliness we expect today. However, privations – and the horrible privies, the "privy privations" if you prefer –

I don't, thank you…

…have been replaced by other, more modern difficulties. The stress of poverty in Victorian York must have been beyond our imagining, and yet we have created our own stresses, from ceaselessly ringing mobile phones to satellite television channels showing so much of so little worth. Where the poor in York used to struggle by on what they could, eating meagre meals in damp, crumbling houses, the relatively affluent in today's city want for nothing except a better sense of meaning to their life. The lack of a higher purpose has, many would say, blighted the great advances history has organised for us.

You clearly feel passionately about this, which is admirable.

Passion, however, can get in the way of historical research. You are finding out much that is interesting. Do not spoil good history with bouts of personal sermonising.

In an attempt to illustrate my points, I intend to develop my thesis by looking at the case of one poor family in York, visited by death solely because of poverty, poor sanitation and the ill luck to be born into a life without prospect of improvement. This story is a shocking indictment of the way Britain used to treat its poor.

Sermonising again but it seems that you are taking your story into interesting territory, although you should be wary of making broad, sweeping generalisations from a singular story. However, good luck on your journey back in time!

RICK Rounder in the gents at the pub by Lendal Bridge. The front and back pages of the Evening Press were placed behind glass above the urinals. The front page contained the latest news, or lack of news, about the disappearance of Polly Markham; and a young dancer from York, who had won a place at college, had been photographed in celebration, legs kicking high. On the back, miraculously, York City had won, just about.

Rick was putting on weight. Doing this job was sabotaging his routines. He was spending too much time in pubs, drinking beer while he watched other lives unfold. He tried to think of this grandly, casting himself as a people-watcher, a sociologist cataloguing the wriggling mass of humanity, ticking off their foibles, charting their oddities. In truth, he was spying on an adulterous couple. What sort of a way was that for a man to spend his life?

At least Malcolm and Wendy chose pubs that sold good beer, hence the layer being added to his stomach. There hadn't been a hint of a belly in Australia. God, he panicked, I'll end up like my brother. And then he thought of Naomi. At first she had liked the beer on his breath, then it came to signify betrayal: she resented Rick's new job because it was too disruptive.

"I never know whether or not you're going to be here," she had said earlier. "You come and go without notice, or you hang around when I'm not here and then shoot out as soon as I get home. A sensitive woman might think you were trying to avoid her."

"That's stupid – I brought you half way round the world, so I'm hardly likely to want to avoid you. I'm just doing my job. It's not a nine to fiver, like yours."

Naomi had started working at a call centre that handled insurance for credit cards, a place that advertised itself as being a business "For people who like people."

"I think my job should carry the slogan: 'For people who hate people!'" Rick had said. He had laughed; Naomi hadn't. She had smiled a smile that didn't last. He had resolved to sort everything out, later, when he had the time, and was frustrated that he still hadn't.

Rick went back to the bar and ordered another pint. The beer, which was brewed locally, came with a decent head that dribbled down the tall glass. He sipped and looked across at Wendy and Malcolm. Wendy and Malcolm – hell, he was thinking of them as a couple, as people he knew, friends perhaps. *We had Wendy and Malcolm over for lunch the other Sunday. Lovely couple...*

Wendy Wistow was a straying woman and Malcolm Hunt her partner in a lustful wander. Their infidelity was his business because he was being paid to watch. Rick didn't fully understand the job, and he couldn't work out why Wendy and Hunt had gone into her house when her husband was there. But the money kept coming, as did the e-mails telling him where she would be.

Rick glanced over the top of his pint. Wendy and Malcolm were sharing an easy intimacy. He was reading to her from sheets of paper. He put amusing emphasis into his recitation, pulling faces to match his words, a mock-serious face, a look of almost comic intensity, his forehead creased into a frown that went as he laughed heartily. He pointed to something on the paper and they both laughed. He had a pen in his hand and he wrote while he spoke.

Rick drank his beer for a moment, then looked up again. Hell, they were going already. He managed another hurried mouthful as

Malcolm Hunt put into his battered leather briefcase whatever it was he had been holding, and left with an arm gently resting on Wendy's back.

Rick left the pub without realising he had not been alone in watching the lovers. Someone else had been observing from a distance, perched at the end of a bench in the small front bar, taking everything in, reading the situation. It was possible to read anything into anything, if you wanted to. All a person had to do was watch and unleash their dark imaginings.

As Rick unlocked his new bike, his fellow observer also left the pub, slipping unnoticed through the arch under Lendal Bridge. He went up the cold stone steps on the other side and crossed the bridge as the lights of a city enjoying itself at night were splashed across the Ouse. Passing between the night crowds, he eventually came to a busy junction near where another river, the Foss, emerged from beneath a road. Then he was gone from view, lost in the shadows of the past. It took him a while to find where he had put the girl, and a moment or two longer to prise open the hatch and slip from view.

RICK pulled on a woolly hat, mounted his bicycle and took a short cut to the top of Micklegate. He remembered the Micklegate run, the beer and the girls. Mostly just beer and looking at girls, but occasionally he had struck lucky. Sam met Michelle on one of their nights out. So Sam had got lucky too, only it didn't look that way any more.

He cycled beneath the Bar walls, looking for other dark places. He skimmed the shadows thrown by walls and trees, switching off his lights so he could be absorbed into darkness. This was a dangerous tactic in York, a city where many of the locals were remarkably hostile to cyclists who shunned illumination. It could only be so long before someone suggested, possibly in a letter to the local rag, that unlit cyclists should be decapitated and have their cleaved heads displayed on Micklegate Bar.

He glanced about, then glided across the road, entering the

darkness again. He waited above the allotments, braced for the wind off Knavesmire. He was near the house and they were coming, he could see them, shapes taking form. A car was slowly mounting the speed-bumps, its headlights rising to dazzle Rick. As he put his hand in front of his eyes, his mobile phone pierced the night.

"Yes?"

"Ah, Rounder…Will Wistow here, your employer, as it were."

"I know who you are and no-one is my employer. Client yes, employer no. But why are you ringing me now? I'm standing outside your house and they're coming, your wife and…the man."

"I know where they are and I know where you are. Look up."

Wistow was in the front window of his house.

"Why don't you come up for a drink? You must be a bit cold out there and it looks like rain."

As if on cue, a large drop hit Rick on the nose. Fat tears spotted the pavement and the wind whipped the rain into his face.

"What the hell are you talking about? I'm meant to be watching, how can I do that if they see me? I'm meant to be a private investigator, not a public one."

"Oh, don't carry on so. Come in and I'll explain everything and you'll still be working so I'll still pay you. How's that for a bargain? You can drink my lovely malt whisky and be remunerated at the same time. Sounds like a win-win situation to me. Stay there, I'll be down in a minute."

Rick stood next to his bike, feeling foolish and vaguely alarmed. Was there anything to be nervous about? He could go now, before they saw him. Wendy and Malcolm stopped, kissed and then went into the house. The door shut and, a moment later, it opened again, once more throwing light into the street. Rick pushed his bike into the small front garden, locked it, and went up the steps and to the hall. He knew houses from his police days, and could quickly determine the types; the posh houses, the dumps; the calm houses, the frayed houses. This house suggested hush and comfort. The hall floor, which would once have been tiled, was covered in gently sprung wood that absorbed the tension of the outside world. There were original paintings on the walls, lit by small spotlights. A long mirror created depth and flipped the paintings. A clock ticked somewhere, a mechanical sigh measuring out the hours. Ten thirty. Naomi would be going to bed, curling up in resentment, hating him and hating York, wishing herself back to a sunny place.

"Come in, come in," said Wistow. "It would oblige me if you took off your coat and let me put a glass in your hand."

Over Wistow's shoulder Rick could see a long room dappled by clever lighting.

"Whatever you wish," said Rick, not knowing what else to say. He followed his host into the room and saw a cabinet filled with bottles of malt whisky. The bottles were ranked on a glass shelf illuminated from below. Notes posted on each label were covered with neat hand-written notes.

Wistow asked Rick to choose a malt, which he did, blindly.

"Cheers. Ah, I see you have noticed my game, a hobby you might call it. I make my own tasting notes, you see, and then stick them to the bottle, so that I can catalogue everything I have drunk. The tongue is such a special organ, don't you think? A fleshy piece of muscle, that's all it is – and yet so versatile. It can be used to taste, for giving and receiving pleasure, for licking and swallowing, to facilitating eating and for the articulation of speech. We would not get far without our tongues, Mr Rounder. Would you not agree with that sentiment?"

"Don't see any reason not to."

Rick sipped the chosen malt, a subtle lowland variety.

"Liquorice," he said, swirling the liquid uncertainly. "At least that's what this tongue finds."

"This well-practised organ," said Wistow, sticking out the tip of his tongue, "uncovers, yes, a hint of liquorice, along with the initial sherried sweetness, a touch of heather and honey, followed by a suggestion of smoke. Mind you, if you'd gone for the 21-year-old instead of the ten, a new array of taste sensations would have greeted your fleshy organ. A hint of musk before the oaky, toasty flavours come through, with malty, smoky, creamy notes and a silken touch of barley…"

"I'm surprised you ever fit that much on one of those little stick-on labels."

"Oh, the pleasures of writing small, Mr Rounder. And the smallness of pleasure."

Wistow was leading Rick by his sleeve and he tried to jerk away the unwanted embrace.

"Politeness, Mr Rounder, that's the thing. Now, of course, we could have gone further north, all the way up to Islay. What pleasures are to be found up there! Laphroaig, with its initial TCP aroma, which gives way to the smoky air of bonfires, then goes on to salty, seaweedy seaspray tastes, with hints of citrus and vanilla and…"

"This one's fine," said Rick, sipping and noticing how the viscous liquid clung to the glass on the way down. He sat on a leather sofa, which was soft and accommodating, and not at all hard as he had anticipated. The room spoke of comfort and detachment, with polished wood floors, thick, expensive rugs, and subtle splashes of light on the pale blue walls. A tiled fireplace contained dying embers that gave off the warm glow of collapse. Hardback books filled the alcoves on either side of the fireplace. Wooden shutters covered the window. Music came from somewhere, an opera of some sort. Rick knew little about opera except that he didn't like it.

"I suppose you are wondering…"

"Too bloody right, mate. This is too odd by half."

"Tongues, tongues," said Wistow. "Accents come off the tongue too, of course. How strange that in a York private investigator I should discover a hint of Australia, the way the sentence lifts at the end, jumping up like a springboard and with a little lithe twang…"

"York born and mostly bred," said Rick. "But I went away and I ended up in Australia for a few years. My girlfriend's Australian and…"

Why the hell was he saying all this? Rick glowered into his

empty glass, then looked up again. Wistow was sitting next to him on the gently creased leather sofa.

"As I said, before we became so pleasantly distracted, you will be wondering. Well, I admit, it may seem odd. But you see, I wasn't seeking evidence so much as corroboration. I know what that woman does. Well, she tells me, so why wouldn't I?

"We have an open marriage where otherwise it would be shut, finished. It is an arrangement that suits us both very well. She has her, her *enthusiasms*, and I have mine. So far as I know, she does not decorate hers with Post-It notes indicating their relative merits."

Wistow laughed at his little joke in a manner that struck Rick as affected and creepy. The wretched man spoke like a prissy teacher or a strict father affecting to be an indulgent one.

"So does this mean that you've proved what you set out to prove and we can settle our account?"

"Oh, Mr Rounder, if only life were that simple."

"What the hell does that mean?"

"Oh, I sense a certain irritation, and I suppose that is fair enough. You feel that I have been playing games with you, perhaps?"

"It's your game to play, so long as you pay me."

"Ah, yes. Well, I have and I will continue to do so."

"So what exactly do you want me to do now?"

"Oh, maybe more of the same, maybe something a little different. A fresh challenge, perhaps. That would be invigorating, yes?"

He reached out and put his hand on Rick's knee. Rick looked down and removed the hand. It was a soft hand, unpleasantly so, the softness of suspicion. Maybe he was just being stupid. After all, if this weirdo wanted to pay him to spy on his wandering wife, that was his own business.

"I need to be going," said Rick, standing up to leave, but feeling the pressure of his bladder. "May I use your toilet first?"

"You will find the lavatory at the top of the stairs, three steps to the left, then straight ahead."

Rick felt woozy after the beer in the pub and a generous glass of malt. He went slowly up the stairs, noticing the brass runners restraining a narrow strip of carpet. The bathroom was a symphony of black and white, with the gold of the taps being the only concession. He lifted the chequered toilet seat. As he relieved himself, he glanced about at the black and white tiles on the floor, laid diamond style, and the smaller mosaic tiles on the wall. It was all very tasteful but he felt like a piece on a chessboard.

As he turned to leave, Wendy Wistow came into the bathroom.

"Oh, sorry, I didn't realise Will had company."

"He doesn't for much longer."

Rick faced the woman he had been watching so intently. Would she recognise him? He had followed her all over York but he had never seen her so close. She was wearing a blue silk kimono, tied tightly at her trim waist. As far as he could tell, she was wearing nothing underneath. He sensed her nakedness and felt a confusion of desire. She stood in the doorway and smiled at him. He squeezed past and she didn't move an inch. Her presence was tantalising. Then she was gone, hidden behind the bathroom door.

Rick was surprised by his erection. Perhaps the surprise would have been if this hadn't happened. He hesitated a moment, arranging himself as comfortably as possible, and while he waited for subsidence, he looked along the landing. There were two doors off, presumably leading to bedrooms, one on the right and the other straight-ahead. The bedroom at the front of the house would have looked across Knavesmire. A third door led upstairs to another floor. Light came down the stairs.

Rick heard the flush and then the taps. He went downstairs as quickly as he could manage.

Wistow was on the leather sofa, his soft hand clasped round a generously wetted glass.

"Ah, Mr Rounder. Here you are again."

"Not for long. It's late, I'm knackered and I want to go home."

"Fair enough. I'll send you a fresh cheque in the morning. And there will be another e-mail along soon. So our association hasn't ended yet."

Rick wanted to say it had, but couldn't turn down his only case. So he smiled tiredly and left, putting faith in the sobering effects of the cold night air.

The flat was quiet. The second floor curtains were open to the ghost of the Minster. Rick went up another floor, undressed and climbed into bed where he lay naked and troubled next to the woman who had inspired in him love, lust and life. Naomi slept soundly, snoring faintly. Rick curled over. The last moments of wakefulness found him clutching his unspent erection as Wendy shed her blue kimono. His final thought, before sleep claimed him, was how can she ever have wanted to sleep with Will Wistow – what has her firm sexuality got to do with his sly softness?

Rick was soon asleep. If he had stayed awake a little longer, if he had not been distracted by sexual allure, perhaps he might have spotted what was coming.

Chapter Eleven

THOMAS Percy had a large family but little love. The evidence of so many children suggested congress in the past, or at least some sort of contact, although Martha could remember little pleasure from him. These days they lived in cold proximity, haunting the same damp rooms, surrounded by the children they had brought into the world, but no longer did anything in unison. Thomas was a labourer who rarely laboured; and a drunk without the means to buy the beer he craved. His life was defined by alcohol, the getting and drinking of it, and the smell of beer lingered about him in a sour haze. Thomas was guarded against his own aromas by the rough cigarettes he smoked, which cloaked him in a tobacco stench.

Eight children could be seen as a blessing or a curse, and Thomas inclined to the latter. He saw his children as a barrier to a successful life. The boys and girls he had filled with blood and padded with flesh amounted only to impediments.

On this late Autumn day in 1901, he had no work and funds sufficient only for later, when the beer house would be full, and where the entertainment to be had might include the getting of more beer than he could afford. There were means other than having the ready money. He knew how to leech beer out of the thin air, or so he liked to boast. Sometimes, he illustrated this accomplishment to his companions by extending a dirty, nicotine-smudged hand to squeeze at imaginary udders and then opening his stub-toothed mouth and going into a pantomime of swallowing. He would then subside into a cacophony of coughs and phlegm-coated rattles.

"Thin bloody air," he would say. "Beer out of thin bloody air. It is a miracle, I tell you lads, a bleeding miracle."

But not yet. He could sit here, in the chair by the range, and such lazy warmth held a strong attraction. Yet she would nag and harry if he stayed. This left perambulation as an alternative and a walk would be good. Besides, he should be meeting the man soon enough. He levered himself from the chair, found a walking stick that had come his way in the beer house, and put on his battered hat. As he crossed the compacted earth of the communal yard, he saw his wife and tried to avoid her gaze. Martha put out a thin hand and halted her husband. He could have pushed her aside but there was power within that frail woman, and besides he did not wish to appear short-tempered, at least, not out here where everyone could see.

"If you are going for one of those walks, you could take the little one with you," said Martha. "I found her playing with that blood again. It's not healthy for a young girl is all that blood. I have told her before but she will be back. Drawn to it, she is. Do not ask me why for I will not have an answer ready."

This amounted to a rare exchange of information, or it would have done if Thomas had contributed more than a grunt.

"She is outside the gate, leaning her back against the wall."

Thomas paused as his wife disappeared into their portion of the big damp tenement. He could go his own way and forget the girl, for it would be easily done. He had the argument laid out in his mind: nowt but a scrap, a twist of a girl, and she could do nothing if he chose to ignore her and went off alone, as a man had every right to do.

She was outside the yard, her bird-boned hand outstretched. Thomas saw the connection. "You have seen your mother do that."

"Ma says I have to come with you on that walk of yours."

"Walk then, girl – and do not be mithering me with your conversation. The mouths of little girls produce a lot of unwholesome noise."

A stranger may have spied tenderness in the scene as father and daughter stepped over the moss-cushioned stones. At least, this person may have done if they had been standing a little behind. From this kindly perspective, Thomas and his youngest daughter Esme could be seen only in outline. He with his purloined walking stick, misshapen hat, tattered trousers and mud-decorated boots; she with her much-owned woollen coat, scuffed shoes and the long dress trailing in the dirt; a happy interlude, father and daughter out for a walk. From the front this assumption would be seen for what it was: Thomas had set his features into a scowl and Esme was silent, her face pale beneath the alley dirt.

They gradually left the crowded houses and dark streets. Esme took refuge in what she saw. She looked in the windows at the goods piled high, the groceries in one window, the material in another, then the household goods, with all manner of tools, implements and fluids for cleaning. Horses clopped by pulling carriages and occasionally decorated the road with great steaming scoops of shit. Soon they walked past the end of the market, and she looked up at the ironmongers, its awning jutting above the wide pavement. A horse and carriage was pulled up outside the ironmongers, parcels and packages piled high on the roof. Esme thought about where those parcels would end up and who had sent them. Then, as they crossed the bottom of the market on Parliament Street, she looked along the wide thoroughfare in anticipation. She desperately wanted to go between the stalls, to take in the smells and noises, to absorb the colours, to look up at all the faces, to hear the shouts of the stallholders, to be lost in it all. She stopped, sensing the edge of wonder, but her father closed stiff, hard fingers about the frayed sleeve of her coat and found the arm within.

"We are not tarrying here," he said, stooping to engulf her with used beer and spent tobacco. "Not tarrying here, girl."

He pulled her away from the market with its friendly sounds and warmth, propelling her past the church, where other carts were parked. Her arm hurt but gradually the pain dulled. She knew this happened with pain, the small hurts and the larger ones; but she did not yet understand fully the way something remained from each pain, some trace of hurt stayed and waited in layers.

"We will walk the long way round," said Thomas, relenting. "The walk will do me good, clear my head and let me forget my luck."

Esme forget her arm as she wandered between the stalls, looking up at all the glories on offer. Sights came her way in half-understood flashes. A man with a big moustache and stubble-rough cheeks smiled down, while his hands clasped his stomach; all around him were piles of fruit, apples and oranges laid in rows and pyramids. At another stall chestnuts were roasting, sweet smoke rising from their black skins. She did not see much more because her father became agitated again, glancing at his stolen pocket watch.

They reached St Helen's Square, where there was much to see. As her father hurried her along, Esme glanced at the window of W. Robinson and Sons, a tailors and outfitters that promised "hats and hosiery by the Best London Makers."

Her eyes were quickly drawn to Terrys, caterers and confectioners, with the promise of chocolates, bon-bons, boiled sweets, nougat de Montelimart, walnut toffee, boiled sugars and peppermint creams. Fancy cakes, pastry and biscuits were advertised, alongside luncheon, dinners and afternoon teas. Esme stared through the painted glass to pink people whose skin was stretched with pleasure to accommodate what they ate now and had eaten before.

He father swiped at her head and pulled her coat.

"Come on, girl. Why did I agree to this diversion?"

In Coney Street, they wove between the crowds, stepping aside for the traffic, and passing Inglis the goldsmith and watchmakers, which advertised "the Ivanhoe watch in 20 different styles". Nearby was Madame Snarry, court milliner and dressmaker. Then a chemist which proclaimed the benefits of Owbridges Lung Tonic, for "coughs, colds, asthma, bronchitis, whooping cough and hoarseness", and Seekamps Lozenges – "For Heartburn, Indigestion, Bilious Afflictions, Flatulence."

Merritt and Co, bootmakers, advertised "boots and shoes for tired feet and enlarged joints," while promising that "abnormal and deformed feet receive special care."

Both now tired of feet themselves, they dropped towards the River Ouse. The river was wide and powerful, a sweeping force beyond anything Esme knew, the water deep and fast and terrible. They joined the crowded quayside, where barges were moored, waiting to dispense their goods or accept other wares, or steamers made ready for the trip to Selby and Hull.

Esme felt in awe of the huge barges and the men who hauled cargoes in and out of the bellies of the mammoth craft. She did not understand the work men did, because she had seen little evidence of it. Her mother worked hard, like most of the women. She always looked tired, even when she woke in the morning. Sleep did not make any difference to women who were mothers; tiredness was written in their faces. The men who worked the quayside had tired faces too, but they were strong men with arms pulled and lifted, arms that made things happen. Her father was strong, horribly strong sometimes; but his arms were not trunk-thick like those of the men here. He was enormous to her but looked small alongside the barge men. This revelation of him as smaller and less powerful made her feel good in a way she did not understand.

Thomas squatted and brought his darting eyes level. He did not look at her properly, because his eyes were flashing from side to side, seeking someone or something else. He told her to walk away and wait, and not to be spying. He turned, took a few steps and stood still, swinging his walking stick in a manner he thought dashing. The sun scattered light across the river as a rowing boat glided by. The light danced and the water looked benign, pleasant, somewhere to escape, until clouds swallowed the sun and the river again flowed without decoration.

Esme then saw the other man. At first, he looked much like the men who went into the beerhouses, but Esme noticed this man was different in ways she could recognise: his coat was cleaner, his boots shone, something sparkled on a finger. He appeared prosperous and yet his face was thin and punctured with bristles. The sparkled hand came up to his shadowed face, two of its fingers closed round a cigar stub. He put the remnant in his mouth and sucked on it so that his cheeks went inwards. The end of the cigar glowed red. He coughed as smoke escaped from his nose and mouth. She could not hear what was being said, only the sounds the words made. The man stepped closer to her father.

The stranger laughed and her father laughed too, making a harsh, rattling sound. Both men were laughing but neither seemed to be amused. Esme wondered at the way laughter could mean different things. Men like her father were always laughing when nothing was funny.

Something was being passed, a package perhaps, but it was only visible for a moment, leaving one dark coat pocket for another. The stranger patted her father on the back. Her father started, as if in pain, then he laughed, emitting the empty sound again. The other man walked off and her father beckoned. Esme looked into eyes that blazed with ill temper.

"You have been spying on me, girl – despite what I said. What sort of a way is that for a girl to behave towards her father? You will find yourself in trouble."

"I have not been spying. Just looking, seeing with my eyes."

Thomas pulled her towards the river. He smiled as he did this, hiding the harm in his heart. Those who walked by or rode on New Ebor bicycles appeared not to notice.

Once more, a stranger glimpsing father and daughter might have supposed they were privy to a tender moment, as a man showed his child the beauty of the great river, pointing out the fleeting patterns made by the sun, or the birds dipping in and out of the water. Yet Thomas had set his face to stone and Esme looked like a snagged creature.

"You will do well to mind your own business, girl," he whispered. Esme knew to be wary of her father, to gauge his moods, to test his temper. Most of the time she was not scared. Like her siblings, she had learnt to keep a few paces off, out of reach.

"You will not be telling a soul about this." His voice was low, his hand still gripped. "You will not tell your mother, or any of those brothers and sisters of yours. You will not tell anyone. By the grace of God, you had better listen to me. Are you clear about that?"

A rowing boat skimmed the river as Esme nodded. She accepted what her father said while not knowing what he meant. She bobbed her head again, thinking this would win her freedom. Yet her father kept her in his grip and took a step closer to the water.

"It is a broad and evil river, the Ouse. A girl who fell in there would be washed right away, all the way to America, I should not wonder."

He pulled her to the edge and her toes projected into air. Another step and she would be gone, swept away.

"Not a word to anyone. I shall not say a word."

Her voice sounded strange and far away, like something overheard in another room. She could not even be certain she had spoken, but words must have forced their way out of her tight, sore throat because her father nodded.

"That is understood, girl. That meeting, the one you did not see, should do me some good. And you may well be able to help me in procuring that good."

Thomas turned his daughter round, released his clasp and rested a fatherly arm on her thin shoulders. He smiled broadly, showing his bad teeth to anyone who cared to look, not that many would. No-one had noticed and the moment was left hidden. They walked towards the old prison. The castle walls could be glimpsed behind the prison wall, which stretched away down the street, forcing them to turn. They passed by the mill, picking up the bar walls again, before passing through the noise and shit-stink of the cattle market. It was an arduous walk to Esme, lacking the shops and the market of the outward journey. Thomas strode on, muttering and laughing to himself, as if at a great and glorious secret. He patted his pocket, checking that what he had put there remained in place.

At around this time in her short life, Esme began to hate her father. Perhaps the surprise is that she did not arrive earlier at this conclusion. Another man might have felt tender towards his youngest child, but Thomas was too much taken with his own concerns to notice the small and seemingly ailing girl who looked to him with love and, finding none there, took refuge in its opposite.

As they reached home, rain fell from a bruised sky. Mercifully free, Esme skipped into the dank parlour and ran to her mother, burying herself in her skirt.

"You are too big a girl for that now."

She looked up at her mother, seeing again her thin face. She had only ever felt love for her mother.

Martha thought of the child she had been herself. Childhood was where she went when she needed to escape. She had been happy on the farm cottage on the edge of York, with the countryside growing tall around her family. Her father had been stern but kindly, and she could see his face now if she closed her eyes, the cheeks full and scratched red with tiny veins, the forehead broad and lined, the hair white at the sides and gone on top. When he smiled, the stern face went and this was the picture she carried now, of her father beaming or reaching out, or picking her up with arms strong from farm work.

Martha opened her eyes and saw her world as it was, the damp kitchen and the darling scrap of a girl hugging her legs.

"Be off with you, and find one of your brothers or sisters. Then in a while it will be time to eat."

"What is it today, Ma?"

"Broth, girl. And the day after that, too."

CHAPTER TWELVE

AT FIRST all was black and then a horrible whiteness hurt her eyes. The black frightened her but so did the white. At home, at night, the toys in her bedroom turned to their dark selves. She had a low bedside lamp that cast shadows. The random, jagged shapes could have been alarming but she knew them all. She recognised the elongated soft toys thrown up against the wall beside her bed and the doll's house that slanted across her duvet.

Sometimes, she woke and cried, and someone would come and cuddle her. Usually it was Mummy because she heard things better in the night. Daddy came sometimes but he worked so hard and wasn't always there. When he was at home sometimes he didn't hear in the night and once, in the morning, Mummy said this was because of the wine. Sometimes he wasn't in a good mood at breakfast. She didn't understand about wine because it looked a pretty colour, purple and juicy, yet it didn't taste sweet or nice; it was horrid and made your tongue curl. When Daddy did come to her in the night he smelt funny and his face had turned to sandpaper but she didn't mind.

She cried for ages but then she didn't cry any more. She was always being told off for crying over nothing, but this wasn't why she had stopped. The tears dried when she stopped feeling. She had felt everything at first: the darkness had shaped round her and she had cried, wanting a light. There was a smell she remembered but did not understand; it was the old shed at the bottom of the garden. It smelt of wet earth and mushrooms. Mummy wanted the shed pulled down but Daddy said it would do just fine. They talked about it in those whispers grown-ups thought you couldn't hear. Daddy got cross and attached a bad word to the shed. The words came back to her as she squinted at the cruel beam of light, trying to make out the shape behind. She couldn't move or get away because her hands were tied and her legs were strapped to the chair legs, which were rough and furred with splinters.

"Fucking shed!"

The words came back, but it wasn't Daddy speaking. It wasn't right and it was a bad thing to say. She didn't understand who had spoken. Someone was swearing, repeating the words again and again, until the light came so close she could feel its heat. The words were in her head and in the darkness. Spit from her mouth hissed against the lens. She closed her eyes but the hard light wouldn't go away and tadpoles of dust swam inside her head.

"That's no way for a young girl to speak."

The words carried on in her head and in the room, going in circles. Polly wished someone would stop saying the words but they wouldn't go away. Then pain came at her from the darkness, a stinging shock down one side of her face. She sat back and hurt her spine against the hard chair. She opened her eyes. The bad words stopped and there was nothing, then she heard a loud wailing that seemed to shake her whole body. She didn't understand how a sound could be doing this to her. The light withdrew and the smell went away. The crying carried on and then subsided. The other girl must have stopped crying, was what she thought. The light was swaying now and the man was making a noise like air escaping from a puncture. The puffing was replaced by a restless creaking. The man was sitting down, making himself comfortable.

"Those aren't nice sort of words for a girl of your age to be using. Not nice at all. In the old days, you would have had your mouth washed out with soap and water for speaking like that. Fancy, a nice sort of middle class girl like you, from a nice family and all, saying words like that. And what's the shed got to do with anything?"

"It's the way the shed smells. It's like this, the same smelly sort of smell."

Polly waited to hear if the other girl would play up again. Instead the man spoke again.

"Well, I've no idea what you are talking about. Sheds and smells indeed! No daughter of mine would be allowed to speak like that. Not that I have children, you see. I've been…saving myself, that's it. Waiting for the right woman. And the right one hasn't come just yet. Perhaps she won't come. I can see her without knowing exactly what she looks like. She looks like a lot of people, a bit like the girl who used to live next door, the one who swapped me a look at her knickers for a few sweets. And a bit like my mother, naturally. When she was young, of course, before me. Yes, I can see her now if I shut my eyes, but I don't want to see her, not yet. Later, perhaps – but not yet."

The other girl started up again but she wasn't speaking, she was screaming. Words came out too, but Polly wasn't sure what they were. Different sounds followed, a scratching and scraping. The man was trying to get out of his chair. The other girl must have heard this so she took a deep breath and stopped screaming. She cried and gulped in mouthfuls of dark nothing. The man relaxed and the beam joggled up and down.

"We don't want a fuss, there's no need for that, no need at all."

She sat in the friendless dark and listened to the man breathing. She could hear other sounds too, a drumming inside her chest and a strange thrumming in her ears, like when you hold up a shell to hear the sea. Her granddad showed her that, the granddad who wasn't here any more.

She knew other people died, but not herself. Her life stretched out all around her. She didn't have to think about things, she just was. She listened to the man breathing, to the sounds of her own insides. She couldn't see much, just the horrible man's shadow, and the lamp, which was pointing down now, casting a pool of light. The floor was rough and hard. A window high up in the wall gave a glimpse of another sort of darkness, the night outside wherever she was. She hadn't come far, or didn't think so. She was still in York, she felt sure. She had been playing with George and Benjy. Something had happened to Benjy but she couldn't remember. It was to do with the man. He had made a funny noise and scrunched his face, which had made George run away. Benjy had been barking and snarling, but the man had had done something and the dog had gone silent. After that, he had shoved her into the back of a car. It wasn't a proper car. There were no windows in the back and no seats, only a metal floor with ridges. She had shouted and the man had stuck tape across her mouth and thrown a stinking blanket over her head. Then the car that wasn't a car had driven off and she had been tossed about. When the car stopped, the man had opened the doors, taking her into the cold air. He had puffed and panted as he pulled something up, and then he had led her down steps into the place that smelt like the old shed. Inside the mouldy damp room, the man had tied her to a chair, taken off the blanket and ripped the tape from her mouth. This hurt so much she had cried out.

"I'll stick this back on if you don't stop that caterwauling! You and me, we'll get along fine so long as you don't go making that sort of noise."

She had no idea what was happening. She must have done something wrong, she must have been really naughty, otherwise there was no reason for this man to be so angry. She wondered if the other girl would scream again. She hoped not, because the man might hit her face again, or tape up her mouth. Her cheek was still warm with departing pain.

The pool of light moved with a gentle rolling motion as the man's breathing went in and out. He must be asleep. She wanted to sleep, but she was too uncomfortable in this chair. Also, she was too scared, and too hungry. She needed the toilet but she didn't want the nasty man to wake up. She felt the warm wee escape and cried because this was dirty. The urine pooled at her shackled feet, its smell rising.

There was a snore and a shudder, like the noise Daddy makes when he wakes up after falling asleep in front of the television. The beam of light lifted off the floor and dazzled her eyes.

"What's that?!"

"You fell asleep..."

"Nonsense..."

"I heard you snore..."

"Well, that's as maybe..."

The man made an unpleasant, dry sucking noise. He picked something up and gulped and spluttered, then made a rinsing, teeth-cleaning noise as he spat on to the floor.

"That's better. Are you thirsty, girl?"

He lumbered towards her. The light didn't hit her this time, but went off to the side, bending the beam up the wall and throwing shadows. He let her drink. The water went down her throat and ran off her chin, dripped inside her fleece sweatshirt.

"What's this!"

The man stepped away in disgust.

"You've pissed in this chair. That's revolting, that is."

"I couldn't help it, I needed to go. I couldn't help it – it couldn't stay in any more. And you're a nasty man for bringing me here and my Daddy will be really cross with you. When he finds out you will be in big trouble..."

Her voice rose, angry and petulant, before falling back to a mumble. "Sorry, that was the other girl again. Whenever she talks loud like that, I get in trouble."

"There is no other girl in here, just you and me and..."

The man fell silent. She could sense his breath on her face and smell his difference. He didn't stink exactly; he just didn't smell the same as other people she knew. Perhaps he hadn't had a bath today. The man made a strange sound. She realised he was laughing.

"No, girl, there's only me and you in here. But you're right in a way, there is another girl, or at least the ghost of another girl. It's clever of you to notice that. Perhaps you're cleverer than I thought. Because the other girl is the reason I've brought you here, to teach society a lesson, and to make up for the sins of the past. The other girl, you see, lived and died a long time ago. A hundred years to be precise, almost exactly. It was important to me, you see, to make that link. We live surrounded by history, especially in a city like York, but so often all we see are the old buildings. We forget about the people, especially the poor people. And we never remember the lost girls like Esme Percy. Or all those children who died because they were poor. Girls like you, you don't understand how lucky you are…"

His voice trailed off and he moved back a little, straightening up.

"It's my back, you see. I can't stoop down like that for too long. Ah, that's better…"

"I don't understand you."

"No, well I don't suppose you do. It's history you see, they don't teach it properly these days."

"I'm only eight. And I've done history anyway, the Vikings and stuff. And the terrible Tudors, we done them too."

"Yes, well, that's all interesting enough. But that's old history, ancient stuff, as you put it. My sort of history is closer and the shadows are nearer to hand. And that's why I've brought you here."

"If I'm good will I go home soon?"

"I don't know about that. History has the answer to that, not me. We are all powerless in the rip of history…"

"That doesn't make any sort of sense? What's the 'rip of history'?"

"Grip, I said – the grip of history…"

"No you didn't…"

"Cheeky, aren't you?"

"And you're not very nice. You're not a nice man to do this to me. Nice men don't do things like steal little girls. Nice men go out to work and come home and open a bottle of wine and things like that. My Daddy's a nice man and you're not…"

The words came out, fluent and fast.

"You'll be needing to sleep, then…"

"How can I sleep without my bed?"

"I've made something up for you."

The man moved away, bouncing light from the torch. He shuffled in the gloom, then came at the girl from behind, resting his heavy hands on her slight shoulders. His grip tightened and she sat upright and dead still, her spine pushed into the rough chair. The hands held her for what seemed ages, then hands lifted and loosened the ropes. She stood, unsticking her urine-damp clothes from the chair. She wanted to run but her legs were weak and nerveless. So she shuffled, following the man's commands.

"Over here, this way, over here…"

The torch threw a long crack of light up the wall, cutting through the blackness. For a minute she could see something that looked like a bed. She fell into a tumble of rough blankets and old newspapers. She hugged herself hard as she curled into a foetal ball. The man's breath filled her rough nest and then he dropped something warm over her. Her cold fingers found the metal teeth of a parted zip. She pulled at the quilted material of the old sleeping bag and tried to find comfort.

As she curled in the darkness, the man's voice said: "You sleep now. And don't try escaping in the morning – there's only one way and I'll block that. And there's no use shouting. No one will hear you at all…No-one round here to hear a thing."

WHAT she heard first was the chatter of her own teeth and she pulled the covers closer, opening her eyes a crack and seeing her breath in the air. In the distance she could hear the shuffle of everyday life, people heading off for the day. Close by, a horse shook the cold out of its mouth and clopped to a weary beat. She heard the plodding of a cow on the way to its death, imagining the docile mass of the huge animal as it passed by in the alleyway.

She heard laughter from downstairs, and the heavy creak of the door to the yard. Someone was heading to the privy. As the sounds mixed, she heard her mother's voice, bright and taut. "Morning time, young Esme. Time to raise yourself from that bed. Your sisters are long up and there you still are, all dozy."

She slipped from the worn sheets and the rough blankets, and sat on the bed, her thin legs dangling. She felt the bed warmth leave her.

"Do not just sit there, or you will catch your death, sitting around like that in the chilly morning air. There is barely meat enough to hold body and soul together as it is, so you need to get yourself up and dressed. Come on, I shall help you."

"Where is father?"

"He has risen and is set about his business."

"Is that to say he is no longer here?"

"Of course it is, you strange child. Now stop worrying and get dressed."

As the two set about getting Esme dressed, their thoughts ran on separate lines. The mother thought about food and how she could manage another day with all those mouths and so little to put in them. The daughter tried to see the shape of the day, a Saturday. She thought of her father and screwed up her eyes, wishing the picture away.

Nightclothes were quickly removed, briefly exposing pale, rib-etched thinness, before second or third-hand undergarments covered her shivering body. She raised her arms and was fitted into a dark, heavy dress that was no longer any particular colour, and was decorated with dirt where the hem trailed the ground.

"There!"

Her mother smiled, sending lines creasing across her thin face and exposing her neglected teeth. Esme smiled back and wondered what it was like to be so old. By a circular arrangement of thought, her mother was trying to remember what it felt like to be nine. She thought again of the farm on the outskirts of York, where they had lived, happily as it now seemed, in a tithe cottage. Martha looked at the pale, unopened face before her. She had always been such a straggle of a thing.

"Just look at you, girl. Sent to try my spirit after Henry, Peter, Rebecca, Mary, Hetty, Joshua and Joseph. Eight children! This body of mine has done its service, girl – done the good work of the Lord by bringing you and your siblings into this world."

She tried to sound cheerful but she was not succeeding, so she rested her hand on the cheek of the child. "Come on, let us see if we can find something to pad out that little body of yours."

In the parlour, Martha scooped lard from a pot and dropped it into a blackened pan resting on the range. When the lard began to sizzle, she put a scrap of fatty bacon into the pan, adding a slice of stale bread as the bacon cooked. She poured thin, thrice-brewed tea into a cup, adding milk that turned the surface greasy. She gave the cup to Esme, along with a chipped enamel dish containing a dollop of grey gruel.

"Eat up and thank the Lord, girl."

Esme wondered why she had to thank a Lord who made her eat horrid porridge for breakfast, but she kept the thought to herself. Instead she did as instructed, eating a mouthful or two of the watered-down porridge and slurping tepid tea.

Her mother slid the contents of the pan on to a tin plate and pushed this in front of Esme. Her daughter picked at the tough, rubber-like bacon and managed to tear free a few strands of meat before she turned her attention to the fried bread, enjoying its crunchy greasiness. She finished the fried bread but left the indigestible twist of bacon.

"Heaven knows, I would give you better if only I could, girl," Martha said. "But the Lord gives what He can manage. At least your father is not here to see you wasting your food."

Esme offered a thin, nervous smile as her eyes darted fearfully towards the door.

"Where are all my brothers and sisters this morning?"

"The young ones are out and about, while Joshua and Joseph are working at the chocolate factory. And thank heavens for that. Lord knows how we could survive without what they bring in."

Martha rested her hand on the rim of the plate. The fat around the uneaten scrap was hardening into ripples. She ought to get rid of this, just in case. She was about to lift the plate when she saw her daughter widen her eyes.

The re-hung door, still too heavy on its hinges, swung open and her father filled the space.

"Breakfast is a gift from on high and an unfinished plate is a sin and an insult to the Almighty Himself."

His instant anger filled the kitchen. He manner of speech was not loud yet his presence could never be missed. Martha turned to face her husband, slipping the plate behind her as she did so.

"Since when have you been worried about what the Lord thinks? You have no more seen the inside of a church than I have the inside of that beerhouse where you spend so many of the hours God sends."

"That is as maybe, wife – but I know what I know."

Thomas Percy moved forward, draining the light. He was not a big man, in a physical sense or any other. However, he was larger than his wife and a giant to his youngest daughter. In general he ate the best of the food, having his pick before anyone else could begin; and the ale he drank, while harmful to his health in many respects, added flesh to his bones. No man in fairness could have called him fat but he had a fullness denied to his wife and youngest daughter. The woman seemed closer in size to the girl than the man, so the females hardly provided a match.

"Let me see what you are hiding, woman. For I know that you are being secret with me."

"Heavens, I have no idea what you mean…"

No-one spoke for a long minute. The coals collapsed in the range and the last steam escaped the kettle spout.

"There is no reason on earth why I should have to put up with…"

Thomas spoke quietly, almost as if he were talking to himself.

"A man has much to contend with in his life as he tries to put bread on the family table by whatever means he can find. God knows, it is not easy. So when I find the food my labours have provided gone to waste, I am much displeased."

Thomas could be quick when so moved, and his hand shot out and extracted the incriminating plate.

"What is this? Food left uneaten in this house, where every last scrap has to be inched out just so that we can gain sustenance…"

The very air around his face seemed to flinch. Martha tried to edge away, her hands extended behind and holding on to the table. Esme looked towards the half open door. A stretch of blue winter sky had pushed through the smog and smoke that hung over York, a dirty city at the start of a dirty new century. Esme took her chance and ran across the cracked flags, heading for the blue safety of outdoors. She might have got away if she had been a step or two quicker, but her father scooped her up and swung her about, almost as if wishing to entertain the girl, twirling her for giddy amusement. But the funfair ride stopped abruptly and in one motion, as the tin plate clattered to the floor, Thomas propelled his wife away and placed Esme in front of him. In triumph, he flourished the uneaten scrap of bacon in the grubby fingers of his right hand, leaving his other hand free to prise open her teeth. He shoved the unwanted food inside her mouth, giving the order that she should eat. Terror and sickness rose as she tasted the vile gristle, trying to chew on the rubbery curl. Tears sprang to her eyes as her father loomed, all bristles and blackened teeth. She caught again the stink of dead tobacco and spent beer. In a triumphant act of self-defence, her poor thin body came to her aid, ejecting everything she had eaten that morning. The vomit spouted from her mouth.

Thomas swore and staggered back, dropping Esme as he tried to wipe his eyes with the front of his shirt. Esme bounced to her feet and darted into the yard. She did not have time to look upwards, but if she had she would have seen that the patch of blue had gone, swallowed by smoke and smog. Her mouth tasted vile and she expectorated onto the wall of the alley, leaving behind a pinkish blob of spit. Then, tiny limbs pumping, she ran, blindly seeking escape.

Some time afterwards, a few days or so later, within the week almost certainly, Thomas Percy, gambler, drinker, and very occasional labourer, would trouble her no more.

LIGHT came into the dark and motes of dust danced on the thin slice of sunshine. Polly Markham blinked and looked around. She could not remember where she was or why she was in this place. Then she saw George running away and poor Benjy hanging from the gate; she saw again the horrible van and the horrible man; and then she recalled being brought to this damp and smelly place.

She sat up. There were no windows or doors so far as she could see. She fidgeted in her cardboard-box bed, rustling the newspapers beneath, and caught a strange stench arising from somewhere. It took her a moment to realise the smell was coming from her pissed-in clothes. She felt pain in her stomach and realised she was hungry.

As Polly stood, freeing herself from the old newspapers, she heard a rustle and saw a movement. The nasty man was waking too, emerging from the shadows to sit up.

So began the second day of Polly Markham's captivity. She was fed chocolate bars and tins of cola, which under other circumstances would have constituted a treat. She ate also an apple, which had tough skin and a bruise; she wondered if the nasty man did not buy his fruit from Marks & Spencer.

The man provided a bucket for her to use as a toilet, and threw her a bag containing clothes he had bought from a charity shop. At first she did not want to put on the clothes as they smelt funny and she could sense the presence of whoever had worn them before; but her own clothes smelt worse, so she put on the other girl's clothes. She wondered who had worn them before, and decided they either had no taste or had been poor. The tracksuit trousers were bobbled and a horrid red, while the fleece top was yellow and worn out.

The man turned his back while she dressed. He would not say much to her that day, hardly deigning to speak at all. He did nothing to frighten her and sometimes she yawned, as if bored; then she would remember and start to cry, thinking of home. Towards the end of the day, as the light faded, the man stood up and came closer, shuffling. She noticed that he walked in a funny way, as if his feet never left the ground.

"You be a brave girl while I'm away."

"I don't understand…"

"It won't be for too long, a couple of hours or so. Something that's got to be done, something I have to do. But then I will be back."

He handed Polly a torch, climbed the rough wooden steps and left through a trap door in the ceiling. After the door was shut, she tried to force it, but was quite unable.

CHAPTER THIRTEEN

RICK Rounder stared at the ceiling and tried to remember what the day held. He reached for Naomi but she was gone. Her tracksuit and trainers were missing, she was out already, running again.

"It's not exactly a beach at sunrise in Queensland, but it'll do," she had said after the first few times. "Anyway, if I sit on my arse too long at work, I'll turn into one of the lard people, and I couldn't stand that."

She made for a striking sight, tall and black. There were women joggers, and a few black women, many of them tourists; but the combination of the two was still noteworthy in mostly white York. Strong and slender, Naomi stood out with her frizzed hair and glowing skin.

She ran round the walls at first, going in the morning, as soon as the gates were unlocked, to avoid the tourists. Then she worked out routes that looped the city, taking in bridges and open spaces, nipping through the Museum Gardens. Soon enough, she began to head to Knavesmire. This was the one place in York where she did not feel confined, as the crowded city withdrew a little and something else opened up for her.

As Rick roused himself from bed, and tried to remember what the day held, Naomi was passing the Odeon, running hard, enjoying the strain. York had been difficult; she felt at first as if she didn't fit in, didn't belong. Even now she wasn't certain. She had come to Yorkshire because of Rick, because of what they had in Australia. It was Rick she loved, not where he was born. Their love had survived much already, but sometimes she wondered if it would survive York.

Naomi turned another corner and was swallowed by Knavesmire, which was hardly pretty but spoke of openness, of unrestricted possibility. Her feet crunched the frosted grass and her lungs pulled deep on the cold air. She looked around, watching out for the dogs. There were too many dogs up here, the "canine crappers" as Rick called them. She wasn't going to let a few dogs spoil her enjoyment.

RICK was meeting his brother later. It had been Sam's suggestion: a drink, something to eat, a chat, maybe even some work to put his way.

"That's if you need the work," Sam had said with a sly sibling sparkle. His expression didn't need a translation, not to Rick. He didn't need to survive on brotherly charity, but he wanted to get on with Sam, or at least to try. He only had one brother and sometimes one was more than enough, but he wasn't going to have any more. So he had agreed and was almost looking forward to seeing Sam.

Rick showered, did the rest, then turned his mind to work. Before thought could progress into anything solid, Naomi returned.

"Good run?"

"Wonderful. You should come with me. Like we used to in Australia, jogging on the beach early in the morning, before the sun got up."

"I seem to remember we got distracted once, when there was no-one else around. We stopped for a rest down by the sea and fell into a different sort of exercise."

"Trust you to remember that, Rick."

"What – and you've forgotten the best sunrise fuck you ever had?"

"Language please. And no, I haven't forgotten. It was lovely," she giggled, "and it also marked my first orgasm with you."

"You mean all those other times before that…?"

"Oh, well, a girl's got to put on a show some of the time, hasn't she?"

Rick looked thoughtful, then smiled. "Damn fine actress."

"Oh, only the best."

Naomi cooled herself then went for a shower. Rick wanted to join her, but she turned him away. "Go and take your one-track mind some place else, Mr Rounder." She laughed. Rick sensed her shape beneath the running clothes, the tautness and the curves, the dark skin and darker hair.

"Away with you – I'm having this shower then it's off to work. So there's no time for what's passing through your mind."

"How can you tell what I'm thinking?"

"Might as well be a bloody great sign up there. Besides, you're a man, aren't you?"

"Was the last time I looked."

Rick went down to his minuscule office while Naomi showered on the top floor. First off, he checked the emails, and found two uninvited communications, one in German and seemingly from a porn site. He couldn't read German but the key words didn't need translation. Rick spiked the email, along with another offering him a guaranteed way to earn a quick buck. Porn from Germany, get-rich schemes from the United States – the cosmopolitan wonders of the modern world.

The third email was from Will Wistow and requested a meeting later that afternoon.

"My dear Richard Rounder…"

Richard Rounder. No-one had called him that for years, not since his parents were scolding him about something or other. He thought about his parents, dead and gone. One more reason to persevere with Sam, to keep something alive.

"I need to meet with you this afternoon. For reasons I cannot go into now, I would like this assignation to take place away from my home. I enclose an address. It is easy to find, so long as you look out for the farm sign as you leave York. You head out along the lane, until you have gone past the church on the left. Soon there is a bend and some more houses, and after that a stretch of countryside. The farm is some way down on the right. It is no longer a farm but is still described thus, as you can see."

Wistow gave the address and signed off, asking Rounder to ring him on his mobile to "confirm his attendance as per the above." A final note offered to pay double the usual rates to "compensate for lack of warning or prior notification."

Rick rang to confirm and asked what was new.

"This is something I would rather not talk about right at this particular moment. When we meet, you will understand my careful circumnavigation. I shall be able to get to the point a little more easily when we meet face to face. Suffice to say that events have moved on and now require further investigation."

"So why aren't you at home then?"

"All shall be made clear later, my dear Richard Rounder. You just need to wait and to display a little patience. Then I shall be able to explain why my nerves have become so embrittled."

"What?"

"Ah, yes, embrittled, a lovely word, don't you think?"

"I'll take your word for that. But if I were you, I'd lay off the dictionaries for breakfast."

"Very amusing, my friend the spectator. And I take it that you observed my note about the extra payment your time and trouble will accrue?"

"Yes, all donations gratefully received."

"Right, until later then."

Rick rang Sam to say he might be late for their meeting because work had come up.

"Ah, so the little spying job is still paying a few bills, is it?"

Rick knew Sam was smiling. It wouldn't be an entirely nice smile. That was the trouble with brothers. However well you got on at any given moment, every conversation had a sub-text, a hidden meaning wrapped in the pocket-fluff of history. Rick liked to deflect sibling hostilities with a smile or a witticism. But right now he wanted to cry out, fuck you, brother, with your lazy, fat-arsed life, with your big house and straying wife. I'm happy and complete, I've got a gorgeous woman, I've seen the world, and now I'm home and you don't like it because it shows you up.

Instead he said: "Yeah, busy enough."

"Who are you going to see – anyone I might have come across?"

Rick didn't want to tell Sam anything, but he relented.

"It's been my biggest earner so far, this case," he said, omitting to say it was his only earner. "Man called Will Wistow hired me to check up on his wife, who has been straying in the direction of a lecturer. He teaches history, the lecturer does, to adults in an evening class. Seems like Wistow's wife hooked up with this lecturer."

"What's she like, the wife?"

"Dark, attractive – rather nice." Rick covered the mouthpiece, and turned to check for Naomi behind him. "I've taken a shine to her while shadowing."

"So where's all this leading?"

"He says he needs to see me this afternoon, but not at his house. So I'm meeting him at a farm just on the outskirts of York, heading towards..."

Sam interrupted Rick. He didn't have time to hear all about this case. There was proper policing to be done.

"Well, look after yourself, little brother. And give me a ring if you're going to be late. Oh, and I'll check out that name. Wistow is familiar for some reason. Can't think why, it's probably nothing. Mebbe I'm imagining it. But this job makes you a suspicious old sod. You spot trouble and shit everywhere. See you later, little brother."

Rick filled out the morning with the internet. Then he left a note for Naomi and wheeled his bike out of the garage. Twenty minutes should do it, easily, fifteen probably. It was surprising how swiftly you could get round York, so long as you dodged the carelessly-opened car doors, the holes in the roads or the pedestrians who never looked before they stepped. He shut the garage door and glanced up at his tall home. He still couldn't believe the place was his, or that he was living there with Naomi. He had carried a splinter of York wherever he had travelled. Now he felt he belonged again and yet didn't belong; somehow, he liked this. He no longer wanted to offer unquestioning loyalty to anywhere; but he did come from York, and that counted for something.

Rick pedalled under Monk Bar, glowered at a driver who had parked in the "bikes only" section. Then he powered past the pub where he was due to meet Sam. He cycled as fast as possible, earning the beer.

Soon enough, the houses started to thin out, giving way to fields. On a straight stretch of road, he saw two buildings on the right, and the second was the farm. He coasted towards the house and stopped in a concrete drive penetrated by intrusive grass. A car was parked in the drive, a Ford of some sort. The windows of the farm were camouflaged in dirt. The place had a forgotten air. Soon enough, Rick would very much like to forget it.

NAOMI returned at four but Rick wasn't there. She had been looking forward to seeing him, as they'd been getting on better again. She changed, made coffee, found his note, and shrugged in the silence. It was so quiet, tucked away in the heart of York – or it was until the Minster bells started up. For now there was the almost perfect quiet of a house occupied by one person. The tranquil interlude was ended by phone.

"Yes?"

"Is that Naomi?"

"Yes."

"It's Sam… is Rick there?"

"No, he's gone out. He left me a note. Gone to meet a client."

"I was afraid of that."

Naomi was alarmed by the edge in Sam's voice. Normally, he sounded conceited or boorishly flirty.

"What's the matter?"

"Well, it could be nothing. It's just that I've found something out about Rick's client. He isn't all he seems – and I think there might be a connection to Rick's past."

"Shit, is he in danger?"

"Don't know about that but this Will Wistow hired Rick to spy on his wife, because he thought she was being an unfaithful little tart and knocking off a lecturer. But it's complicated. Not the situation Rick thought it was at all."

"Hell, Sam, what are you going to do?"

"I'm on to it – the trouble is, I don't know where Rick is. He didn't tell you, did he?"

"No, he just left that note saying that he'd gone to meet a client."

"I'll send someone round to look at Rick's computer. There might be something buried in there, especially if he's been getting emails from Wistow."

The silence returned after the call but was no longer any comfort.

RICK locked his bike to a rusting drainpipe. When he straightened up, Will Wistow was standing behind him.

"Ah, greetings, Mr Rounder. You could always put the bike away, safely out of sight. Bicycle theft is a problem in York, or so I understand. Not that I own one myself. Not my cup of cappuccino at all. Nasty rattling things that do something unspeakable to one's behind."

"The bike will be all right here. It came with a good padlock, and, anyway, it's insured."

"Well, well – come in then."

Wistow went into the house. Cars were speeding out of York at the end of the long drive, and a dog barked in the garden of the other building, straining at its leash. Rick ignored the hostile canine, entering the house, which was neglected on the inside, too. This struck Rick as peculiar.

Wistow was a man of taste and refinement, a man who liked good whisky, fine literature and art. He had withdrawn into his comforts as a way of escaping his wife's infidelity – that much was perfectly clear. You didn't need to be a degree-wielding psychologist to work that one out. His younger, very attractive wife had started seeking her pleasures elsewhere, so Wistow had done the same. She went for the flesh, he withdrew into malt whisky, books and operatic CDs.

Rick tried to imagine what had brought such a disparate couple together. There must have been fire and passion, there usually was, at least at first. He was still puzzling over this when he stepped out of the threadbare hall and into a large empty room. Once this would have been a room to show off to friends; the ceiling was high and a mock-medieval stone fireplace dominated the far wall.

The floor was partially covered by a moth-eaten carpet that had rotted to expose wooden blocks laid in a herringbone pattern. The shabby curtains might have been knitted from dust. Although they looked as if they might fall apart if touched, they kept out the light. The dim room felt musty and shut up, unused for years. The smell of damp rose from somewhere deep below.

Rick walked through the abandoned room, looking for Wistow. He hadn't seen him since he entered the house.

"Mr Wistow…"

His voice rang out and disturbed the dust. Rick could hear his heart rushing and pumping in his chest. His ears popped and crackled, his throat and nose protested at the dust. He coughed and sneezed, then heard a voice.

"I'm in here, Mr Rounder, just fixing us a drink. We have much to talk about and I find a drink helps."

"No whisky for me." Rick said to the unseen Wistow. He didn't fancy the sour slosh of whisky in his belly as he cycled home. He was still puzzling over something: how did a man like Wistow hook up with a woman like Wendy? The thought turned on its suspicious axis as he rounded the corner into what had probably been the kitchen. On the floor was a mark where a table had once been, the tiles shaded darker. Rick heard the tinkling of a spoon against a cup or a mug, so he supposed he was about to be offered tea or coffee. Naomi wanted him to cut down on the coffee so perhaps he should ask for tea, which was supposed to be better for him. He preferred coffee and almost resented Naomi's insistence on tea, although he liked her fussing too. At least someone cared enough to worry. Such were the mundane thoughts forming in Rick's mind when he felt a whoosh of air followed by pain, then nothing.

SAM had always resented having to look after his kid brother when they were young. He was the big sensible one, Rick the cute younger sibling who could get away with murder if he smiled. Sam had always felt much older than the two years that separated them, and the difference stretched tighter still when Rick came back with a tan, a rucksack full of stories and the lovely Naomi. Sam hadn't believed it at first. Even now his eyes were drawn to where they did not belong. Talking to Naomi on the phone had been thrilling until he recalled again the danger Rick was in. Then his policeman's brain had clicked in.

Superintendent Pierce hadn't been keen at first, citing tight budgets and a lack of regard for snoops.

"They get in the way, make things messy," he had said. "Tramping all over the proper procedure. What's more, we've got that lost girl to look for." He had a point: it was the largest investigation that Sam had ever been involved in, a real media circus. But Pierce had relented when Sam had explained the history and the long resentments.

"Get on with it then," Pierce had said. "But watch the mileage and the overtime."

RICK had no idea about anything when he came round. All the reference points had gone. The fuzzy room was new to him, as was the throbbing. He wanted to touch his head and feel the skull beneath the skin. His hands were tight, his wrists burning from whatever bound them. He took a deep breath and winced. There was another pain in his side, where he felt he had been kicked.

Standing sent small agonies darting around his body. The pain pulsed from his head to his arms, into his hands, through his bruised ribs. Panting with the effort, Rick tried to concentrate on his surroundings, then realised his eye was hurting too. His ankles were tied loosely and this gave him some mobility, so he hopped towards the window.

The room was small and desolate. Wallpaper peeled in sagging curls, pink roses adorning a once cream background. Rick craned his neck and pain reverberated round his skull. Sour petals of damp decorated the ceiling, which was violated by a jagged crack. The plaster around the fissure was piss yellow, the white ceiling paint had dried to dust.

He nudged the curtains aside and tried to part the rotten material with his teeth, which set him coughing. The harsh sound came back at him in the small, empty room. He heard a noise downstairs and steps starting up the stairs. Rick tried to work out where he was. He saw flat, uninspiring fields, cows, a house or two. Cars passed along a road. Rick looked for a means of defence. Then he laughed, which wasn't smart as it hurt too much. There weren't many options open to a man with his head bashed in, hands lashed behind his back and shackles round his ankles.

A man came into the room. "Ah, Mr Rounder. I do hope the accommodation is to your liking. I apologise for the restraints, but I didn't think you'd stay without a little persuasion."

"Any chance of telling me why you've got me trapped in this shitty room?"

"It isn't the best of locations, is it? But it suits my purposes. A family lived here, until they all died or departed, leaving an old woman to fend for herself. When she died, the house died with her. Her children squabbled over what to do. While these deeply tedious people indulged in a sibling slagging match, the house began to fall apart, and eventually fell into my hands, for a ridiculously cheap price. All of this makes for a sad story in a way, although not so sad as the story which brought you to me."

"What the fuck are you on about?"

"I must say that your language leaves a lot to be desired."

The man stood a foot or so away, meticulously prising dirt from beneath one of his fingernails with the blade of a penknife. One of those Swiss jobs you shouldn't be without: two sharp blades, a thing for getting stones out of a horse's hoof, a corkscrew and no doubt a special attachment for inflicting pain on private detectives.

"When I first employed you, you were politeness herself – and now listen to you, cursing away like a common man."

He inspected the blade of the knife, then snapped it shut. "You have to be so careful with these things, you know. Terribly sharp. A man could have a nasty accident."

He dropped the knife into his shirt pocket, where it lay, a

weighted smudge of red showing through the pale blue shirt. The man's voice was precious and strayed towards the camp.

No, it didn't stray, it skipped in that direction with glee. The intonation was annoying and false, as if exaggerated for effect. The voice awoke a memory. This man had hired him, had paid him to follow someone. But who and why? The memories came back in such a muddled rush they made Rick's head hurt even more.

"You hired me and your name is West or Wist or something. I had to spy on someone, your wife, I think, and..."

"Dear me, your memory is still a little shaky. Perhaps I was a little too enthusiastic with the violence. Better safe than sorry, though. I didn't want you escaping. You are bigger and fitter than me. What I did took courage and, do you know what, I rather impressed myself. Went out stone cold, you did. Didn't know I had it in me. And you wouldn't believe the effort it took to get you up those stairs, you great lump."

"So when are you going to tell me what all this is about?"

Images swirled through Rick's mind. There was a woman – smallish, dark, curved in all the right places.

"Wendy!"

"Ah, your memory is returning. So I can't have destroyed too many brain cells."

"Your solicitude is very touching."

"You are right, there is someone called Wendy. My wife, yes, my wife! What an amusing notion."

"Wistow, Will Wistow..."

"I see your cognitive powers are regenerating nicely. You'll be reciting that poem you learnt at school soon."

"What poem?"

"Oh, just an image that came into my head, a playful scenario, a fancy that fluttered by."

"You don't use one word where half a dictionary will do."

"Very perspicacious. You seem quite bright for a copper..."

"Ex-policeman..."

"Ah, yes, sorry I forgot. When you spend so much time thinking about the past, it is easy to become muddled. Past and present – what is the difference? Only, perhaps, that some people who used to be here are no longer with us any more."

Wistow dipped his hand into his shirt pocket and the red smudge became a penknife again. He flicked open the longest blade and rested the cushion of his left thumb on the keen edge and moved it along the steel inches from Rick's face. A bubble of blood rose from the skin. Others followed as a tiny wound unzipped the flesh.

"How careless. As I said, a man could have a nasty accident."

The blade came closer, dribbling blood. Wistow sucked his injured thumb. Rick couldn't take his eyes off the flash of silver.

CHAPTER FOURTEEN

WOULD the darting blade be the last sight he saw? The thought was terrifying and absurd. The blade was small, designed to cut apples or whittle a stick. Sensible people who hiked bought such a knife, not those with thoughts of inflicting harm.

Rick Rounder tried to imagine Wistow buying the knife. Perhaps he had visited the huge hardware store that went on forever. It was an unbeatable place, if useful objects were your thing. Had Wistow opened the different blades and inspected each one, wondering how good they would be for the job at hand? The knives would have been locked up, for safety; so he would have needed to find an assistant to open the glass case. What would he have told the assistant? I'm looking for a useful knife that will slice tomatoes on a picnic; oh, and the blade needs to be sharp enough to do possibly terminal damage to a private eye against whom I have an unexplained grudge.

Rick saw Wistow exchange money for the small red knife. The knife was put in a paper bag until Wistow could inspect what he had bought: the sharp blade, the stubby blade, the bottle-opener, the corkscrew, the minuscule tweezers, a tooth-pick and the tiny scissors. Rick had such a knife at home and its weight had been a talismanic presence on his travels. Why the hell didn't he have it now?

The blade was an inch or two from his face. Rick looked at the fidgeting silver, then into Wistow's eyes. He never thought death might look like this, puffy flesh and tiny red lines. Death's eyes were small and round yet cast in the clearest, nastiest blue. Death smelt of old whisky and older after-shave, and had yellow uneven teeth.

"You could do with a good dentist."

"Ah, still the little jokes, Mr Rounder, even though I have the advantage. This blade is very sharp. I have kept it that way, dutifully tending to its keen edge."

"Are you going to tell me what all this is about? Or will I have to wait until I'm looking back from the other side, whichever one I'm booked in for?"

"Heaven or hell – which one of us ever knows, aside from the terminally religious? But I have my reasons for hoping it might be the hotter and less comfortable location."

"There you go again, dropping hints about why you lured me here, beat me up and tied me up in this vile room."

"It could have been so much nicer. I had plans for this place. But property is a bother. Now, where were we?"

Wistow stood in a pantomime of indecision, his left hand cradling his chin, his small eyes glinting inside tight sockets. Rick twisted his hands, hoping to loosen the binds. With free hands he would have a chance. Wistow was round and slightly bloated, as if too generously inflated. He did not look strong and yet he could inflict damage, as testified by Rick's cuts and bruises.

"I suppose you want me to tell you what all this is about, don't you, Mr Rounder?"

"It had crossed my mind."

"Your dry wit is admirable in the circumstances. If our roles were to be swapped, I would – to use the vernacular – be shitting myself. But you, you seem to be keeping your head."

"Bits and pieces are floating around in my skull again, Wistow. You had me spy on your wife. I've been following her for ages. I had almost grown fond of her, from a distance..."

"Are you trying to make me jealous? Wendy is your sort, is she? Well, I hate to disappoint you. No, actually, I don't – I love to disappoint you, it gives me the most tremendous pleasure. Anyway, I thought you went for something a little more exotic."

"What are you talking about?"

"Oh, merely a passing observation on your choice of partner. Anyway, before I explain, let's get one thing out of the way. Wendy is not my wife. So you can forget trying to make me jealous by saying that you find her attractive. She may well find you attractive, but these matters do not concern me one ugly little iota. So, to the truth, or a bit of it. Wendy is my lodger, not my wife. Perhaps you would have found this out, had you been a more assiduous investigator. Luckily for me, you took me at my word. And, my word, that was very foolish of you."

Wistow chuckled for a moment, enjoying the verbal fun.

"So why did you want me to spy on your lodger?"

"It was all a distraction, an elaboration to keep you occupied and within the orbit of my influence. You see, it suited my purposes to have you fully employed. I wanted you to look in one particular direction, which you did most diligently. I couldn't fault your reports at all. But my grievance with you goes back much further, all the way back to before everything else…"

"What the hell are you talking about? I don't have a clue why you are doing this – are you going to tell me?"

"Oh, when the time suits," Wistow sang, enjoying the power. He snapped the blade shut, and began to back out of the room. "Don't do anything I wouldn't."

Rick slumped against the wall beneath the window, exhaling in short, panicky bursts. Then he bent forward and threw up on the threadbare carpet.

"YOU can find all sorts in here. Computers keep their secrets well. Sometimes you just have to look in obvious places, sometimes you have to try a little harder. What I am doing now is going through Rick's e-mails. He communicated with Wistow this way, didn't he?"

"As far as I know. I mean, I only know a bit about his work, what he chooses to tell me."

The police computer expert tapped on the keyboard and squinted at the screen; then he tapped again, screwing up his eyes.

"I think I'll go upstairs, leave you to it. Can I get you something? Tea or coffee?"

"Water, mineral if you've got it. Caffeine tends to irritate, or so my wife used to tell me; not sure if it was me or her it was supposed to irritate. Anyway, she got me to drink water and the habit stuck. Even if she didn't."

By the time Naomi had walked upstairs, taken chilled mineral water from the fridge, and descended again, the computer expert was triumphant.

"I've found the email, easy as anything. I didn't even need any of my technological cunning, which was disappointing, because I like a challenge. You see, the thing with a really thorny problem is..."

"Look, I don't care about all that. What have you found?"

"Well, you read that on the screen while I ring Sam Rounder, then..."

Naomi read the first part of the message and touched the mouse to scroll down. The address lay off the screen, one click away . The computer expert – Naomi hadn't asked his name – was talking into his mobile. His hair was thinning and needed cutting; dandruff decorated his jacket collar; he appeared neglected. These thoughts flashed through Naomi's mind without stirring up enough interest to require a question. She went to click the mouse, and just as she pressed the button, the image vanished into the blue screen of death.

"Bloody Bill Gates," said the computer expert, as if referring to a troublesome colleague. "His programmes are always doing that. Soon have that fixed..."

RICK ROUNDER already smelt of old blood and sweat, now vomit had been added to his personal fragrance. His heart was pumping in panic. Most of your life you don't worry about what's going on inside, but there are times when your heart can't be ignored, when its urgent plumbing becomes the only rhythm in the world.

He breathed deeply and listened. There was a dog barking. There had been a dog as he had locked up his bike. That seemed months ago but it could only be an hour or two. His watch was stuck behind his back. He wondered what Wistow was doing, why he had left him. There had been footsteps but nothing for a while.

Rick shuffled and listened. And worked his wrists, twisting against what bound him.

"SO where is the fucking thing then?"

It was a moment before Naomi realised what she had said. She never swore in front of strangers. She was about to apologise but the computer expert batted away her words.

"It's the tension, I imagine," he said, his voice slow and deliberate. "First rule of computer maintenance: switch if off and turn it on again."

The computer went dark and the policeman drank from the bottle of mineral water. His Adam's apple bobbed as he swallowed. He hadn't shaved well and a stamp-sized patch of stubble lurked under his chin.

"Sorry, I don't know your name."

"Warter, as in the Wolds village, not what I'm drinking. DC Dick Warter. And I've heard them all. Warter under the bridge... Warter, Warter everywhere... bridge over troubled Warters. Yes, you think of a joke concerning water, I've heard it."

"I'm sure you have. Does it usually take this long?"

"Ah, computers have a mind of their own. Either that or they've got Bill Gates' mind."

"That's the second time you've mentioned Gates."

"Oh, me and him go back a long way. Seems like I've spent half my life working his bloody software. Ah, something's happening."

Impenetrable codes marched across the screen, then a message indicated a "fatal exception error." The screen went blue and DC Warter tutted, swigged at the bottle and tried his on-off cure once again.

"It's sure to work in a moment."

IT WAS all he could manage not to throw up again. He must have nodded off and now the stairs were creaking. The steps came closer, accompanied by heavy breathing. Confused and pained, Rick still felt affronted. His fitness should have counted for something, yet he'd been trapped by a wheezing soft man. His head hurt and his wrists were bloodied raw. The rope was coming looser. If only he could...

"Those stairs…will be…the death of me…You will have to pardon me for a moment." Wistow stood outside the room and leant against the doorframe, panting.

"Why don't you do me a favour, Wistow, and drop dead of a heart attack right now? That heart of yours isn't in good shape and must be desperate for all the bothersome pumping to end. So give in to the inevitable and die…"

Rick didn't know where these words had come from. Sheer naked panic – and the thought of being beaten by one so flaccid. Yet for a soft man, Wistow knew how to inflict pain. Rick couldn't remember the last time he had hurt in so many places. Wistow lunged into the room with ungainly menace, covering the distance from the door in a rush.

"That tongue of yours will get you in trouble, Rounder. Perhaps I should cut it out for you…?"

Wistow was a spit away. His small blue eyes bulged maniacally and his skin had an unhealthy sheen, as if the unused grease in his body had risen to the surface to glisten. A dribble of sweat ran from his forehead and down the side of his nose, diverting round the curl of his lips, and dripped off his chin. Wistow put the knife in his other hand so that he could use his shirt-cuff to dab at his face. Rick sensed his chance and propelled himself forward in a mad hopping motion. With his wrists and ankles bound, it was the only action he could take. The two men collided and staggered around the room in a huddle. Although still in the room, they were only a few feet from the top of the stairs. Rick sensed the luck turn his way. Another shove or two and Wistow would fall down the stairs and break his fat neck. He smelt the other man, smelt his own fear rising. It was now or…

"Shit!"

How had he forgotten that knife?

He hopped and staggered back into the room until he was back where he had started, leaning against the window sill and looking across the room at his captor.

"You stabbed me, you puffy-faced shit."

"Only a flesh wound. Didn't want to waste my opportunity. No good..."

Wistow couldn't breathe and talk at the same time and gulped air instead. He grew calmer and the colour began to return to his face, but just then he lurched forward and grabbed at his chest, swearing. Sweat broke out all over his skin. Groaning, he doubled over, clutching at his rib cage. Rick didn't notice at first because he was concentrating on his own pain, the sharp new sensation that had joined all the other hurts and aches. He felt a spreading warmth and looked down at the blossoming crimson. He saw the other man bent over. His concentration drifted and he didn't understand. He'd been hurt and yet Wistow was acting as if he were the injured one. Perhaps natural justice had intervened with that heart attack, right here in front of his eyes. Oh, sweet unexpected fate.

The spasm passed and Wistow straightened up and gulped in the stale air. "It will go and I will feel better. It always goes and I always feel better."

He took a few more breaths and spoke again in sentences that were short and ran into each other, as if leaving a space in between would be a waste of breath.

"We have much to talk about, you and I. We go a long way back, and you don't realise how far back, or how much you have cost me," Wistow flashed the knife. "You will know pain before you die, Rounder."

DC WARTER continued to struggle as Naomi stood at his shoulder.

"Perhaps you could give me a bit of space. There's not a lot of room in here." He put his hand in the air and made a disparaging motion, as if to embrace the smallness of everything.

"Sorry. I'll step into the street for a while. Get some fresh air and leave you to it."

Naomi walked outside. Clasping her right foot in her hand, she pulled it gently up to her buttocks and then held the posture for a moment, standing slender and erect on one leg, stork-like. Then she released the foot and repeated the exercise with the other foot. Soon she found herself going through the whole pre-run routine. She stretched and bent, twisted and turned. She must have been working for a while because sweat was starting to dampen her forehead. Her skin began to glisten. A bead of sweat rolled into her eye, then off down her cheek; or maybe she was crying. No, she wasn't crying, she wasn't going to cry. She was going to be strong. There had to be a simple explanation. He can't have come to any harm, not Rick, not her Rick. Her Rick, not the private investigator who had gone missing, but her Rick, the man she had followed halfway round the world.

A sound broke through the shell of her thoughts.

"Hey, missy. What's your name? I think we might be getting somewhere…"

CHAPTER FIFTEEN

THIS was often the way: nothing for ages, a few stolen cars, a mugging or a break-in, a scuffle in one of the streets where trouble congregated, and then suddenly this.

"All hell's broken loose."

Sam Rounder had used those words at a briefing a few minutes earlier and now, sitting alone in his office at Fulford Road, he mumbled the phrase again, finding comfort in its familiarity. His father had used the same expression. He could see the shape his father's mouth made when speaking, the grey stubble moving while the words whistled through ill-fitting teeth. Would his face collapse in the same manner when old age mugged him?

Sam took a deep breath and tried to relax in the way his wife had taught him in the days when she still took an interest in his well-being. Then he muttered "bugger relaxation" and poured another coffee as he thought back over the conference.

"LADIES and gentlemen, we now have two missing persons. One, as you know, is my own brother, Rick Rounder, who has set up as a private investigator in York. Now normally I take a dim view of the sods. Last thing we need is some half-arsed pseudo-copper making our life difficult. But this one is flesh and blood. We thought we had found a lead on Rick's computer but the bloody thing has crashed. Dick Warter is doing his Jesus act on the bloody thing as we speak. We've got teams out looking and you lot will be out again, once you're done listening to me."

Sam took a breath and tried to exhale a sense of his own futility. He felt haunted by his own lack of use, but wasn't about to show it to these buggers.

"Now the other case, that's particularly worrying. Polly Markham was playing outside her home when she disappeared. The friend she was playing with told her mother she had gone with a man who called himself 'Uncle Pete.' Polly has no uncle of this name. This is not, as far as we can tell, a domestic. The Markhams seem a happy, successful couple. Pauline is a teacher who has spent the past eight or nine years looking after their two children, the missing girl and her elder sister, Samantha. Graham works in Leeds for an IT firm. He was in Leeds at the time of the abduction. We have no reason to suspect that either parent is involved."

Attention was straying in parts of his audience, so Sam increased the volume and glanced darkly about the room. His scan took in Valerie Rodgers – Sergeant Val soon enough, from what he'd heard. He still couldn't see her without remembering what she looked like naked, so slim and shapely, and one of many pleasures now denied to him. The affair had been brief but passionate, a round of clandestine meetings and forbidden sex. She had left as quickly as she had arrived, moving on to someone her own age who didn't have a swollen belly, grey hair and what Val had, on their last night, described as "the sag of disappointment." He had responded by calling her the "slag of disappointment." His words were stupid, but it had been too late by then.

Sam found another face to look at.

SAM gulped more coffee. It was vile and tasted as if it had been on the boil since the week before last. His brother knew about good coffee, having a way with the finer things. Sometimes this annoyed Sam, making him feel stupid or blundering. Then he would make a joke, play the buffoon or say something nasty. Yet whatever strategy he chose, it always made him feel inadequate. Sam may have been the eldest but Rick had always been the coolest, the smartest, and a magnet for the girls when they were teenagers. Now he was living in that Ogleforth love-nest with his gorgeous girlfriend, while he was trapped in a marriage gone sour and resentful, and...

He shook away the bitter reverie. Rick wasn't in his flat with Naomi, he was God knows where with God knows who: but he felt sure Wistow had something to do with it.

Sam pushed the door and barged into the central area, punching the air and rallying his troops. "Right, people, let's get looking, let's scour every inch of this city and..."

The room was empty. Everyone was out following the orders he had given earlier. He was alone. He rang Dick Warter and set off for the car park, shouting into his hand as he went.

"Well, make sure the bloody thing is resurrected by the time I get there."

GRAHAM Markham's eyes flicked from one pale face to the other. His wife and daughter were sitting on the sofa in the lounge, gazing at him. He fell to his knees and embraced them.

"I know, I know," he said.

Pauline could only sob; Sally, upset by Polly not being here, by her mother's tears, by everything she didn't understand, cried too. Graham tried to make sense of what had happened yesterday. He was absent a lot, working long days, playing away when he felt he could; but he had always felt his other life, his family life, was getting along nicely. All he had to do was return when he felt like it and the picture was complete.

"How did this happen?"

"That fat policeman explained it all to you."

"I want to hear it from you, in your words, not theirs."

She told him again, the story coming in gulps. She was haunted by what she imagined was grief, yet this couldn't be grief, she kept telling herself. There was no loss to grieve. Everything would be all right. Polly would be found and life would go back to how it was meant to be. She would never moan about another mundane thing; she would never again resent anything. Her life would again be whole and she would embrace the completeness.

Graham took his arms away.

"So... you let Polly play outside by herself..."

"She wasn't by herself. She was with George. George is a girl, Georgina really, but no one calls her that, aside from her Mum and Dad. They were together, they always look out for each other and..."

"You let her play outside by herself..."

His words rolled on, unaffected by anything his wife said. He had told her so many times, reminded her so often that he did not approve of the girls being at the front of the house by themselves. She had told him, as many times as he raised the argument, that the girls didn't want her hanging around.

Graham spat out his words. The more he spoke, the harder and more distant he sounded. He didn't look at Pauline at all, directing his gaze to a foot or so above his head, looking into the dark mirror of the window, gauging his own reflection.

"All you have to do, your only part of this relationship, is to look after our girls. And now you've failed. Failed Polly..."

"I didn't fail...it happened when...the dog, poor Benjy, the dog you wanted so much...it all happened. And I thought I was doing what was right. Anyway, you're never here so you don't know, you've no idea what it's like. You don't know anything about me any more. You're too wrapped up in being the big self-important man."

Pauline was shouting. Graham turned away, wanting to leave. Pauline tried to stand but Sally was clinging hard. The girl's eyes darted between her parents.

"I just want Polly back," Sally said, her voice so small it was barely audible.

"Me too...me too."

Pauline could feel the girl's heart pounding. She hugged her and wondered if she would ever stop feeling so lost and lonely.

SAM Rounder stewed through York. The traffic was hellish: it always was. He put on a tape, some Phil Collins. He listened for a while, then switched to the radio, skipping stations until he turned that off too. He surrendered to the stop-start motion of the car and the agitated rhythms of his heartbeat.

There was nowhere to park in Ogleforth, one of many York streets which hadn't foreseen the invention of the car. He slipped his car into the back yard of a shop, sticking an 'On Police Business' note on the windscreen. Lifesaver, that.

He stood outside, craned his neck and looked upwards, admiring the vertiginous rise of the old bricks. His own house was much bigger, and worth a sight more; but he couldn't help feeling the old prickle of envy. Rick's life was so much freer and more interesting. He may not have achieved as much, he may not have as much salted away – but Rick seemed to have more, and to have a better grasp on what he had.

Sam looked inside himself and did not like what he saw; then he shrugged his heavy shoulders and rang the doorbell for a second time.

Naomi answered, twitchy with anxiety.

"Any news?" she said.

"I've come here to ask the same question of DC Warter."

"He's still cursing Bill Gates."

She stayed by the open door as her lover's brother took his sour aura down the corridor. She supposed lover was one description for Rick. "Boyfriend" seemed too girly, "partner" too dull and businesslike, but besides she liked "lover", suggesting as it did passion and friendship.

A sound boomed down the corridor, a voice, two voices. "Halle-bloody-lujah! It looks like we've got something here!"

She rubbed her salted eyes and rushed inside.

AS THE police tried to build a picture of what had happened to Polly Markham, a sense of drama leeched through the suburb where she lived. Neighbours who knew the little girl shared in the shock, and held their own daughters and sons closer. Playing outside was banned, at least for now. Those quick to judge observed to themselves, and occasionally to others, that such things happened when children were given too much freedom.

As questions were asked, and answers left wanting, the traffic continued up and down the road outside the Markham house. Ordinary life went on as it always does, navigating tragedy or trauma.

After the police had come and gone again, Pauline Markham stood by a window and gazed trough the mottled raindrops. She didn't see her reflection or the rain. All she could see was the daughter who was no longer there. Polly's life came at her in flashes – the buried agonies of birth, baby faces, birthday parties, tottered first steps and later loud exuberance. She heard Polly's laughter, felt her hot, impatient breath, smelt all her warm life. She had never prayed in her life, but she was praying now.

SAM patted Warter on his thin, dandruffed shoulders. "Keep it up, lad," he boomed. Warter, made nervous by the rough bonhomie, said: "Glad to help, guv."

"Guv? Don't think you've ever called me that before."

"Sorry, must be all those old episodes of The Sweeney I've been watching. Not much else to but watch television, since she left me and…"

"Yes, yes, let's get on with it. No time to hear about the ups and downs of your personal life. I've got to insert myself back into York's never-ending traffic jam and grind my way over to Knavesmire to see if Wistow's at home."

Sam doubted he would be.

CHAPTER SIXTEEN

WENDY was happy to have the sunshine but not the wind. Out on Knavesmire, they had huddled against the cruel gusts. The shared warmth had reminded her how lucky she felt in her choice; except that she hadn't chosen him so much as chased him, brazenly. It had always been that way with her: when she wanted something, she had to have it, or so her mother said. She had wanted Malcolm from that first day in his classroom when she had heard him speak. She had set herself, heart and mind, and had made sure he noticed her, or so she had told herself. Malcolm had corrected her later, when they were in bed for the third, maybe the fourth, time. She didn't have to make him notice her because he couldn't stop looking.

"Magnetism," she had said.

"Enough to pull a car," he had said. "And just look at you."

He had pulled the covers from her, exposing her breasts; and she had tugged the covers back, laughing and telling him off. Weeks ago, months ago, and they were still happy.

Malcolm carried in the coffee which they drank, squashed against each other on the small sofa by the window. The sash rattled and Malcolm pointed out the age of the glass, how it appeared slightly uneven, beautifully faulted in the tiniest way, a piece of ice perhaps rather than a clear, flat, straight plate of nothing-to-see glass.

Wendy laughed and teased. "Oh, the things you come out with. Once I would have said glass was glass, and now you've got me looking at it to see if it has a story to tell."

"Everything has…"

"…a story to tell!"

"Well, it's true."

Malcolm hoped the wisps of steam would hide his displeasure; but there was no chance.

"There's no use burying your face in your coffee and pretending not to sulk. I can spot that a mile off."

He smiled back over the rim of his mug. "A good choice, this one. Rich and creamy but with a nice, undercutting edge of bitterness. My spot, I think you'll find."

"True, you chose the coffee," said Wendy, leaning over in search of his coffee-warmed lips. They kissed and tasted each other and the coffee.

"We could always…"

"Finish our nice coffee first, and then…"

Wendy ran her fingers over the stubble-pricked flesh of his cheek. "What's this, Mr Hunt? A few weeks ago, you'd have been ripping the clothes off me and never mind the coffee. Now you're wanting to finish your coffee first."

"That's true," said Malcolm, taking a final gulp. Putting down the mug, he leant over and kissed Wendy again, then reaching down he pulled up her pale-pink fleece and the T-shirt underneath, freeing both garments in one go and dropping them to the floor.

"You're getting too good at that."

Wendy leant towards him, her nipples hardened. "And if you think that's brought on by your electric presence, you're wrong. It's bloody freezing in here."

She ran to the bed tucked against the wall and under the slope of ceiling. A slanted window let the sky into the room, giving a sense of openness whenever they were safe in bed exploring each other. They had grown close under this patch of York sky; fallen in love beneath its passing clouds; coupled and writhed in pleasure in uninterrupted moments of blue.

Malcolm pulled off his own fleece, which was purple and hadn't even come from the same shop as Wendy's because, hell, you didn't want to get into all that same clothes, share-and-share-alike shit. He fumbled at the buttons of his jeans and she leaned over to help.

And then they heard the doorbell.

"It won't be for us."

Wendy ran her hand over her flat, goose-bumped stomach and undid the button at the top of her jeans, then eased open the zip and exposed the white of her knickers.

"Oh God!" Malcolm felt his erection rise with impatience.

The doorbell rang again.

"I suppose we'd better have a look." Malcolm looked out over Knavesmire, kidding himself there was no disturbance, that he could admire the familiar flatness of the racecourse, then return to bed and to Wendy. Then he peered down and saw the police cars.

"Bloody hell! It's the police. Two cars, flashing lights, the lot."

SAM rang the bell again. He had traced Wistow to this address but wasn't expecting to find him at home. He wanted to check out the house, to make sure. Something about the man was puzzling him. From what Naomi had said, Rick had gone to meet Wistow at an address on the outskirts of York. That ruled out Wistow's home, which wasn't that far from the centre of the city. Mind you, nowhere was far from the centre in York. A small place and better for it, Sam reminded himself. He had never lived anywhere else and that was good; staying put, that's what you were meant to do. It carried on the tradition, kept the family alive in the city they had always come from. Sam took comfort in this notion, even as his personal life disintegrated.

"They're taking their bloody time."

"Who, sir?" said Sergeant Wold.

"I don't know – whoever is in this house."

There were two more officers behind them, another driver apiece in each of the cars. He hoped this wasn't going to prove a useless visit.

A figure loomed in the glass behind the door, then the figure divided into two as the door opened. Sam wondered if he had disturbed them; what the hell, it served them right – what sort of person has time to fuck away the working day? This prickly thought took no account of his own indiscretions and Sam spotted the irony without caring.

"Wendy Wistow?" he said.

"You're half right there," said the woman. She was dark haired and attractive, as Sam absorbed in a downward glance. She returned the look with fire.

"How do you mean?"

"The Wendy part – that's my Christian name. But Wistow, no you're well off beam there. My surname is Barrie, Wendy Barrie; and you are?"

"Sorry, madam, I forgot the pleasantries. Chief Inspector Sam Rounder and this is Sergeant John Wold; and the others, well they don't really need to trouble us. May I come in? It's freezing out here."

"This is a little difficult," said Wendy Barrie. "This isn't my house – I just live in the flat upstairs, which I rent from Will Wistow. Oh, and this is my friend Malcolm – Malcolm Hunt. Sorry, I forgot to introduce you. He's just visiting and…"

"And we disturbed you at an inconvenient moment."

"Something like that, inspector – copperus interruptus, perhaps."

"Quite so, though I've no idea what you're talking about. Anyway, this hall will do fine, so long as Sergeant Wold shuts that wretched door." Wold did as instructed and the house quietly reasserted itself. A clock was ticking in another room. Paintings lined the hall. Sam didn't know much about paintings and didn't like the look of these. Looks more like an art gallery than a home, he thought.

"Right, there is something I must get out of the way immediately. I am looking for my brother, Rick Rounder, who is a private detective here in York. An ex-copper from this city and a good one too. Travelled the world a bit, came back and set up as a private dick. And his biggest payer to date, quite possibly his only one, had been your Will Wistow."

"He's not my Will Wistow – he's just my landlord."

"Sorry, but I'm confused. Perhaps I'm being dense. But my brother was hired by Will Wistow to spy on you – his wife."

"Whose wife! Will's?"

Wendy giggled, then laughed.

"Oh, that's a good one! Me married to Will. Sweet enough man and all that, but no thanks. Besides, I'm not sure he's even interested in women.

"Don't get me wrong, I've not witnessed him shipping little boys into this house or anything; but I just sense he is not that bothered with female company, especially of the more intimate variety."

"That's all very interesting – but Mr Wistow hired my brother to observe you and Mr Hunt here. And he said you were his wife and that he wanted confirmation of his suspicions."

"Why would he do something like that? I've already told you I'm not his wife. The very idea is just too ridiculous for words. And Malcolm's just my boyfriend – a girl's allowed to have a boyfriend, isn't she?"

"Mind if I ask what you do, Mr Hunt?"

"I teach history and do some work at the university but mostly I work with adults in the city. I take them back, teach them about the history of their city, that sort of thing. Help illuminate the past for them."

"And how did you two meet, if you don't mind me asking?"

"Well, you know chief inspector, I think I do mind. I don't see that it has anything to do with what you're asking me."

"Oh, Malcolm – just tell him, there's no harm in it."

Instead of letting him have his say, Wendy told the story herself, about how she attended one of his classes and fell for him straight away, and set about capturing him for herself, and…

"That's more than enough detail. Do you have any idea where Mr Wistow is at this moment? I believe he has gone to meet my brother and I think my brother could be in danger."

"What – from Will; surely not?"

"Did Mr Wistow say where he was going?"

"No, I've not really seen him today, only to nod to."

"Did he ever in the past talk about an old farmhouse, somewhere on the outskirts of York? Maybe it was somewhere he visited or somewhere he thought of buying. Anything come to mind at all?"

"Oh, gosh, I don't think so. We have sat and talked sometimes. He's given me some of his whisky and we've talked about this and that. But I don't remember much about a farmhouse." She stopped as if trying to grasp a lost thought and frowned in concentration.

"There might have been something. One race day, perhaps. There'd been cars all along here and lots of drunks tumbling about. He said something about getting away from it all, but not too far – just out of York. But no, I can't think of anything more at the moment. He gave me rather too much whisky that night and I woke up the next day with a mouldy old slug for a tongue and a head that felt like it had been used for drum practice."

"Now this could be really important – are you sure you can't think of anything more specific?"

"Sorry, I can't."

Sam glowered and turned to leave. Then he swivelled back: "If you remember anything, give me a call on my mobile. Anything at all, just make that call."

He handed over his card and left, shutting the door forcibly.

In the hall, Malcolm grasped Wendy from behind, letting his hands rise up her stomach and towards her breasts.

"Hey, where do you think you're going?"

"Oh, I just thought we could get back to what we were..."

"You can think about it as much as you like, Malcolm Hunt."

She pulled his hands away and turned to face him.

"I don't much feel like it. I want to try and remember that conversation I had with Will in which he burbled on about a farmhouse somewhere or other near to York."

"But my firm friend is ready and waiting," said Malcolm, putting on a private, soppy voice.

"Oh, never mind about that – go away and masturbate or something. I want to concentrate."

Wendy went back upstairs to her flat and Malcolm, once the moment had passed, went back to his own house in a foul mood that was still in place when he went to teach a class that evening.

CHAPTER SEVENTEEN

POLLY Markham shouted until her throat hurt and cried until her eyes were dry. Then she nibbled another piece of chocolate: it didn't taste right so she spat it out. She pointed the torch at the slit in the ceiling. The beam had been bright, sharp as a knife, but it was blunting against the night.

She was scared and sick; her eyes itched from watching the fading beam. All around her, not far from her impromptu prison, normal life continued. The police hunted in empty houses and ransacked barns in the green belt or old industrial buildings closer to the city. They dredged streams; they peered inside rusting car wrecks; and they broke into boarded-up houses. They came close to where Polly was incarcerated, driving within yards of her basement prison, which was barely a mile from her home, in an area marked for redevelopment. Headlights from a passing squad car swept the ground above the basement, illuminating the cracks in the ceiling. Polly shouted but the tyres crunched away, unhearing.

As the police hunted for Polly, they also sought Rick Rounder. DC Dick Warter spent hours battling with Rick's computer. He did not mind because the flat he had been forced to rent after his wife left him was cold and musty. Good coffee rewarded his work and kept him going, while further compensation was found in the private detective's girlfriend, who Warter concluded was "a real looker", letting the thought condense into a droplet of envy. He had never made love to such a woman and wondered at the difference. The erotic thought made him feel daring, and he cherished the fantasy, enjoying private images. Then the thought came back: he had only ever slept with one woman and she had left him.

Yawning, Warter rang Chief Inspector Rounder, who had gone home intending to have a rest. Instead, he had argued with his wife before slumping into an armchair, which was where Warter's call found him.

"I think I've cracked it, sir. I've got an address for you, or at least a description of where the farm is. Should be easy enough to find, by the sounds of it."

Roused, Sam drank half a glass of water, splashed the remainder over his face, and drove the half a mile to his brother's flat.

Within minutes, he was heading out of the city again, summoning help on his radio.

THE two men glared across the cold room as their breath smoked the air. Neither was looking his best. In the tableau they presented, there were few clues as to who was in control. The puffier man was slumped against the wall two or three feet from the stairs; the leaner, fitter man was arranged in an uncomfortable curl beneath the window, hands tied behind his back. Normally the weightier man had an air of urbanity, suggesting a life spent in comfortable softness, with long meals, re-filled wine glasses and malt whisky to follow. The other, fitter man was clearly in pain. Blood was wet and dark on his side, the wound still weeping fresh over crusted, dried blood. On a good day and in a flattering light, his face might qualify for that old-fashioned description of chiselled, but today the chisel had bitten deep. His face was grey and drained, and one thought was going round and round his head: I feel like total shit.

Will Wistow took a deep breath and broke the hostile silence.

"I said we go way back, Rounder, and that you had no idea what you had cost me. I want you to know what pain really is, before I use this on you again." The blade flashed, hungry.

Rick rested against the rotten windowsill. An icy draught cut across his neck but he welcomed the discomfort as a distraction from the pain coursing round his body like liquid barbed wire. His dazed eyes again took in the wallpaper, which bulged and sagged from the damp walls. Someone had chosen this paper from a shop, Laura Ashley by the look of it, in the 1980s. The wallpaper seemed a summary of lives forgotten. Pink roses had once graced a creamy, top-of-the-milk background. The pain made his mind wander. You didn't get top of the milk any more. He was taken back to his childhood and the sight of milk bottles on cold mornings. A frozen stalagmite of cream rose from the bottle, forcing up the tin lid.

Wistow's voice quavered before finding its usual irritating pitch. The cadence was careless, falling and rising as if in expectation of having fun; yet there was nothing amusing about the words coming out of his fleshy mouth.

"We never met, but when I first knew you, you were a bright young copper, progressing quickly up the career ladder – in your twenties and with everything to play for."

Rick sighed. "I don't think you lured me here, beat the shit out of me and then stabbed me, just so I could hear a recitation of my old police CV."

"Very perspicacious of you. But you have to know, Rounder, what pain is. So I shall finish my little re-cap of the situation that brought us together, in a Rounder-bout sort of way. Ha, ha! You see, I can keep my sense of humour even in difficult situations. So there you were, with everything to play for – and yet you left, disappeared off on your travels, winding up in Australia, or so I am given to understand."

"Yes, yes – but where is this getting us?"

"Have patience, my well-travelled friend. I shall arrive at my point in a while, when this point will arrive at you." He indicated the blade, and Rick remembered its kiss as his side ached.

"As you would have guessed if you were possessed of a little more wit, I am not much of a one for the women. Thankfully, you didn't spot this elemental aspect of my character or else my little ruse with the lovely Wendy would not have worked at all. Nice girl and all that and it was mean of me to hijack her sexuality for my nefarious purposes. Mean but necessary, I fear.

"In my life, I have travelled from being more or less homosexual to nothing much at all in sexual terms – retired, you might call it. Or all buggered out – if you'll pardon my little anal joke.

"No, the sex thing has receded in recent years. Oh, it wasn't always like that and I've had my lusty moments with all sorts of delightful boys. It is surprising what you can find if you know where to look, even in dear old York. But before I arrived at my more or less happy state of homosexuality, I had a few exploratory flings of a heterosexual nature. Or to speak more succinctly, I fucked a few girls to see what it was like. It wasn't really to my taste, but I wanted to make sure. That's how I met the lovely Sonia..."

Wistow surrendered himself to the uneven whoosh of his heart. He wondered about the state of his arterial plumbing. Not good, he suspected. A fatty overburdened organ. Somewhere, head or heart, wherever these memories lurked, he saw Sonia across the years, before she grew pale with misery and lost her shine.

He started up again, disliking the silence.

"Well, I thought she was lovely for a month or two. She was different from the people I knew. She was working class, from a different background. Friendly, in good shape physically if you liked that sort of thing, which I did ever so fleetingly, and very eager. Oh, my, was she eager – but sexual enthusiasm has the obvious penalty, as I was to discover. Much to my surprise would be one way of putting it.

"Sonia fell pregnant. I've always liked that expression, by the way. It is so apposite, suggesting as it does a degree of horizontality that normally precedes pregnancy. Anyway, she swore I was the father. I did not deny this likelihood but I had to explain my sexual predicament. I warned her that marriage would therefore not be a sound notion. She understood, although only after a lot of shouting, a fair few tears and the deliverance of what turned into a real shiner of a black eye. Lasted for days, it did – quite iridescent it was. She could hit that girl could – had a forceful punch on her.

"Anyway, a little girl was born and I became, well, not so much a father as a distant uncle. As she grew up, she knew me as Uncle Will. We grew to love each other, that girl and me. My little Tanya. It was not a name I would have chosen but under the circumstances I felt an objection would have been unreasonable. Besides, I grew accustomed to the name and came to love it – for all of the poor girl's short life. She wasn't granted long on this shitty, forsaken earth..."

The name made Rick dizzy with half-understood knowledge. It must be a coincidence. There were other Tanyas. But it was no good, Rick's mind raced. For a year or so afterwards, there had been no escape. Her face had loomed into his waking mind and invaded his sleep. Whatever he had done, wherever he had gone, she had followed him. He had travelled to escape, but some memories cannot be slipped.

"Tanya, did you say Tanya?"

"I did, Rounder. And now at last you are furnished with an explanation for all this – all engineered, rather smartly I hope you'll agree, via that clever little charade I built around my lodger. Dear Wendy was merely a means of entrapment."

"So..."

The past rushed up like a speeded-up film. Rick saw again the dead-white face. So much failure had afflicted the poor girl and his shortcomings had hastened her death. His best had been inadequate, a useless thing. The girl was dead by the age of nine, and he had never been able to escape his guilt.

"So you are Tanya Smitten's father? That's why you've orchestrated all this, just to get what you see as your revenge? Bloody hell, I suppose it makes a sort of sense, but I don't really understand..."

"Shut up and listen then."

Wistow continued his story, the light faded and a November chill seeped into the dank bedroom. As the narrative unfurled, Rick, resisting interruption, listened and waited, planning what to do next. He feared he might not survive another injury.

They had had a good relationship, Wistow and his "girlies." That's how he had always referred to them, as the girlies. It had been a fruitful arrangement for a while. Wistow's hidden family allowed him contentment of a sort he had neither sought nor expected. Everyone had been happy, until the arrival of Arthur Smitten.

"A thug and a moron, you see. And I don't just say that with hindsight. I knew he was no good from the start." A single tear navigated the wrinkles round Wistow's eye. He wiped it away and the knife flashed before his own eyes.

Sonia married Smitten on a cold February day at the registry office on Bootham. Wistow attended as an old family friend, enduring for the sake of his girlies the scorn of Tanya's new stepfather. Smitten had no time for Wistow, calling him a "fucking soft old poofter," a phrase he uttered a number of times during the reception, which was held at a pub near the registry office. At one point Smitten had grabbed the lapel of Wistow's new suit, crushing the buttonholed rose. Wistow had smiled and brought himself close to Smitten and told him, in his best mincing lilt, "not to be such a silly boy."

Smitten never knew, Wistow was certain. During her short, unhappy marriage Sonia maintained Tanya was the product of a one-night stand after a drunken night out on the Micklegate run. This was as likely as any other story because Sonia had been a bit of a girl. Smitten had his suspicions, but he mistrusted everyone and everything, and lacked the wit to pursue his dark thoughts. He accepted Sonia's explanation or at least could not be bothered to question it. Wistow was able to support his daughter from a distance, giving the money willingly. He had the funds, thanks to bequests from relatives of convenient distance and wealth, whose deaths had caused him little grief – quite the opposite. He had earned more, from antiquarian books and antiques, and property deals. He had been, and remained, a ways-and-means man, as he told Rick in the tenebrous light.

"Benevolent fate and a little bit of hard work have seen me through in fine style," he said. "You've seen the house, it's worth a bit and it's all mine. I've another two in York, rented out, plus this pile of dilapidation in which we now find ourselves. A bricks-and-mortar pension. A safe bet what with the way property prices have been going."

Rick was tiring of Wistow's self-serving narrative, but he

calculated there was safety in words. The longer Wistow talked, the more time he had to gather what was left of his strength.

The story wandered to another frequency and Rick felt drowsy with pain. But he came to, alerted by movement. Wistow was trying to stand. "Bloody pins and needles," he said, wheezing and puffing as he pulled himself up. He hopped about on the bare floorboards.

"That's better, much better." Wistow spoke as if addressing his partner or perhaps his cat. Rick drew in his legs, pushing the knees up and resting his heels on the floor, steadying himself.

"So you see..." He was chatting to a friend again.

"So you see, as I was saying...I couldn't blame Smitten, could I? Well, I did, many times; how I cursed his nasty little soul. But there's not much mileage in blaming a dead man. Smitten was a selfish, stupid man – and in his inadequacy he killed the daughter I never meant to have, but ended up loving with all my puffed up old heart. You don't get used to that, ever. It haunts your every waking moment. But you have to go on, have a survival strategy."

His fingers flexed around the knife's smooth handle, the blade still dancing before Rick.

"My aim was simple in a way: find someone to blame for poor Tanya. Smitten had done himself in, so there was no mileage there. So I started thinking about the stupid policeman whose lumbering actions gave Smitten no way out. Vengeance is what I'm after."

"She was dead long before I got to the flat, you know. Tests proved that. The coroner said so. Smitten had already..."

"There you go, trying to find a way out. Be a man, why don't you, and accept what is coming."

The floorboards creaked as Wistow lumbered forward, red penknife in hand. Rick pushed himself up, using all his remaining strength to stand. Wistow was inches away, puffing and snorting. Sweat ran off his brow and snot sputtered from his nose.

"I told you you'd feel pain before the end, Rounder. Losing your child...if you'd done your fucking job properly, my girl, my little darling..."

The blade slashed out and cut Rick's cheek. Wistow pulled the knife back and lifted his arm before letting the penknife fall in a hammer blow. Rick lurched and dodged the knife, which sliced into his shoulder. He yelped in pain and rolled forward in the hope of unbalancing his attacker. Wistow raised his arm again and watched the blood from the blade drip on to the other man's neck, leaving a necklace of red dots. He steadied himself. He could do this thing, he could bring events to their proper conclusion. As the blade came down, he was distracted. There was a flicker of blue somewhere outside. He blinked, focused again, on nothing. Rick had rolled into the shadows away from the window. A pulsating blue light was picking out the dead wallpaper roses.

Rick lunged at Wistow's legs, screaming with pain as his injured shoulder made impact. He curled into a knot of agony, a useless thing, unable to fight further. Death was a thought that came more often than in the past. He did not obsess about it but his mind would roll in that direction, following the inescapable groove. Is this what death looks like, coiled and beaten in a damp room? He was having one of those revelatory moments, life flashing before his eyes. So it really did happen and wasn't another myth. He blinked and tried to see what was happening. Sweat obscured his vision, reducing Wistow to a smudge that filled his eyes and was gone.

THE cars came, squealing and skidding. Doors opened, officers jumped out. Sam Rounder reached the door in two or three long strides, directing officers carrying battering rams. The rotten door offered no resistance and fell into the hall. Officers rushed forward, torchbeams lasering the darkness. Sam was halfway through the door when one of his team shouted and pointed to an upstairs window. A spotlight from one of the patrol cars picked out a solid black shadow. Sam craned his neck, trying to make out the shape. The silhouette held still and then the picture changed, and the dark outline moved forward, falling against the glass. The damp-racked window gave way and the loosened frame fell to the ground, showering glass. The dark shape followed, tumbling through the air before hitting the concrete path with a hollow smack. Sam rushed forward, shouting for an ambulance, and crouched. The fingers of one hand felt for a pulse in the neck, while the other hand brushed a blood-soaked fringe from a grotesquely misshapen forehead. Sam felt a faint pulse, then nothing. He looked at the white flesh and shivered.

"I don't know who the fuck this is but it's not my brother."

Sam went inside the farmhouse and found the unstable stairs. As he climbed he thought of his brother in a thousand infuriating ways. Anxiety and panic mixed with irritation. Rick couldn't be dead, that was too awful to entertain. His own brother couldn't die on him – not like this, not so soon.

Yet wouldn't it be like Rick to be the centre of attention, the little brother in another of his scrapes? It would be the wall all over again.

Sam hadn't wanted to walk along the wall, telling Rick it was too high and looked dangerous. Rick had laughed and said he was no coward, before scrambling up the friable bricks, sending out a cloud of dust and brick splinters. Rick caught his knee and blood welled from the gash. He had not noticed but had walked along the wall, singing and laughing.

"I'm the King of the Castle and you're a useless bastard..."

Rick's face is pink and soft and shines in the afternoon sun as he trots along the wall behind the boarded-up house in The Groves. Sam stands below, face spotted with anger. He is furious to be mocked by his younger brother. He runs on the uneven ground beside the wall. Now he is close enough to see the tiny blond hairs on his brother's legs picked out by the sunlight. Up ahead is the abandoned house, slates slipped from its roof and the upstairs windows put in, leaving it open to the wind and rain or, on a day such as this, the caressing sunshine. Sam takes all this in before he slips and falls headfirst into a bushy plant that thrives in the wasted garden. For a moment he can see nothing and then he rolls over and looks up through the green fronds into the painted sky. He sees his brother, looking down from the wall. Then Rick disappears from the sky.

Sam was at the top of the stairs, panting from the exertion.

"He's in here, sir."

"Is he all right?"

It was Rick who answered. "I'm not dead or stupid, you know."

"Now, now, that's no way for a little brother to speak to his big banana policeman brother. So can I take that as a yes – you're all right?"

"No, I'm not – I feel like total shit. Covered in cuts and bruises and there's a bitch of a cut on my shoulder. I feel sick, knackered and knotted with pain."

"You should see the other fellow."

"Not good?"

"Dead."

Sam helped his brother downstairs and on to the drive, where two ambulances had joined the police cars, one of which conveyed Wistow's remains to the hospital. Rick, limping and with his brother's shoulder for support, was led to the other ambulance. Sam told one of his officers to drive his car to York District Hospital and got into the back of the ambulance with Rick. The back doors were shut and Rick lay on the stretcher as the ambulance sped towards York, at one point passing the comfortable house where, until yesterday, a young girl had lived with her family. Sam was on the cusp of telling Rick about Polly Markham, but thought better of it. He looked across the bright, swaying insides of the ambulance. Outside the siren blared and beneath them trouble-bearing tyres sped towards the hospital.

"So what's all this about, Rick?"

"It's a long story, going back a few years and…"

The paramedic butted in, telling Sam that his brother shouldn't talk.

"It's all right," said Rick. "Here's the potted version. You're not going to believe this, but it's all to do with poor Tanya Smitten."

"Who?"

"Christ, Rick – Tanya Smitten! You can't have forgotten her. She was the reason I left the police, the reason I took off and explored the world. And now, all this time later, she's the reason I nearly got killed during my first case."

"You mean the girl who…?"

"Yes, Tanya Smitten, the girl who was stabbed in that flat after I failed to talk her father round. You remember, Arthur Smitten… killed his daughter, then turned himself into a human firework."

"So what's all this got to do with that body we took away from the farm?"

"That's where the story gets long-winded."

The paramedic cut in again. "The full explanation will have to wait. We're at the hospital."

Rick was stretchered, undressed and had his wounds inspected. He was given a blue gown that fastened round the neck but exposed his arse to the world, and was left to wait on a narrow trolley-bed. There, before time gummed up, the way it does in hospitals, he remembered Naomi.

"Shit, you'd better ring…"

"That girlfriend of yours? Sure. My phone's been off, messages only – I wanted to concentrate on getting to you. Let's see…"

Sam fumbled for his mobile, which he handed to his brother.

"You've got messages."

"Never mind, ring, er…"

"Naomi, her name's Naomi."

"I know that. My mind just went a bit and…"

Naomi, roused from a sleepless sludge of coffee and anxiety, berated Rick for not telling her he was at the hospital, burst into tears, swore, said she loved him, called him a bastard, then set off on foot for the hospital, jogging.

Rick, handing back the phone, felt tiredness wash over him. He held up his hand and imagined it was fading before his eyes.

"You have a rest. I'll wait here until Naomi arrives. Then when the docs have finished putting you back together, you can tell me the full story."

"It's a good one – better than Corrie, although perhaps not so bloody..."

"What are you on about?"

"Not so sure any more."

Rick stared at the ceiling. Soon he was asleep, pale beneath a sheen of sweat. Sam paced the curtained-off area. The soles of his shoes carried out a squeaking conversation with the shiny, scuffed floor. He was wondering what to do when the curtains opened, admitting a doctor and Rick's girlfriend. The doctor didn't look old enough to recognise the sticky side of a plaster. Naomi looked like she had just met one of York's many ghosts – which might almost have been the case, if the police had been any slower.

"Christ, Rick! You look terrible."

Naomi sat and sobbed on the trolley-bed, which woke Rick and brought the baby-faced doctor out in a flutter of tutting.

"I really don't think Mr Grounder is robust enough for ..."

"It's Rounder not Grounder – him and me both."

Sam turned from the doctor and put out his hand to touch Naomi on the shoulder. His hand hovered towards solicitude but withdrew. He wanted to do what was right but ended up feeling clumsy. He hid his embarrassment with a few words.

"That brother of mine will be fine, just you see. Tough old lot, the Rounders – full of York obstinacy."

"What's all this been about, Sam?"

"I haven't got the full and grisly out of Rick yet. Anyway, I must go. I'll phone you later. Bye."

Naomi held Rick's hand, watched as he was wheeled away to have his shoulder sewn up. Exhausted by the rush of emotion, she went to the waiting room and fell asleep in front of a Clint Eastwood movie: one of the old spaghetti westerns, she wasn't sure which. Her eyes didn't stay open long enough.

A MILE or so from the hospital, a similar distance from home, Polly tried to shout but it was no use. No-one could hear. She was completely alone now the nasty man had abandoned her. She had been happy to see him go, but now she felt so lonely, like the only person in the world, as if everyone else had left her in this stinking place. She didn't understand what she had done wrong. Nothing made any sense. She wondered if she had offended God, who she only half understood anyway. Perhaps He had arranged for her to be put in this horrible dark place. She had no idea what could warrant such a punishment. Perhaps God was only another adult.

CHAPTER EIGHTEEN

MALCOLM Hunt sat at the old desk in the scuffed classroom and waited. He was still annoyed by the police's interruption earlier, and now he had to take this wretched evening class.

Malcolm enjoyed teaching adults, as he sometimes had to remind himself. He felt he had much to offer, although he worried he had squandered his talents, fearing in the darkly wakeful dawn that he could have done so much better. The world was full of people who could have, he reminded himself; it was over-populated with "maybes" and "what ifs"; surely he was more than another clapped-out half-achiever?

He read the Evening Press spread out on the desk. News of the snatched girl filled the front page, underneath the headline: Girl, nine, kidnapped. There was a photograph of Polly Markham, taken during a family holiday. She smiled out from the crumpled newsprint, pretty and carefree. A caption said the photograph had been taken in happier times, a statement Malcolm thought fell into the category of the bleeding obvious. Still, he read the story and felt suitably alarmed.

He put down the paper as his students started to arrive. "Students" hardly seemed the word for this bunch, especially Frank Helmsley, who always looked more like a down-at-heel caretaker than a student. He looked particularly down-at-heel tonight. Perhaps he had been up late worrying about the poor of York at the turn of the last century.

Malcolm took the marked essays out of his briefcase, feeling a pinprick of guilt at the comments he had written on Helmsley's work. He would stand by every acidic annotation, yet he knew he had been playing a game, flaunting his superiority to impress Wendy. He had shown Wendy the essay and the comments. This wasn't ethical, but how they had laughed. The essay had been another impassioned but stilted account of poverty, based round what Frank insisted to be a true story. It concerned a girl called Esme Percy, who had died of consumption in 1901. He surveyed the class, counting them in. Frank sat at the front, unshaven and shifty. Beads of sweat decorated his forehead, although it was not warm in the classroom, which was heated by one ancient, dust-wrapped radiator. He looked even more ruffled and unclean than usual. Drank too much beer, no doubt – the cheap stuff sold in big plastic bottles.

The usual suspects arrived, one by one.

The frustrated librarian who never had time to read; the earnest widow who wanted to better herself; the house-husband who was desperate to "squeeze some life out of his washed-out, ironed-out, cooked-out brain"; the clever, articulate woman in her sixties who had been a secretary all her working life; and the fifty-something businessman who woke up one morning and wondered if business was all there was. A late middle-aged couple ran a post office and needed to escape all the red tape; the former publican with a drink problem; and the retired nurse recovering from a life spent being professionally brusque. And Helmsley; who did what exactly? Malcolm wasn't about to ask. As for Wendy, she had stayed away from tonight's class, and he still felt angry with the police for spoiling his afternoon.

"Right, good evening one and all. I have your essays, all marked and ready to return. I'll hand them out during the tea break, then I'll make myself available for discussion when…"

When Frank bloody Helmsley will bore on about the twin iniquities in his life: the horrifying unfairness of the Victorian class system in York; and the even more horrifying unfairness of the way in which his essay had been marked. Malcolm put the thought away and told himself to be positive. He had read an article in one of the weekend newspapers by one of those life-style gurus. This particular trendy charlatan advocated the "halo technique," whereby you dismissed negative thoughts about people by sitting them under an imaginary halo. "Place the shining ring above their heads and feel its positive pull, see the way that the halo relinquishes all negativity, replacing such harmful feelings with aeons of bright optimism…"

Or some such rubbish.

"Right, tonight I thought we could start by looking at the history of open spaces in York. First off, I would like you to think of all the open spaces you can imagine. York is quite a closed-in city, a walled city with a tight mindset and what you might call a suspicious mentality and..."

"Who are you calling suspicious?"

John Street, the retired landlord. His life in assorted York pubs had left him with two broken marriages, a drink problem and a confused sense of bodily self. Having started out thin, he had swelled on a diet of beer, crisps and assorted dishes from the microwave. Bulbous with crisis, he had lost his second wife to a passing tourist from Bournemouth (of all the southern places.) He had also been clinically declared an alcoholic, confirming what could have been diagnosed by any one of his regulars, had they not been hiding behind their own half-empty glasses. The specialist told John that his predicament could be summed up in three short but direct words: drink and die.

On hearing this prognosis, he had told the doctor that not drinking would be a sort of death anyway. The specialist had shrugged and said: "Just don't book a summer holiday."

John stopped drinking, sold the pub (without telling his already departed second wife), lost weight and returned to his former slim shape, and took up local history. He missed his second wife and his old stomach, occasionally assuming both were still present. He would find himself talking out loud to his wife, as if getting ready for a good old argument; and he would put out his hands, as though expecting to find a comfortable mound of flesh. But his wife wasn't there and his hands fell into his unfilled lap.

"I don't think it's fair, all this talk about a closed-in city. We've lived a lot of history in this city, we have, you know..."

"Well, I do know that as I teach the subject, you know, John..."

"True, but I don't think you understand us. You're not from round here, are you?"

"Oh, let's not get all personal. My origins needn't concern us..."

"So you're not then, are you? Knew I was right. So…"

"Oh, leave the poor man alone, why don't you…"

Long years of unruly emergency had given Mary Lewis a voice that could cut across a crowded hospital ward. Still booming, she added: "We should be able to talk to each other in this class without getting cross."

"Quite so," said Malcolm. "I wanted to introduce this topic to see if the geographical, physical shape of York shaped the sort of city it became – or if that shape grew out of historical necessity. This city started life as a fortified community and you could argue that everything grew from that defensive need. So in that context a discussion of space has some relevance."

"There's Knavesmire, the racecourse," said Lillian Crayshaw, the librarian.

"The Ascot of the North, as it is known," said Jeffrey Smithson, the house-husband.

"Ascot of the North, my arse," said John Street. "I reckon Ascot is the York of the South."

"York has such a long and proud history, yet here we all are, being parochial all over again," said Jeffrey. "I mean, the thing is, York has so much to be proud about, and people come here from all over the world to explore our history, and yet we can all be so inward looking, so wrapped up in our own suspicion about the wider world."

"Or even just about Leeds," said Malcolm, glad of some like-minded support. "I've heard the way you go on about Leeds."

"It's being parochial, as you call it, what made this city great…"

"Yes, Frank? That's an interesting spin on matters. So what is the point you are trying to make?"

"Being parochial, closed in and with…" Here Frank looked down at the notes he had written. "With 'a tight mindset and what you might call a suspicious mentality.' Well, all of that's what has helped to make this city great. You've got to be suspicious of someone what wants to invade your city. Pride in who we are and why we are here is what has kept us going down the centuries."

"Yes, well, we don't have to be suspicious of people nowadays, do we? I mean, the only invaders now are tourists and we need them here to support us all, don't we?" said Sandra Graham, who, with her husband Paul, ran a local post office.

"Sandra's right, you know," said Paul. "She's got a point."

"Yes, that's true," said Malcolm. "And we've all got a point – more especially, you've all got a point and that's why you're all here, to learn and to share.

"Right, we have got off to a good start, but we do seem to have wandered from discussing open spaces. Now, of course, York is surrounded by open space, with countryside and moors accessible in all directions, but the city itself is, I think we can agree, fairly crowded. And this is especially so nowadays when every available bit of land is used for building…"

"And usually to build rather nice looking flats that none of us could afford – at least not on a secretary's pension," said Elizabeth Marsden, crisply. "Still, mustn't grumble, that's the life I led." The last sentence was spoken aloud but seemed to be just for her.

"You have raised an interesting point, there, Elizabeth. The use of space in modern York reflects, and indeed intensifies, the historic use of space. The developers putting up flats today try to squeeze profit out of every square inch.

"The other day I walked down a street where a friend lives. There's a main road on one side, a side street on the other. An old shop – I think it sold bikes – has been knocked down and ten flats put in its place. How can the space occupied by one small shop be turned into ten flats? This seems to me to be a perfect illustration of the importance of the history of space in York…"

"So they don't pay you enough to buy one of those there flats then, do they?" said Frank.

Malcolm took a deep breath. Stay calm. In and out, nice and controlled.

"Very amusing, Frank, yes. But let's keep this away from the personal and…"

Malcolm looked away, casting about for a more sympathetic face.

"So…"

Whatever thought Malcolm was about to impart never got further than his lips. There was a great crash. At first he had no idea what had happened because his brain had been wired to think about space in York, and to avoid thinking about Frank bloody Helmsley. Now he saw that it was Frank who had caused the commotion. He had fallen to the floor and was lying face down, hands spread out, as if he had collapsed while trying to do a push-up. His face was hidden and it was hard to tell if he was breathing. As Malcolm crouched, panic and distaste coursed round his veins. Even in this extreme situation, it was difficult to get close to Frank. He smelt like he had been out somewhere damp all night; he smelt like he hadn't washed in weeks; he smelt like the invention of deodorant had passed him by. The whiff of 'eau de desolation', as he would later tell Wendy, trying to make her laugh, but failing. Perhaps the joke was a mistake, all things considered.

Mary Grace stepped in, becoming once again the efficient nurse who sorted everything out, the one everyone relied on. As she hurried towards Frank, as brisk as she was fat, Malcolm offered up a prayer to the patron saint of retired nurses. He gave Mary room to do whatever it was she needed to do.

"Phone for an ambulance," she said and Malcolm pulled out his mobile. Mary swung her great bulk downwards in one swift, graceful movement. She did not flinch at Frank's odour. Such smells had been common on the wards and she had sniffed much worse in her day. Pink clean fingers went in search of a pulse.

"He's still with us but he doesn't look good," she said.

"And he doesn't smell so good either," Malcolm said, the words slipping out. He hadn't spoken loudly, only Mary heard.

"Well, that's as maybe. I don't like a bad smell myself but this isn't the time to be worrying ourselves about that, is it?"

"Sorry, the words just came out, and…"

"Make amends by giving me a hand. We need to roll him on to his side, and put him in the recovery position."

"Sort of like the foetal position?"

"That's the fellow."

Helmsley lay in a curl, his breathing erratic, his skin pale and sweaty.

"He looks kind of wounded, like a hurt animal or something," said Malcolm.

"That's because he is," said Mary. "Heart, I expect. He doesn't look like a man who takes care of himself. It catches you out in the end, does the heart."

The class looked on anxiously, caught in a moment of collective social indecision. Should they stay or should they go? No-one seemed to know.

"I suppose class is dismissed," said Malcolm. "I don't think we'll be doing anything else tonight. You can all go if you like. Or, of course, you can stay around to…well, to be with Frank. Yes, to be with Frank in his, you know, moment of need. To see if he is going to be all right, which I'm sure he is. Well, I'm no expert of course, but we'll have to see and…"

Malcolm shrugged and frowned, his face went blank and his mouth gave up attempting to make useful sounds.

Everyone stayed silent, waiting for the ambulance, stuck fast by uncertainty. A crisis was a sort of embarrassment, until it happened to you. Malcolm wondered if this was what death looked like, pale and lardy. This was death from the outside, Malcolm reminded himself – quickly adding that Helmsley wasn't dead. He led his mind into a philosophical cul-de-sac. In any subjective sense, death could not be that bad, because, after all, being dead was just like being unborn – to die was to return to that state of nothingness from which we all came. We arrived out of glittering blackness and we went back there. Life and death, you couldn't have one without the other – the connection between the two was what made us human, alive and sentient. We don't do death well nowadays – we keep it hidden, forgotten and feared on the quiet, the last great embarrassment. The Victorians did death terribly well, trussing themselves in the stiff social etiquette of mourning, yet they kept sex hidden. We flourish the sex and keep death under wraps.

Yes, Malcolm thought, there was a theme there, for a lecture or an article perhaps. He really should start reading up on the Victorians again, Dickens and Eliot, a bit of Wilkie Collins perhaps. And maybe…

A siren intruded and a blue light strobed the walls. The ambulance officers bustled in. Frank was turned over to professional solicitude, his pulse monitored, his breathing checked; he was transferred to a stretcher and carried out. The mature students of history started chatting. John Street felt the sudden call of alcohol, but then he remembered with regret that he didn't do that any more. Some of the others, unencumbered by alcoholic restraint, headed for the comfortable fug of the nearest pub. John went home alone to make a cup of mint tea, which was said to be good for him.

Malcolm hung back and, almost too late, decided (as teacher, and therefore some kind of position of authority) he ought to go to the hospital. He chased after the stretcher, catching the ambulance as it prepared to leave. He sat in the back opposite Frank Helmsley. The inside of the ambulance was bright and full of medical equipment he half-recognised from television dramas. The siren wailed and Malcolm imagined cars getting out of their way. He braced himself as the ambulance was thrown into a corner. An ambulance officer sat in the back, her hand resting on Frank's forehead.

In a few moments they were at the hospital. The stretcher was briskly lifted out of the ambulance and Malcolm jogged along as Frank Helmsley was taken into the accident room. Bright lights and swift care took over. Frank was wheeled along a shiny, scuffed corridor and disappeared behind curtains.

Malcolm was directed to a waiting area, where he sat in front of an over-sized television screen. He picked up a crumpled two-day-old copy of The Sun, and then swapped this for a Cosmopolitan from the summer before last, which was full of sex and sun (neither of which he had experienced today). On television, a Clint Eastwood film had given way to the late-night local news. There had been a car crash, one person dead, another injured. An old woman had been mugged. The disappearance of Polly Markham was mentioned and Chief Inspector Sam Rounder appeared on screen to appeal for information. "Polly Markham is out there somewhere," he said. Malcolm stared blankly before making the connection: this was the same man who had interrupted his sexual encounter with Wendy. The memory caused him to scowl.

A nursing sister swept in, young and trim in her uniform. She smiled briefly and then didn't. There were bags under her eyes and her skin looked like it could handle a shot of neat daylight.

"Now did you come in with Mr Helmsley?"

"Yes, I did. Is he...?"

"We're doing what we can for you... is he a friend or a relative?"

"Er, neither. I'm his teacher at night class. I teach history and..."

"Well, Mr Helmsley would like to speak to you."

Frank had suffered one heart attack, another was feared. He was on his way up to surgery for a heart bypass, but had wanted to speak to Malcolm first. Malcolm wondered what on earth Frank could want to say. They hardly knew each other. Frank had been connected to assorted pipes and he was breathing through an oxygen mask. He indicated the mask with an agitated shake of his thick wrists. A nurse removed the mask, his face looked deathly white.

Frank started to speak, his words coming in hushed bursts broken by pain. What he said was garbled and concerned one girl, then two.

"I discovered so much about Esme Percy, the lost girl who died in 1901. There was so much about this girl that wasn't fair or right and that's why..."

A wave of pain silenced him. The nurse told Frank he should rest; it would do him no good to get agitated. He breathed in short gasps, as if each mouthful of air contained a thistle.

"This won't do you any good at all, Mr Helmsley, a man in your condition."

"Some things need saying." Frank delivered the words in a whisper. Then, turning to Malcolm, he held him with his bloodshot eye. "Fuck, this hurts. Feels like I've got a fucking giant kneeling on my chest."

Frank fell quiet. The nurse mopped his brow. "We'll be taking you upstairs in a moment, Mr Helmsley. Just a minute or so, then you'll be whisked away to where the surgeons can do their work."

"I want to talk, things to tell." Frank spoke with the urgent brevity of a man who could no longer afford to waste words.

"Esme Percy, you see. That's how I got into all this. What had happened sort of took me over. The injustice of it all. A hundred years ago. But we can't forget. History is about remembering, isn't it? I'm not an educated man. Not by today's standards, not by your standards. But I know what's right and what's not. What happened to Esme Percy, that wasn't right. Not right at all. Something had to be done to make up for the sins of the past. That's where the other girl…that's where she comes in."

"You keep talking about the other girl, Frank. Who is she?"

"Esme Percy died because she was poor and because she lived in the slums of York. I wanted to make…what's the word? Reparation. I wanted to put things right. That's why the other girl had to become involved. She had to come from a good family. A well-off family, as that made sense and…"

The nurse stepped in. "The porter will be here in a moment, to take you up to the surgery, Mr Helmsley. You really should stop all your agitating. It's not good for you."

She went off, whisked to other business, perhaps bored of deathbed confessions.

"Perhaps I shouldn't have done what I did, but it was done for a reason. To make amends. To put history right. To correct the balance of injustice. Those are the reasons why it was done…"

"Why what was done, Frank?"

"The other girl. Haven't you been listening to a thing I've been saying? You could be the last man on earth I speak to. You with your smart words and your complacent ways. You with your cocky southern airs, you with your leather jackets and…"

"Now look here, Frank, I don't think…"

"Oh, shut up for a minute. My words are more important than yours at this minute. My words are more than just words. They have been given force by my actions, by what I have done."

"Go on, Frank."

"You will need to tell them where to look."

"Tell who where to look?"

"The police…"

Images bumped into Malcolm's mind. There was a missing girl, kidnapped from outside her house. Frank's skin was deathly white, his eyes unnaturally bright.

"Are you trying to tell me you're some kind of paedophile? You've been kidnapping girls so you can …?"

Frank had been born with strong hands. There were powerful now, even in his final weakness. He grabbed Malcolm by the wrist.

"Shit, Frank!"

"Shit yourself, you bastard. I might be many things but I'm not one of those what goes round interfering with little girls. Haven't you understood anything I've been telling you? And you a history teacher too. Some teacher you are…"

Malcolm brushed away the insults, trying to understand what he was being told.

"There's a girl, Frank. You've been trying to tell me about her, haven't you?"

"Ho-bloody-ray! You've got it…"

"Who is she, where is she?"

The curtain was pulled back, heralding the return of the nurse. "The porter's here for you, Mr Helmsley. Let's get you upstairs."

"Can't this wait a minute, he's trying to tell me something important…"

"Nothing is more important than getting this patient into surgery."

As the porter stepped forward, Frank said: "I'll be ready for you in a second. I have something to tell my friend here."

Malcolm's wrist was beginning to hurt. He leaned forward, putting his ear close to Frank's pale, stubble-pricked face.

"Unburden your load, Frank."

Two pairs of eyes locked in unlovely gaze. Neither man liked the other but circumstance, fate, call it what you will, had thrown them into this moment of finality.

"I took the girl. She's all right, like. I've not harmed her, like. Just kept her somewhere, somewhere fitting, somewhere with a parallel. When you think of Esme Percy there was only one place I could keep her, really. And that's what I did."

Frank started to gabble.

"I'm running away, chasing. The blackness is after me. This is my time."

He sat upright, animated by a final surge of life, his hand still clamped round Malcolm's wrist.

"You're the historian so you can work it out for the police. If they want to find Polly Markham, they need to follow a trail from their history books. Find Esme Percy and you'll find…"

Helmsley collapsed into the hospital trolley, leaving Malcolm to touch his chafed wrist. Frantic activity swept in. Doctors and nurses ran to help the history lover and kidnapper of an innocent girl, but he was beyond the intervention of medical science. He died on that hospital trolley at the age of fifty-six. His early death could have had many contributing factors, from poor diet – salt with everything, hardly anything fresh to eat, only the cheapest convenience food from the cheapest supermarket – to lousy genetics: his father's arterial plumbing had given out at the age of fifty.

Malcolm Hunt left the hospital wanting desperately to find Wendy and to take her to bed, to restore blood and life to his body, to embrace the quick and the living (and Wendy was both of those.) Instead, he started to research the most important history lesson of his life.

THE lost girl gave up shouting into the darkness. She was afraid the nasty man would come back and scared he would not. She hated that man with his nasty smell and his funny-coloured teeth.

Mummy wouldn't like the nasty man at all. Daddy wouldn't like him either, but he wouldn't be around. He'd be off doing whatever it was Daddies did when they got up to no good. She'd heard Mummy talking to Grandma about the no good thing. Mummy cried. Polly couldn't work out what being up to no good involved, but she guessed it was like what happened in the soap operas on the television, when Daddies went off with the wrong Mummies and had sex they shouldn't have been having.

No, she didn't like the nasty man at all, because he had snatched her and brought her to this horrible place. But if the nasty man didn't return, then no one would know where she was at all and she could die in this place, cold, hungry and alone.

Polly screamed again but her voice did not even dent the darkness. She was quite alone and, though she did not know it, abandoned by a dead man.

CHAPTER NINETEEN

SAM Rounder yawned across the desk at the teacher, or lecturer or whatever. He thought of the American use of the phrase – "what-*ever*" – used by his daughters. Sam Too said it most often although Lotte said it too, usually as she wrinkled her nose and dispersed the freckles.

Sam yawned widely. "Sorry, I'm knackered, but I'm always knackered these days. I guess I owe you an apology of sorts, Mr Hunt."

"Why is that?"

"Oh, I think I put myself in the way – inserted myself between you and well, er..."

"Not sure that's any of your business, inspector."

"Chief inspector, actually – but, yes, you're right. Not my business. Nothing to do with er, that, seems to be my business these days, but that's another sad story. So how do you think you can help me to find Polly Markham? Oh, and sorry about bringing you in here, but my office was being used."

Sam didn't mention the office was being used by a policeman to catch up on his sleep.

"So I thought we might as well sit in here. Nothing formal, no tapes on or anything like that."

"Yeah, I've seen rooms like this on TV dramas. In the American ones there's often some sort of cage in the corner. And maybe a black guy with a thick lip who's just been done over by one of the NYPD's finest."

"Oh, we tend to leave all that violence and intimidation to the *New* York boys. Anyway, how do you think you can help find Polly?"

"It's a hunch, I guess you could call it an historical hunch. You see..." Hunt settled in the police chair, as if he were about to deliver a lecture. He had the air of a man on the point of imparting a bit of education, whether or not the person listening was open to elucidation. "York, you see, was a very different sort of city in

1901 – outwardly respectable and boasting much of the magnificence it has today, but so very poor. The poorest people led a life you or I could hardly contemplate…"

Sam wasn't in the mood for an academic ramble round the old houses, yet there was Hunt, his face suffused with the joy of telling someone something they ought to know. Everything about his appearance – the longish sandy hair, the almost invisible freckles, the slight furrows of the broad brow, the bright blue eyes – seemed calculated to annoy the hell out of Sam. He took a deep breath. "Look, Mr Hunt, it's very good of you to come in here and offer to help, especially so late at night. At less urgent times, I would be thrilled to hear your lecture on York a century ago – but I'm living in the here and now. And the here and now I'm most worried about is the unexplained disappearance of Polly Markham."

"Ah, but you see, the past is often with us, Chief Inspector. History is with us all the time – other people's pasts, our own past. You can't escape history, you know."

"That's as may be, but how does all this help me find a poor, terrified girl who is being kept prisoner somewhere?"

Hunt rested his chin in his hand, cupping his own face lovingly, as if facing a photographer who had been hired to take the dust jacket photograph for his latest book. This was a favourite fantasy, and certainly fantastical as, strictly speaking, he had yet to publish anything, discounting the occasional snooty admonishment in the letters pages of The Guardian.

"Ah, but you see, the past is with us all the time. And I think that the way to find this poor girl is to go looking for another girl who lived a century ago."

"So what's the connection?"

"I was teaching poor Frank Helmsley just before he died tonight…well, I say 'poor Frank' but he was a bit of a weirdo, if you ask me. I always thought there was something not right about him – something not quite connected. He didn't make the link with other people – but he was obsessed with history, especially the inequities of the past. He did a lot of research in his own way –

nothing quite properly academic, of course – nothing up to the rigours true history demands. But he made quite a few discoveries. He became much taken with a girl called Esme Percy. He found out much about her short life."

Hunt paused, seeing Helmsley's face, as grotesque in death as it had been in disputatious life.

"It was a strange business, all this, you know, Chief Inspector. I knew Frank because he was one of my adult pupils. That was my only connection to him – and yet I was privileged, if that's the word, to attend his death. You know, I didn't even like the man – I mean, hell, he smelt and didn't look like he knew which end of the toothbrush to put in his mouth. He was pretty much a disgrace. Yet he had a life and fate put me there when he left it.

"And as he lay dying, he was trying to tell me something. He kept going on about running away. And he said: 'The blackness is after me. This is my time'. After that he sat bolt upright, animated by the life that was leaving him. His hand was gripping my wrist. Look, it's still chafed from his grasp. He may have been dying but he was bloody strong. This is the bruise I got from a dead man, which is a strange thought, the bruise outlasting him. Anyway, his last words to me – his last words to anyone on this earth – went something like this: 'You're the historian so you work it out for the police. If they want to find Polly Markham, they need to work it out from their history books. Find Esme Percy and you'll...' That was it. The words petered out and he was dead. I'd heard about the missing girl and I guessed that was what Frank was talking about."

Sam scratched at the stubble decorating his too-pendulous chin. How had so much flesh found its way on to his face? He frowned and looked again at the lecturer.

"Helmsley kidnapped Polly?"

"I think that's what he was trying to tell me when he died."

"Any idea why?"

"Fuck knows...oh, pardon me, Inspector...Chief Inspector... that just slipped out, I didn't mean to..."

"There's a girl gone missing and you might have the key to

finding her. A spot of swearing is hardly likely to bother me. You should hear the language in this police station – quite a fucking lot of it from me."

Hunt smiled at that. "Fair enough. Why would Helmsley kidnap Polly Markham? I can't say for sure. He took his reasons with him when he died. But I think he was trying to put right what he saw as an historical injustice. He found out about this girl, Esme Percy, who lived a terrible life of poverty and died young, probably of disease brought on by poverty and malnutrition. And he felt that kidnapping a girl of a similar age would somehow put things right. That's my guess."

Sam sighed. "I've come across all sorts of warped explanations for crimes, but that one takes the digestive. Well, you may well be right – and I can't afford to ignore the only lead we've got. Are you willing to help us look for this dead girl from a century ago who could help us find Polly Markham?"

"Yes, of course."

"Right, first up I'm sending a team round to Frank Helmsley's house, to take the place apart. What a day this has turned out to be. All this, and my bloody brother too."

ESME Percy feared one face more than any other. It may have been accounted a strange dread because she was accustomed to all manner of unpleasant visages – faces dirty and ravaged, badly assembled around gap-toothed, black-pegged mouths; she was used to unwashed and sometimes diseased flesh; she knew rottenness in its various forms. There were many faces even less wholesome than that of her father. Darting in and out of the alleyways near where she lived, she would come across all sorts of everyday demons. Some of the shadowy people were harmless; others were brothers to the devil himself. She may not have known this for a fact, but she had such a strong sense of their malignancy that she felt confident in the truthfulness of her fears.

These slums were her world, the only one she knew. She could find her way about by herself or with her brothers or sisters. The

Percys were numerous and there was comfort in being one of many.

Since the day of the gristle, Esme had tried to avoid her father. In her memory the indigestible rubbery curl took on a greater significance, coming to represent the loss of her love. Her father became a figure of fear and loathing. Esme, as the youngest child, would have kindled love in the heart of another father, but not in Thomas Percy. To him, Esme stood for all the limitations of his life; she represented his burdens, and he hated her for this.

In the small, damp rooms where they lived, avoidance was not easy; but Esme mostly managed to find separation, thanks to her father being absent from home. Her days settled into a pattern of self-preservation. Her mother and siblings observed and protected her, especially the oldest boys, Joshua and Joseph, whose dislike of their father had grown since they started working, fulfilling the paternal role by bringing money into the family. The boys were bigger than their father and would brook no nonsense; and however much Thomas might swear and shout, he would always back down, made sour and sullen by failure.

In all this Esme did not exactly thrive, but she seemed well enough and flickers of vivacity would illuminate her paleness.

She took to sitting outside. She had a favourite spot of wall, a short distance from the back door, across from the midden privies shared by the families. The stench could still reach her, but she would try to forget the smell, enjoying instead the sunshine that penetrated the gloomy yard and painted her stretch of wall, while also burnishing the weeds that filled the crevices between the cobbles.

Esme sat in her favoured spot on one of those bright November days when autumn seems unwilling to let go. She was warm and busy with her secretive task. In her hands she held two objects, one hard, dense and solid, the other slender and quick. Her fingers brought the two objects together with a sound between a slither and a scratch. She would let no-one see what she was doing, not even her mother. If someone came too close, she would hide the two objects down the front of her washed-out, colourless dress. When she felt free to start again, the objects would come out and the job would continue. She looked like a child preparing a secret gift. Perhaps this was so.

She was in the yard when her father came home. Her fingers froze in their clandestine task and were then busy with hiding. She glanced around, looking for somewhere to run, but there was no way out.

Thomas Percy smiled at his daughter, which was not something he often did. The smile God had given him had a suggestion of deviousness, and with a slight change it could become a sneer; but it was a smile right now, there was no arguing with that. As for his mood, that was expansive and happy.

"Come indoors, lass, and share in my good fortune," he said, extending his hand. Esme flinched, then stood with care, hoping to dart away. Yet her father caught her with unaccustomed gentleness, and guided her into the parlour, his rough hand weighted on her slight shoulders.

Thomas Percy was in general a stranger to cheerfulness and when his temperament swung from hostility to happiness, his family did not know how to react, nor what to expect. Happiness, being a mood that could not last, was feared the most. On this November day, Thomas Percy had about his person what could without exaggeration be described as a sparkle. His cheeks, usually sallow and bristled, shone pink and smooth; his wayward, lank hair was slick with perfumed oil. He wore on his back a new garment, which until yesterday had graced the shoulders of a wealthy and respectable man from Fulford. Such wealth and respect, as Thomas Percy now explained to his wife in the parlour, where damp bloomed on once-white walls, that could be his for the having.

"We live in a new century and a man can make great things of himself," he said, tugging the lapels of the coat with his thumbs. "There are opportunities for a gentleman in this twentieth century." He released the coat and the folds of material fell back, as if seeking the rounder contours of the previous owner.

"Here, feel this," Thomas said, grasping his wife by the wrist. Martha Percy flinched but his hands did not hold her with cruel intent. He guided her hand towards his smooth cheek. Martha laughed nervously.

"Why, Thomas your face is as smooth as the behind of a baby. It must be an age since you were that smooth."

"I have been at the barber off Coney Street. For a lather and a shave, like a proper gentleman."

He crouched on the stone-flagged floor, where the fringe of his newly acquired coat trailed in the grease-moulded dust.

"You feel it too, Esme – touch the smoothness of my cheek."

Esme held her breath as her father grasped her wrist and placed her fingers on his unsplintered cheek. He smiled and exposed green-furred teeth, strands of tobacco. Only when he released her and stood up did Esme take another breath.

"Now that my luck could be changing, what with me having found a benefactor, I could do with some help from this young lass here. Our Esme could aid in my good luck."

Esme stopped breathing again, as if a stone of anxiety lay across her lungs. Her eyes darted, seeking escape. She took a shallow breath followed by a deeper one. When she spoke all that came out was the one word: "How?"

"Oh, do not worry yourself about that. Your mother can smarten you up a bit, give you a wash or such. Then you can come out with me on a trip to a grand house. We'll go on one of them trams. You will like that, I know you will."

Her heart beat like a trapped thing. She did not want to leave the house with her father.

She feared his cruel tongue and his harsh fingers. She feared what he might do to her.

"Are you sure one of the other girls would not do as well, Thomas?" said Martha, standing in front of the girl. "Our Esme is so young still; what good can she be to you in this matter?"

"Oh, you will just have to trust me. I am going to Fulford and the girl is coming with me. It is a grand house, the grandest you have ever seen. Esme will come into that house and help me make something better of myself."

"How will she do that, Thomas? How can our scrap of a lass help you?"

"Her presence has been requested, that is all I can say. She can be a playmate for one of the rich daughters, yes, that will be it, I am sure of it."

"The rich tend to play with their own," said Martha. "What would a wealthy child want with our Esme?"

"Never you mind about that. She is coming with me and that is the end of the matter."

Esme Percy, smartened up and wearing a dress borrowed from her sister, who in turn had inherited the garment from another girl, stood in the parlour while her mother brushed her hair, seeking shine. Martha let her hand rest on an insubstantial shoulder.

"You be a good girl for your pa," she said, smiling as best she could. "He will look after you, lass. Then you come back to me and I will prepare you a treat. Bread and marmalade, I know you like that. Just think on that and keep the picture in your mind. And keep a picture of me in there, too. Your old Ma, waiting here for you."

"You are not old, Ma," said Esme. More than ever before, she wanted to stay with her. She wanted to remain close to those familiar, worn features, the face pinched by unseen fingers, the forehead lined by an invisible pencil; and yet how the lines, the cracks, could heal over when her mother smiled, for which expression she did not often find time enough, nor reason.

Thomas Percy stood in the doorway and blocked out the light.

"Come on, lass, it is time to go on our adventure. What a fine thing it is, for a young girl to be going out with her father for the afternoon. A fine and proper thing."

Martha wondered when it was that her husband had started to talk in this manner; perhaps he had borrowed some high-sounding words along with his new coat.

Esme looked between her parents, wanting to stay with the one but forced to go with the other. Her genial captor extended his hand and escorted her into the yard, where the late November sun painted the grubby walls.

"So let us go to Fulford, my sweet lass," he said.

"Did you say we could go on a tram, Pa?"

"I did, lass, I did. And I am a man who is good to his word."

Esme Percy stepped along with her father in fearful wonderment, trying to imagine when he would turn back into his harsh self. Until that moment should arrive, father and daughter were composed into what may almost have passed for a picture of happiness.

CHAPTER TWENTY

WHICHEVER way he turned, Rick Rounder could find no comfort. The hot, dead air of the hospital weighed on his lungs and he woke from the last short sleep to find a nurse asking what he wanted for breakfast. Breakfast – he didn't want breakfast, he wanted the dream she had just violated, he wanted sex, he wanted a drink, he wanted to be somewhere else, anywhere else.

In his sleep he had been in Australia, making love to Naomi on the beach, until his brother had walked in on them. This made no sense because Sam had never been to Australia. Rick blinked away the confusion of sleep, said he would like the finest cornflakes the hospital had to offer, then noticed Naomi, her eyes shot and tired, her mouth caught between a smile and a yawn.

Rick grinned back.

"What's with the smirk?"

"I had a dream. It was nice, you were in it. You and me, on the beach. Then Sam spoilt it."

Naomi kissed Rick's forehead: a mother's kiss, a sister's kiss. He closed his eyes and conjured a passionate meeting of mouths and the thought let warm life trouble the hospital sheets. Musing on the irrepressible nature of the male erection, he unglued his eyes.

"Remind me that we are due to have sex when I get out of here."

"I've been worrying myself half to death and you've been lying here thinking about sex."

"Well, the thing is, sex just does that. It occupies the male mind when nothing else is there."

"Is that so?"

Naomi lay her right hand on the sheets, finding just the right location.

"Shouldn't you, er, draw the curtains or something? That old lady over the way doesn't miss a thing. And, oh…"

"Just checking everything is still in working order. Well, seeing as you appear to be on the mend, I'll leave you on that beach with your brother. Now I know you're alright, I think I really, really have to go home for a shower - it'll do us both good! See you later, lover man."

She kissed him and was gone.

POLLY Markham lay on the rough concrete floor. Her body was curled in defence, seeking safety in itself. Apart from the choreography of dust, there was no movement. Time stretched into something beyond time and Polly lay like a dead thing. Then she found the energy to pull herself upright. She had been glad when the horrible man had gone away. Now she felt so alone she almost missed his funny smell and the pencil-pricked skin of his face.

Polly stood and walked unsteadily about her cell, her legs weak with hunger. She had never been so alone. There had always been someone a shout away, someone to watch over, to return her smiles or offer a cuddle.

Cars were driving along a road a short distance from this hole in the ground. Life was going on so she couldn't be dead. She pictured the cars, saw the wheels spinning, going somewhere or other. She tried to imagine which road the cars were driving along. She shut her eyes and concentrated on the noise, trying to work out where she was. Nothing came. No-one came. Her stomach ached deep down, as if her insides were trying to eat themselves. She tried to cry but had nothing to spill; she thought about having a wee but there was nothing left inside her.

A CENTURY apart, Esme Percy sat up high and watched the huge, busy arses of the two horses. The tram was full and the burdened beasts moved with weighted slowness, pausing occasionally to shift their tails and release a steaming load of mustard-coloured shit. Esme held her nose against the stench. No-one else seemed to notice and the tram trundled on. Her father did not speak and peered ahead with unseeing eyes, while biting his bottom lip with the top teeth he still possessed.

"It lies this way, lass," he said, stepping from the tram and striding off in the afternoon sunshine. Esme walked as quickly as her ill-fitting dress would allow, keeping sight of her father as he pushed through the people on the wide pavement.

Everything here was grand; the buildings were huge and daunting; the people were pinkly fleshed and wore clothes whose colours were rich and full, instead of lost in dirt and wear.

Her father stopped outside a house that rose like a cliff made of red bricks. On the other side of a wrought-iron gate a long path went up to the house, passing through a garden as lush and green as anything Esme had seen. She touched the black curls and swirls of the gate, but her father pulled her away.

"That entrance is not for the likes of us, nay."

His eyes flickered as he spoke, as if in expectation of being caught somewhere he should not be; he grabbed his daughter by her thin arm and took her into a gloomy alley. The sky disappeared up the brick canyon between the house and its neighbour. Esme tipped her head to see clouds float between the chimneys, then she slipped on the mossy stones as she tried to keep up with her father.

"Come on, or else we shall be late and the master does not hold with tardiness."

She did not understand who this master was or why he would want to meet her. Maybe her father desired her to work at this grand house, perhaps in service. She had heard of service but was not sure what it meant. She tried to ask but her father told her to be quiet and continued to drag her until they reached a wooden gate next to a round metal plate with a bell-pull at its centre. Thomas Percy stretched out an arm clad in the cloth discarded by a man of greater importance, and pulled the bell. Esme heard a distant peal as she stood in this place of shadows on a sunny day. Out on the busy street, the world minded its own business.

The door was opened. A manservant looked at Thomas Percy with a disdainful superiority that had no call on words. His eyes rested on the scruffy man in the once-fine coat, then moved up and down in the performance of an almost imperceptible nod. He turned briskly and Thomas and Esme Percy followed, passing along the edge of a garden that flourished within warm walls.

Esme did not know houses had such gardens. To her eyes, the garden, collapsing but still lush in November, looked like Eden, at least from what she had learned about it in Sunday school. Ahead was a large dark-wooded door with four panels of stained glass, each depicting a season of the year.

Sunshine from the garden lit up the year, throwing colourful shadows on the wall behind, but then the manservant led them away from this cheerful place into a tilting, brick-lined passageway. They passed an opening from whence escaped great amounts of heat. Esme saw a place of spitting fat and furious steam. She was frightened by the noisy busyness, yet mesmerised by such a blur of activity; she had never seen such a kitchen and did not understand how or why it could take all those people to cook a meal. Esme found herself at the foot of stairs that twisted and turned in alarming ascension and gazed up in dizzy apprehension, before tagging behind her father, who followed the disdainful manservant. The shadowy stairs were steep and the three of them were panting when they reached a cramped landing. A tiny window admitted a grudging amount of light through dirty panes.

The manservant spoke. "He awaits you in there," he said. Duty done, he twirled round, nostrils flaring, and descended the narrow corkscrew stairs with a quick, confident step, his shiny shoes beating out a brisk rhythm, glad to be gone. He left behind a male aroma Esme did not recognise. It was, although there was no reason Esme would know this, the smell bequeathed by hot baths taken with the slippery remnants of a rich man's soap; it was the smell of cleanliness and of small favours having been returned. The manservant disappeared, his eyes turned blind.

Thomas Percy brought his fist down on the door. A voice from within granted admittance and Thomas propelled Esme before him. The girl blinked in the half-light of a small room whose one window was shrouded in heavy velvet curtains that hung like a dead animal. The sunshine in the room was thin and filtered, and an unsteady crack of light fell at the feet of a large shadow that turned out to be a man.

"So this is the girl of whom you spoke, eh Percy?"

The voice was deep and rich and lardy, like the sound a cake would make if it could speak. At first the words came from high above, then they boomed towards her, as if from somewhere closer. The gentleman was looking down, eyes glittering from inside a pink-cheeked face like over-sized currants in a ball of dough.

"Your father informs me that you are a goodly lass, who likes to help her father whenever she can."

Esme did not understand but nodded, too afraid to do anything else.

"I have a…"

The gentleman moved his mouth without saying anything, as if the word he sought had to be tasted before it could be uttered.

"A venture…yes, a venture. One from which your father could benefit in fine style, should I wish to extend my patronage. I am a gentleman of means and also certain needs. There are things that happen of which no-one should speak, but they happen none the less. And when these occurrences have, well, occurred – then I am likely to find myself in a mood of some beneficence. A girl who does what she is asked to do could help her father get on in the world. Is that not right, Thomas?"

"It is, sir. Sure as I am standing here in this fine house of yours. And I am proper grateful that you are giving me this chance to…"

"Yes, yes…that is enough. You should leave the grandiloquence to me. I believe I have more of an ear for the language. The words enjoy themselves in my mouth, whereas they shrivel in yours, for lack of literary nourishment. If you could perhaps now remove yourself from this room for a certain period of time; shall we say ten minutes? I shall call when I wish you to return. So disengage yourself from my presence, if you please."

Esme was left quite alone with the fleshy, statuesque stranger. She felt an urgent fluttering in her chest, as if something were trying to escape.

"Come over here, my girl."

The lardy cake voice was thick like something that could be cut with a knife. Esme did as she was told, scared into obedience. In the corner of the small room there was a chaise-longue, a once-elegant piece of furniture transported here from a more respectable quarter of the house, and the gentleman sat on this, releasing from his expansive person a series of noises as air was expelled from uncomfortably displaced flesh.

He indicated that she should sit also and she settled on the worn-out fabric. She sat as still as she could, a thing of frailty next to the monumental gentleman. She did not understand what was happening or why the gentleman was fumbling with his clothing, but after much wheezing his manoeuvre was complete. He spoke again, this time with a squeak of urgency in his clotted-cream tones.

"You know what to do now, girl. You poor little lasses always know. You see all sorts in those squalid places where you live. So grab hold of me and start the action, as if you were pumping up the tyre of a bicycle. In and out, up and down...in and out, up and down..."

Esme lived in a large household with brothers and an intermittently present father, so she had some understanding about men and boys. She understood men were different between the legs and she had glimpsed her brothers when they washed in the tub. She had, however, never seen anything like this. By some horrible magic, the flaccid sausage she recognised as being the male thing had transformed into a throbbing pink stick. The gentleman captured her thin hands in his porcine palms and made her grasp the stick, moving her up and down inside his unshakeable embrace. She tried to remove her hands but the man was too strong.

"You may kiss me there, you slum bitch wench, kiss the magnificence of my manhood!"

Esme pulled her face as far away from the vile manifestation as she could manage, but still she could feel its salty heat.

"No matter, no matter."

The voice was different, higher in pitch and distracted, and the breathing was faster, as if the gentleman had been walking upstairs too quickly. Her imprisoned hands continued their piston task. She shut her eyes but the gentleman ordered her to look, before his power of speech subsided into a series of moans, which grew in volume and pace.

Esme looked at the floor with its worn rug, at the shadowed recesses of ceiling, eyes anywhere, but now she addressed what her hands were being forced to encircle. At that moment, as the gentleman began to pant with an unstoppable rhythm, Esme saw a pearl barley speck appear at the tip of the flesh-stick. This stayed for a moment, a tiny white decoration. Then thick milky liquid spurted forth, soaking her hair and her face. Esme screamed and still the gentleman held her. Then, as he subsided into the chaise-longue, he relinquished her hands.

"Go, girl," he said. "A maid will be waiting. She will convey you to your father."

Sobbing at the horror of what she did not understand, Esme left while the gentleman stretched and fell into a satisfied slumber. He awoke sometime later, tidied his disarray and descended from his private eerie to enjoy a four-course lunch containing a profusion of roast lamb, munificent seasonal vegetables and his favourite steamed pudding, washed down with plentiful claret.

As for Esme, she was taken to a tiled laundry room where all sounds assumed twice their normal volume. A young maid, her eyes cast to the floor, used a flannel dipped into warm soapy water to wash away the stickiness. The maid averted her eyes and avoided looking directly at Esme, not wishing to awaken her own memories. It would only get worse for this girl, she knew, until the girl became a woman, and was discarded, as if broken, or dirty.

Cleaned up and with a shine of sorts brushed into her hair, Esme Percy was delivered to her father, who shifted nervously from one foot to the other, before making what he hoped would pass for a gesture of heartiness, resting a hand on her slight shoulder.

As they were shown out of the grand house in Fulford, Thomas Percy patted the pleasing swelling in the inside pocket of the coat once owned by the fine gentleman. He raised his head a little higher and told himself that his daughter had done him a grand favour.

Esme walked in a trance. She did not understand what had happened, but she instinctively understood that, somehow, she had been done a great wrong, and that her father was to blame. She stayed quiet all the way home, so that Thomas Percy gave up his attempts at joviality, something to which he was not much suited anyway, and retreated into a self-satisfied silence as the money in his pocket was spent many times over in his mind.

On the tram, Esme did not notice the solid, tired magnificence of the over-worked horses or the huge, cliff-high houses. Instead, she stared into nothingness while her thin hands played inside the front of her dress, turning a hidden object over and over. She had her talisman and it would look after her.

CHAPTER TWENTY ONE

THE two houses were not far apart, being at different sides of the Groves, a district just out of the centre of York. A tangle of circumstance connected the two houses, occupied by people whose lives had never overlapped.

The first house was deeply untidy, as if its owner were planning to audition for one of those before-and-after TV make-over programmes and had been working especially hard at the "before" requirements. The front room was so monumentally messy that people would stop and stare. Sometimes onlookers caught their own reflection in the time-mottled glass of a dislodged mirror facing the street. Chairs were stacked upside down on an uneven table; a heap of newsprint tottered above the windowsill, stealing light from a shrivelled rubber plant.

Inside the room, the mess proved to be even more elaborate. Yellowing paperbacks, once arranged in precarious towers, lay where they had fallen, backs broken and pages turned over, their words going to waste. The door was propped open by a supermarket carrier bag containing bottles to be recycled. Thick dust coated every surface and gathered itself into weird caterpillar shapes, as if waiting to take on new life.

Someone had once spent time choosing paint and paper for this room, turning it into a happy retreat, a place of comfort. Hardly any of the painted wood remained visible, but a short, exposed stretch of skirting board displayed a colour that might once have been cream. The walls had been covered in paper with a bold green and gold design falling in wide vertical lines. Much of the paper was ripped or damp and some came away from the walls in large curls.

A single light bulb dangled from a wire insulated in dust. Once there had been a shade but it had been made of paper, and paper does not last. The hallway was scuffed and tatty, paint chipped, carpets worn. A bike stood in the hall and, unlike almost everything else in this house, it shone with newness. A door at the end of the short hall lead to a small dining room, which in turn gave way to the kitchen, smaller still. There was not a clear or clean surface in either room, although the kitchen, being a place of occasional activity, was the messier. Dust and grease, crumbs and discarded scraps of food had coalesced into a furry tackiness that touched everything. The sink contained a pool of grey water. The pots and plates on the draining board had been washed up, although the tardy baptism had not granted much in the way of cleanliness.

Upstairs there were two bedrooms and a small bathroom. Of the three rooms, only one held any sort of surprise. The main bedroom, at the front of the house above the front room, was unkempt. Clothes were scattered everywhere. The contents of a make-up bag had been spilled across the dressing table and lay where they had been abandoned. The carpet may once have been blue, now it was no particular colour. Newspapers lay where they had been dropped by the bed, alongside mugs containing evaporated tannic dregs of tea. A bedside table housed a lamp, an alarm clock and a wineglass crusted with sediment.

Amid such mess, the small back bedroom was a picture of order. The room was pink. A single bed was made up but never slept in. Pictures of a girl adorned the wall facing the window, below which there was a small desk. A child's toys were carefully arranged on the polished desktop: assorted dolls, a plastic castle for a princess and a teddy bear with one ear chewed.

The woman stood in the room for a moment, her eyes closed. She opened her lids and her eyes sparkled moistly before reverting to their normal dullness. Grief and resentment had aged her and she hardly recognised the person who haunted the mirror. She dabbed at her eyes and then ran her hands over her uniform, tugging the skirt into tidiness. She turned from the photographs on the wall and looked at her reflection in the window.

"It'll have to do," she said, either out loud or to herself, she was alone so much she forgot the difference. She gazed through her reflection, out into the night. She saw her ghostly self again and fussed over the ghostly uniform. It would have to do. The uniform was clean enough and she had thrown cold water on her face. She looked presentable and what if some of the younger girls at work tittered? What did the little bitches know about anything? They came and they went, off to better jobs or to have babies; but she stayed put.

Her baby should have been their age, she could have been working in the hospital, giggling and learning and growing up.

Before leaving for work on her bike, she took from the kitchen a small but sharp knife she had spent the last few nights keening as she sat in front of the stupid soap operas. She had swished the blade up and down, stropping it against the stone and testing the edge against the flesh of her thumb. The blade was sheathed in cardboard from a cereal box. Its presence gave her strength and hope as she cycled the short distance to the hospital.

SAM Rounder yawned widely; when would this day ever end? He was tired beyond endurance. His body felt like an alien weight. He tried to concentrate. He had never been in this small terraced house before, but it was familiar. He had been raised in a house such as this; grandparents, aunts and uncles had all lived in similar houses. He had inserted himself into such houses a hundred times as a policeman on duty; it was a typical terraced house, unremarkable but solid.

The hall had the original tiles, Victorian or Edwardian, he wasn't sure where the one crossed into the other. They were brown and red and blue, with the squares arranged in a recurring pattern of diamonds and stars, with larger tiles that featured a fleur-de-lys or something similar. He did not know for sure. There was much he did not know; but he knew that somewhere in this house there must be a clue to the whereabouts of Polly Markham. The year 1901 was connected with the girl's disappearance, according to Malcolm Hunt. Only a dead man knew for sure and his house would have to have to speak for him.

Sam moved weightily forward and looked up at the stairs, before turning through the one doorway off the hall. This led into one large room which had once been two; there was a window at either end, one facing the pavement of the tight, constricted street, the other a tiny yard. A small kitchen lay beyond the extended room.

The house was tatty but neat; everything had its place.

"CDs and books all arranged in alphabetical order, sir."

"What's that?"

Sam was known for his occasional abruptness. His friends thought this a sign of distraction, saying he was lost in thought; those less kindly disposed said he was a rude bastard. Sam had no idea his behaviour divided opinions. He considered himself to be decent enough, heavy-handed when duty required. If he thought about such matters for too long, he came to the gloomy conclusion that he was a middle-aged copper with a voluminous belly and a wife who had stopped loving him, possibly before or maybe even after she started an affair with a younger man.

"It's all arranged, sir."

"Yes Sergeant, I heard you the first time. Any clues in the ordered world of Frank Helmsley?"

Sergeant Lockwood, Sandy Lockwood, the Sandy being short for Sandra. Short was the word for her: cropped hair, stocky build, she barely came up to his chin. As they talked in this dead man's lounge, Sam looked down, as he might at a teenage niece, or even at his own daughters, if they hadn't grown tall and disdainful. Other officers moved around the room and looked through books and newspapers, or catalogued the contents of an upturned bin.

"That lecturer fellow's upstairs, sir. In the study, if you want him."

The stairs were steep and Sam's breath was short. He was huffing by the top step.

Malcolm Hunt was in the tiny study, leafing through computer-printed pages held in a cheap-looking blue folder, packed to the point where the springs could hardly contain the pages. There was barely room for the two men. Sam Rounder leant against the doorframe.

"Any answers yet?" He dreaded the question, suspecting it would trigger a long-winded explanation. He wasn't wrong.

"Lots of pointers, lots of possibilities. You see, what we are dealing with here is an interesting mind – crude, a little unschooled, but certainly interesting. Frank Helmsley had a chip on his shoulder. Resentment stews and stains everything he touches, yet his research, while lacking in historical exactitude, does have a certain rough-edged passion. We are dealing with a man who had a huge inferiority complex – and yet, he was dangerously confident, too. Cut off from the ebb and flow of everyday humanity, and yet oddly so certain in the rightness of what he was doing. His research, well, some of it really is shocking, and yet he felt certain that he was on to something the professionals had missed. Here was a man who did not like being told that he was wrong or that..."

Sam had had enough.

"No, Mr Hunt, what we are dealing with here is a poor scared child stuck somewhere in York, terrified out of her wits and starved half to death. That's if we're lucky. Believe me, I've seen what happens when the luck runs out. And I don't want to see it again. There are some sights a man can't shake out of his head, however hard he tries. So what have you got for me?"

"While your impatience is understandable, Inspector..."

"Chief Inspector."

"Well, yes. Although we shouldn't let a little matter of rank impede our important discussions, should we? Now where was I?"

"With your arse on the end of my foot, if you don't get a bloody move on."

"I am sensing a little tension here, *Chief* Inspector, and I would remind you that I am a member of the public helping your investigation thanks to an awareness of my social responsibility. I am attempting to do my best to help find this lost child."

"Fair enough, *Mr* Hunt. But what have you got for me?"

"Hungate, I'd say. That's where Esme Percy lived, the girl whose story Frank Helmsley became so interested in. The house where she lived – well it wasn't so much a house, more of a tenement block – will be long gone. There's probably a disused warehouse on top of it now. You know the story – old industry dies and the building lies empty, until someone wants to build trendy flats no ordinary person can afford. It's a familiar tale these days."

"That's as mebbe, but all I've got time to care about is the girl. All the rest can go and hang itself for now, much as I may like to agree with you, if we were sitting around having a nice chat at one of those dinner parties you doubtless like to inhabit."

"A man's got to eat, Chief Inspector – and to converse occasionally, too."

"I'm sure you are skilled in both arts, Mr Hunt. But have you got any more ideas about how we can find this girl?"

"I'd start looking round Hungate if I were you."

Sam heaved himself from the doorframe and reached for his mobile. He arranged for a search party involving every available officer in York. It was going to be a long night.

He walked along the narrow landing to the bedroom at the front. He had never become fully accustomed to the guilty thrill of walking in on a life just departed.

It was a perverse sort of privilege to root about in the still-warm remnants of a life. Houses possessed a palpable sense of their dead owners. The rotten old bastard was here, in this room, taunting them with his shitty secrets.

This was the all-so-familiar part, leafing through what the dead left. The room, with its meagre carpet, limp, defeated curtains and lumpy double bed, made up with sheets and blankets instead of a duvet was a scrappy receptacle of a person's life. Frank Helmsley had lived in this room, in this house, and then he had died with his life unfinished, as most lives were. The room, like the house, spoke of loneliness and the hermetic life; and there were also the usual signs of the final interruption, the cold, half-drunk cup of tea by the bed; the bedside book that would never be finished; the pristine newspaper that would never be read. Perhaps it didn't do to get too carried away with that last one, Sam thought, because half the newspapers found in his house were recycled with their words untroubled.

He inserted himself by the bed. Aside from the bed, a small, cheap-looking wardrobe and a modest chest of drawers, the room was filled with books and tidy piles of newspapers and magazines. Shelves ran from the floor to the ceiling containing books that were neatly arranged and free of dust. If the house was threadbare, the books, papers and articles were all cared for beautifully.

Rounder dug his hands into his jacket pocket and pulled out the thin rubber gloves he was supposed to wear. He struggled to get them over his sausage fingers, but eventually his hands were safe from contaminating anything.

Funny thought, really, that he might cause contamination in this horrible place. As if to confirm this line of thought, his hand, which had felt beneath the pillow unearthed a crinkled, stiff hankie.

"Bloody hell!"

He struggled with an evidence bag and then dropped in the hankie. "The dirty old sod hadn't been using that to blow his nose," he said, half out-loud.

He'd made his discovery on the left-hand side of the bed, which suggested that was where Helmsley slept. With a sigh, Sam put his hand under the other pillow and found what he had been expecting.

He had been certain Helmsley would have used pornography, and here was the evidence. Sam flicked through the pages, taken back by the raw gynaecology, legs spread and everything on show. He wasn't prudish, but some sights were better left unseen. Top halves certainly; a nice arse for sure; but not all that doctor's surgery stuff.

As he flicked over another page, his eyes beginning to glaze, as physical distaste met queasy fascination. He was wondering how a model got her legs arranged like that when he noticed the face. There was something wrong with the face. It had been covered by that of another girl, younger and yet much older. A girl from a different era.

He took the magazine into the study to show Hunt.

"I don't usually go for this sort of stuff myself."

"That's what they all say. But never mind that, take your eyes away from all those fleshy crevices and have a look at the face."

"Oh, I see what you mean. He's done a spot of snipping and gluing and put another girl's face on top of this naked girl. It looks like the face has been blown up from a photograph. It's all grainy and pixelated."

The girl stared out of the page, a little serious and concerned; her long fair fell to below her shoulders, only they weren't her shoulders, belonging instead to the model.

"Bit of a sicko, wouldn't you say, chief inspector?"

"Lots of us are."

"If you say so. Perhaps your line of work makes you a little dyspeptic."

"Do you think there's any relevance to the picture? Why did he choose this girl to stick on top of a porno model? And to, you know, entertain himself with?"

"So this is what you might politely call a sleeping aid?"

"Yes, Mr Hunt, your mature student wasn't so mature that he didn't like to wank himself off to a picture of a Victorian girl stuck on to that of a thoroughly modern madam."

"Interesting that you should say Victorian. I would posit that the period might be the next one along."

"What?"

"Edwardian, I'd say. And, you know, it's just possible that this is a picture of our long-lost girl."

"The one who so fascinated Helmsley?"

"That's the one."

Sam placed the magazine in an evidence bag. He wondered how much this knowledge would help. Helmsley had been a history-besotted lonely weirdo who liked to masturbate to a doctored pornographic picture containing the face of an impoverished girl who had lived and died a century earlier.

"Your Frank Helmsley seems to have taken his love of history in hand, as it were," he said, going downstairs before Hunt could respond.

CHAPTER TWENTY TWO

THE two knives are divided by a century. One is a short kitchen knife, lovingly keened, although not with affectionate intent; the other a fragment, the bone handle worn slippery, the broken blade worried into an unnatural claw. Both are properly concealed: one hidden inside a uniform that suggests a duty of kindness; the other bound in grubby cloth and tucked down the front of a worn and tattered dress. Both wait to do damage, one in the name of injustice, the other in the pursuit of self-preservation, although no such refined words would arise in the girl's mind. She has her special thing, her bit of sharpness.

RICK Rounder lay in hospital, confronted by his own foolishness. How had he imagined he could return to York and make a go of being a private detective? This city was his home and he felt proud of the place, but he no longer fully belonged as he had before he went away. He had changed and the city had changed. York was a confined city, walled in by the past; friendly when you knew where to look, but still with a certain gruff isolation, a passing suspicion of the outside world (which was unfortunate, when a place at history's high table drew in people from around the world.) Was there a contradiction in there somewhere? Rick's brain wasn't up to exploring the paradox.

The theme had been on his mind when Naomi had visited earlier. His mind flashed back to their conversation…

"It's all that time I spent in Australia," he said. Naomi was calmer. She had slept well, felt better. Her skin shone, her surprisingly blue eyes sparkled. She brought radiance into this dead-eyed place, with its draining light bulbs and worn-out air.

"What are you on about, Rick?"

"Oh, I was just trying to think things out and I concluded that having spent too much time in Australia hadn't been good for my powers of cog – something or other."

"Cognition. Well, I guess that's the word you're after. Anyway, are you insulting me, Australia or my fellow countryfolk? Or half-countryfolk. Remember, I can switch and be American when I want to..."

"Oh, I dunno really. I've been lying here thinking about whether or not I'd been an idiot to imagine that I could make a go of being a private detective in York. It's been a long time and people don't remember me."

"Don't remember you! Every time we go out you keep bumping into someone or other you were at school with, or arrested once, or used to play football with or used to go and see York United with back in the old days when they were good."

"City, York City – haven't you been paying attention? Anyway, when on earth did I say that City used to be good?"

Rick screwed his eyes to banish a ghost. There were too many ghosts in this city. Naomi slipped across to perch on the bed. Rick opened his eyes and smiled.

"There was a man who smiled a crooked smile."

"I'd never noticed until you said."

"Oh, don't give me all that false modesty shit. I've seen you looking in mirrors or smiling at yourself in darkened windows."

"Just checking – you know, to see if you were right. No one had ever said that before and..."

"Oh, you poor neglected man."

Naomi cuddled Rick.

"Shit, that's my stabbed shoulder!"

"Sorry, I forgot. Well, I didn't forget, how could I? I just wanted to give you a hug and..." The tears surprised her. She thought she had herself under control.

"You could have been killed, you stupid, lovely bastard."

"You should have seen the other guy. Besides, I know what I'm doing, walking down these mean streets of York."

"Are you sure about that?"

"I'm sure."

"At least you're safe in here."

"So long as I don't pick up MRSA, or something. Risky places, hospitals. You come in with one thing wrong and get sucked in. Next thing you know you're..."

She silenced him with a kiss.

"Next thing you know, you'll be back home with me to look after you."

"Have you checked my messages and e-mails?"

"You're not doing any work at the moment. Just get yourself better before you start playing at Marlowe again."

"I think Marlowe was a bit more successful than me."

The curtains round the bed agitated apart and a youngish male nurse inserted himself into the small, private space. There was stubble on his chin and his eyes were tired from too much looking. "Hello, Mr Rounder. Glad to see you looking a bit brighter. I'm off in a moment. Back home to collapse into my bed before everything starts up all over again.

"A doctor will be coming round to see you soon. I think they would like you to stay in for one more night, just for observation."

"I don't want to be accused of bed blocking or anything, you know. I might find myself in the Evening Press."

"Oh, I think you'll find that you are there already. I'm off soon and you'll be looked after by..."

Rick didn't catch the name. Sister someone or other. The male nurse nodded towards a middle-aged woman. She smiled the sort of smile that was hardly worth the effort.

The male nurse turned back. "You'll be in good hands, don't you worry."

Rick nodded, watching the nurse. He wondered if he was having one of his York flashbacks. Her face held some meaning but he couldn't say what. His memory was trying to put together a mental photo-fit, but whoever it was had gone.

All he could see was another nurse with a tired face. She had more excuse for it, this one, than the young lad. The male nurse went off, away to his bed.

"Are you all right, Rick? Only you look like you've seen..."

"Another one of my ghosts? Maybe. It's just that nurse, the one who is taking over. She looked familiar for a second or so. Then she was gone."

"You're getting paranoid, that's your trouble."

"You should go off now, go home, go for a run or something. Put those tight shorts on and give the old pervs of York a thrill."

"Oh, it's more the young pervs I had in mind. At least they're worth the effort."

"Watch yourself."

They kissed and, with a smile and a parting glance, she was gone. He watched her dodging the trolleys and weaving in and out of the nurses. Through a window on the other side of the ward he could see a patch of November blue. He longed to be out of here, to breathe again the clean air outside. This was a fond delusion. The air outside was dirtied by the traffic queuing along the busy road. Behind the hospital a diesel train burped fumes. A mile or so across the city, the sugar factory exhaled burnt-caramel smoke.

Rick thought of leaving, busting out of the hospital like a proper private eye. But he was tired, his shoulder hurt and he would be safer in here. Just for now, until his strength returned.

He tried to drift off but sleep wouldn't come. Soon it was the middle of the night in this time-stalled place and his memories were keeping him awake. He rolled over and over, grimacing as he twinged his shoulder, trying to trick himself into sleep.

ESME Percy could not forget the man with the vile pink spurting stick. She worried at her guilty hands until the palms bled. She did not understand what she had seen but knew she should never have been left alone with that man. Something foul and ungodly had come her way and her father was to blame. That much made sense. Yet she told no-one and clutched her horrible secret to her chest, turning it into a pearl of hatred. Her mother noticed the palms, a day or two later, grabbing her thin wrists.

"What have you been doing, our Esme? Your poor hands are all bloodied."

"Hurt myself playing, is all. Fell and scratched myself in the alley."

Martha Percy felt overwhelmed by the frailty of the child. The wrists she held were thin and insubstantial, hardly more that flesh-covered sticks. She worried, as she had so many times before, about the hold on life her youngest child had.

"I am all right, ma." The girl was speaking but Martha did not hear. She was away in her mind, fretting and ferreting, as Thomas used to say in the days when he still took notice of her. Martha did not understand the ferreting but she took it as a criticism, something else she had done wrong.

"Just make sure you are all right, my girl."

She released her grip and the girl ran off, such a slight thing, bonny if only she did not always look so tired.

Esme was short of breath by the time she reached the alleyway and she felt the thumping inside her chest, the racing drumbeat that came when she ran too fast. She slumped against the mossy wall until the rush slowed. As she waited, she scratched at her palms until her blackened, chipped fingernails drew fresh blood. Then she spat into her upturned palms, so that bloodied spittle joined the blood coming from the small wound. The pink spittle was another secret, to keep the sharp secret company. Her bird-like eyes sought out her talisman. Her heart settled again into its usual fragile rhythm.

As she pulled away from the wall, a change in the light told her someone was approaching. She knew the shape before she knew the man. Samuel Smithy lived in the basement next to her family. Not all the children liked Samuel, calling him Smelly Smithy and the like. It was true that he stank, but there was much competition for smells in this part of York, so a person would have to have a particular nose to pick out that which Samuel owned. His skin was rough with stubble and dark with dirt, his teeth hardly showed when he smiled, more black than white. He stooped towards Esme, giving his gapped grin. The smile animated his face, banishing the dirt and the tiredness.

"Got something for you, little 'un."

Smithy held both hands behind his back in a stance that pushed out his small stomach and exaggerated the ill fit of his rough woollen trousers. He had not been the first man to wear these trousers, possibly not even the second; but he would be the last. Baggy and without shape, the trousers had gone through at the knees while dirt ringed the hems. They had the appearance not so much of a garment once cut and tailored, but of something that had grown about the wearer in an organic manner.

As he brought his hands round to the front, Esme Percy froze with anticipation. She looked along the alley, glancing past Samuel Smithy and whatever it was that he held. She had known this dirty, kindly man for as long as she could remember. There was not a fleck of harm in him, she felt sure, but suddenly she felt so alone. She turned and looked the other way, towards the abattoir. Blood was frothing along the drain.

"Are you not looking at what I have for you?"

Esme turned back and squinted up at Smithy and in her nervous state, her right hand found her talisman.

"You see, I have a hoop for you. Not a proper one, like what the rich children have. But it is one I have fashioned for you. It is the ring from a barrel, probably one of the barrels emptied by your father down at the public house!"

Smithy laughed as he said this, making a sound somewhere between a neigh and a cough. "Here, girl, have a look."

It was black and shone with the cleaning he had lavished on it. He gave Esme a stick too, a slat from the same barrel, smoothed free of splinters.

"A hoop, a hoop – cock-a-hoop. Something for you to play with."

Esme looked up, her eyes animated by suspicion.

"And it is for me?"

"Course it is, girl. Have you not been listening?"

He lay his large, rough hand on her head. She flinched at its callused weight, pulling instinctively away from its strength.

"Thank you sir, Mr Smithy is what I meant to say."

"Go on, be off and play."

Esme rolled the improvised hoop along the alleyway, only to

watch the black circle fall and clatter to the stones. She picked it up and had another go. Again the hoop fell and again she picked it up, trying once more to propel it with the smooth stick. It fell once more and many times after that. With time, the hoop began to stay up longer, holding upright for a few feet before tumbling. Esme played with the hoop for hours until she began to master its rebellious nature and started to understand, without knowing exactly what it was that she was learning, something about momentum and the nature of gravity. She did not know the word or what it stood for, but she did know that things stayed up and then fell down, and that some mysterious force, something powerful but unseen, pulled the hoop down.

She was rolling the hoop in the evening when her father came for her. Her mother had said she could play in the yard, but Esme had gone a little further, into the alleyway. The sky above her was clear and bright, the cleanest thing around. Stars punctured the blackness, silver slits in velvet.

Esme's quick, shallow breath smoked as she sprinted down the alley. The hoop was on its longest run yet, keeping balance as it skipped the cobbles. A slight incline favoured the hoop, which gathered speed and sent out tiny sparks. This hoop would run for ever, it would never fall, it would roll merrily on until whatever happened when time stopped. Esme clapped her hands with glee, hardly noticing her breath came in painful bursts. She spat pink again but did not see the colour in the evening shadows. She chased and the hoop sped on until it hit something and clattered to the ground, disappearing into the dark.

"Never mind that hoop, girl. I need you to come with me." Thomas Percy stepped out of the darkness. "There is something that needs to be done, something a girl can do to help her father as he tries to make his way in this world."

"But Ma said I was not to go far. She said it would be time for bed soon."

"I have told her and she understands."

This was a lie, Esme was sure of it.

Thomas Percy was not tall but he seemed so to his daughter, especially as he leant towards her, smoke rising from the cigarette in his mouth. He smelt of beer and tobacco, the only fatherly aroma Esme had ever known.

"Your mother understands and she knows what is right and what is not. There is a difference between the two, as you will learn one day, girl."

Thus delivered of his brief sermon on morality, a subject about which he had never before spoken, Thomas Percy made to grab his daughter.

"My hoop, you must let me have my hoop!"

"What?"

"The hoop what Mr Smithy made for me. He made it out of that bit that holds a barrel together."

"I have no time for this, child."

"My hoop – it cannot be lost. My hoop cannot be lost."

"It is not your place to talk to your father like that. A girl should owe respect towards her father."

Thomas Percy clenched his fist but did not act on the unkind thought, reasoning that it would not do to damage the girl tonight.

"Please, Pa."

He bent and his hand fumbled in the shadows until he found the improvised hoop. He stood with the circle in his hand and threw it into the air. The hoop disappeared into the dark and clattered into the yard.

"There, girl. Your hoop is safe. Now be going."

As they found their way to the tram, Esme felt no excitement, no thrill at the unknown. She took no pleasure in anything she saw. She did not marvel at the way the lights from the houses and shops warmed the darkness. A tram ride on a fine, chilly November night should be a treat above all other treats, yet for Esme it was not so.

Once again, she and her father presented a happy picture to the unknowing eye, a child out with her father. Watching them, a fellow passenger of the tram might have supposed this to be the case, and it would have been an easy mistake to make. Even the most cynical of strangers might not have imagined the truth, as some truths do not bear thinking about.

As before, the great-arsed horses walked towards Fulford without any sense of urgency, flicking aside their tails to deposit straw-bound shit. In summer, the tram would approach Fulford under a panoply of leaves, with, on a sunny day, a pretty dappling of light. By the winter the trees were mostly bare, the stripped branches spread against the sky like capillaries. Esme felt the sway of the tall trunks as they disappeared upwards.

The short journey was over and the passengers left the tram. Thomas Percy's thoughts were measured in pints as he walked towards the house, his hand on his daughter's bony shoulder, apparently resting there in a gesture of concern, but in fact guiding the girl with a forceful grip.

They reached the house and Thomas bent to towards his daughter to inspect her face. He spat on grubby fingers and rubbed at a patch of dirt on her face, moving it around somewhat before declaring she would have to do. Then he turned from the warm light of the street and marched Esme along the dark passageway between the two houses, seeking out the back entrance.

Esme looked up at the dark cliffs of brick each side of her. There were chimneys at the top of the cliffs, one for each house. Smoke from the chimneys smudged the sky.

Thomas Percy stumbled as he approached the gateway, losing his footing for a moment. He would have been better on his feet if he had taken a drink earlier, instead of holding off. Not having a drink had been a bad idea and he swore now as he attempted to rise, reaching out his hand, muddied from the alley floor.

"Here, girl, give your father a hand. And be quick about it, or I will show you what my belt is for. I cannot appear muddy and dishevelled, not when there is important business to be done with the gentleman. Come now, your hand, before you make me give way to my temper."

Father and daughter were lost to darkness and there would be no witnesses to what happened next. Had a passer-by stopped to peer into the passage between the two grand houses, they might have seen a struggle of some kind, a puppet show in the shadows. They might, too, surely have heard the scream that rang out, before ending as abruptly as it had begun. No-one did see anything and the broad alleyway, a road almost, just wide enough to admit a horse and cart, held on to its secrets until the following morning.

CHAPTER TWENTY THREE

RICK Rounder slept fitfully. His shoulder hurt and his head was dizzy dull. Dreams in and out of sleep brought back his hours as a hostage and he saw Will Wistow fall from the window. He saw this clearly, recording the exact moment when the window gave way, marvelling at the splintering frame and the shattering of the glass, and looking down afterwards to see his captor dead on the concrete. Yet at the time he had seen or understood little of this, only grasping later what had happened when Sam filled in the details. His brain was putting everything together, developing a devious photographic truth, every frame in part a lie.

He saw the lost girl, eyes upturned in the darkness. Her name, what was her name? He couldn't remember in the middle of the numb hospital night, but his mind pinpointed her, his eyes peeling back the concrete until she looked up at him, hands raised in supplication.

Other images intruded, superimposing one on the other. A figure fell, unfurling in flames and this man was dead too, along with the child he had stabbed.

Rick rubbed his eyes and wondered if he had been asleep. He didn't feel as if he had, but dream negatives were still superimposed on his mind. His eyeballs were prickly with exhaustion and his head buzzed with redundant thought. Yawning, he sought comfort in the utilitarian bed. Around him the hospital carried on the night's work, providing busy proof that illness and misfortune kept untidy hours. He heard doors open to admit the dying wail of a siren, followed by activity and voices, as a stretcher wheeled close by.

Drifting off, he was jerked awake by shouting. Someone was drunk and rowdy and a nurse was trying to talk brisk sense. The drunk voice made one last roar, accompanied by the metallic clatter of something being dropped, or thrown. A voice complained about the rank smell, then later, a few seconds, perhaps a minute or two or more, the snoring started. It was to prove a steady snore, loud and regular, the sort that would keep up its circular cacophony all night, going round and round with only the shortest occasional pause, providing false hope for the tortured listener.

He slept for a while, this time he was sure he slept, escaping the snoring, and then he was awake again, fully and hopelessly.

The voice surprised him.

"What was that?"

"I said it's hard to sleep in this place, what with so much going on. Working nights, I've seen it so often. People never sleep in here. Sometimes I wonder if they dare not sleep, for fear of not waking up."

The sister laughed at what she said but there was little amusement in her voice. Rick squinted and tried to place her. It was the nurse he had seen earlier, the middle-aged woman who had replaced the young male nurse.

"I've see it so often, the unwilling night owls, stuck in here when they'd rather be somewhere happier. Or maybe just outside for a while, away from the stuffy old hospital. I would understand if you felt that way, Mr Rounder. Perhaps you would like some fresh air."

"Well, there's certainly not much of it in here."

"Oh, nasty and full of germs – that's the air in here."

"Tell me about it," said Rick, which was a surprise because he hated people who said "tell me about it." He really wasn't at all well.

"I could take you outside for some fresh air, if you wanted me to…?"

"Is that allowed?"

"Oh, we sisters make our own rules, you know."

She laughed again, another mechanical tinkle.

"So how about it then, a little spin outside?"

"You make it sound like a date."

"Oh, don't tease me, Mr Rounder. I've seen that girlfriend of yours. Pretty thing, isn't she?"

Rick watched the woman's face as she spoke, sensing the effort she was expending on being light and conversational. She looked towards him but not at him, her eyes darting and distracted. Perhaps Rick should have read something in those eyes but he did not, and instead agreed to her suggestion.

"Oh, go on then."

"I'll get a wheelchair and a blanket, then we'll be ready to go."

"I'm not that much of invalid."

"Oh, better safe than sorry. You put your shoes on. Just wait for me for a mo." A mo. The word sounded alien, as if borrowed from the lexicon of a more naturally cheerful person.

Rick did as he was told, tying up his trainers, fumbling slightly and wondering at the obedience that came with being a patient. The nurse – Nurse Smith, he saw from her badge – returned with the wheelchair and blanket.

"Hop in," she said, bright and brittle.

Rick put on his cycling jacket, checking his mobile phone was in the pocket. The touch of the jacket on his bruised shoulders brought his bike to mind. Where was it?

The air outside tasted wonderful, which was strange as it was only the same old York air, polluted by cars, buses and lorries, and tainted by the city's many competing smells. But compared to the hospital, this was heady stuff, nectar for the lungs, and Rick breathed deeply and sat back in the wheelchair while Sister Smith pushed him. Her breathing deepened with the effort and perhaps he should have felt guilty, but injury had removed the last traces of gallantry. Let her push, it was her job.

Rick glanced up at stars pricking the dark, then looked down as they crossed the passage that ran alongside the hospital and led to the footbridge over the railway line. On match Saturdays this route was thick with York City fans on their way to Bootham Crescent, with their scarves, hats and hopeful faces. A couple of hours later they would return with their scarves and hats, but often without much hope in their faces.

They passed into the dark road with a high a brick wall to the left, and nurses' accommodation to the right. He had been smuggled in there by one of his earliest girlfriends. He remembered the encounter, urgent and explosive on his part. She had cried afterwards, sitting half dressed on the narrow bed. He hadn't understood why and, shrugging on his T-shirt, had gone home.

Behind the high brick wall stood a row of handsome terrace houses, two of which had been for sale shortly before Rick had left on his travels. He could have sold the flat and bought the pair. They would have been worth a bomb now, he reflected. Still, he had his flat, bang in the middle of York; his flat, his girlfriend, a new life as a not spectacularly successful private eye. What was there to complain about?

At the end of the road, they turned into the grounds of Bootham Hospital. To his left in the shadows he make out the old tennis courts, gone more or less to ruin. Ahead he could make out the dark outline of the hospital, which looked like the sort of stately home that didn't invite callers. One of his uncles had ended up as a patient after "a bad spell that left his mind all put out," as his mother had put it.

Twenty yards or so further, they turned into the park. By day this was a verdant backwater, a rare spot of open space in a crowded city; by night, it was dark and quiet. Just beyond the old church, which was now used as offices, Rick thought he should say something to this panting woman who was pushing him.

"There's no need to go any further, you know. This is very good of you, I really appreciate it. Fresh air's doing me the power of good. Should sleep like a baby when you get me back to that ward."

Sister Smith said nothing. Perhaps she was out of breath, Rick thought. After all, he must be quite a weight, although nothing like Sam. Hell, his brother would take some pushing these days. Funny the way he had stayed slim and fit while Sam had expanded.

He was about to say something to this effect to the nurse, pointing out that she was lucky not to be propelling the fat Rounder brother. That would really have knackered her.

He was about to say something, but he did not: Sister Smith had a knife in her hands and she was holding it close to his neck. So close that if he turned too quickly, the blade would slice him into silence.

SOMETIMES events rub across the grain of time. So it was that the fate of a young girl at the turn of the twentieth century should lead to another girl being gravely imperilled one hundred years later. The first girl cannot help the second; and the modern child cannot know the earlier girl. Yet chance has toyed with their lives, making one dependent on the other. The second girl cannot survive without help from the first, although she has been dead for one hundred years.

The link between the two girls leads down a broad alleyway between two large houses in Fulford, just outside York, on a cold November morning in 1901, when a discovery was about to be made. The head gardener, Fred Hamilton, had slept in his potting shed, thanks to drinking too much beer with his friend the butler, Harold Fountayne. He rose early and in extreme need of relief. He did not want to go into the big house. His dishevelled appearance, thanks to rough sacking for blankets and the stale beer of the previous night, would cause unkind comment among the other staff. So he scurried across the garden to the back gate. His fingers fumbled in the cold, trying to free the bolt. As first he could not get the metal rod to move at all but eventually, at about the point when he felt certain he would in shame piss himself, he gained his escape and tumbled into the alleyway. So urgent was his need that he neither felt the extreme cold now assaulting his exposed member nor saw the frost-furred shape lying a few feet away. Instead he indulged in the exultation of a man emptying a bladder fit to explode. His urine steamed in the fresh morning air and splashed against the bricks of the next grand house. After a surprisingly long interval, Fred Hamilton sighed with the gratefulness of one born anew and buttoned his trousers, noticing as he did so the sacking threads he had picked up in the night. Glancing down the alley towards the road, to check that he had not been seen, he cleansed his fingers by rubbing them across the frosted stones on the ground. After that, he turned to go back through the garden and thence to the house, in search of breakfast. Fatty bacon or a slab of black pudding, served with stale bread fried golden in lard. Such a feast would ameliorate the effects of too much beer.

Then he saw the shape and stopped. What his eyes witnessed his brain could not immediately acknowledge. Shock can slow the reactions, giving time for the inescapable to sink in. Hamilton stared for he could not say how long, taking in the clothes and the way the limbs were uncomfortably arranged in a manner suggesting rest had not been gently come by. He swore under his breath, then over it – "Bastard-hell-Jesus-Christ" – the words linking into a chain of profanity.

His brain soon caught up with his eyes. It was a body, there was no denying that truth, a body covered in a fine filigree of frost. The body belonged to a man of middle years. Although the coat he wore was fine, the cloth was beginning to wear thin, suggesting another man had owned this garment in fuller days. Now he thought about it, the garment looked strangely familiar. There was mud on the coat tails and a large dark patch of what must be blood up around the collar, with frost settling on the stain. Frost also decorated the dead chin stubble. The face was grey and the eyes, although open, would never see again. Fred Hamilton, wondering if the dead man was staring into the recently stolen past, scurried towards the house to raise the alarm.

MARTHA did not miss him for a while, and why would she? He often stayed away without revealing what he was engaged in. So she was not surprised to find him still gone in the morning, even though she half expected to discover him in the chair by the stove, asleep in his clothes. The chair was empty when she entered the parlour and she enjoyed the quiet of the early morning. As she set about her work, she yawned so impressively her jaw seemed to crack with the effort. She had not slept well because her mind had been in a whirl of anxiety; not about the errant Thomas, great heavens no, the lumpen bully could look after himself. Her youngest daughter had provided the worry fodder. The girl had returned late and alone, too tired for speech. She said her father had made her walk a long way. Esme had gone straight to the bed she shared with her sisters, where she fell asleep immediately. A dozen questions had queued in Martha's mind but she had left off the asking, reasoning that morning would do.

Peacefulness was not hers for long. The younger children would be stirring soon, getting up in readiness for the Board School. Six of her children were still at school, Henry, Peter, Rebecca, Mary, Hetty and young Esme. Joshua and Joseph would rise first, and it was them she could hear now; they would have to leave soon for their shift. The older boys came down, jostling for first use of the outside privy. They pushed and shoved into the parlour, filling all available space, then leaving through the door into the yard, racing for the privilege of the first visit of the morning. Josh won and left Joe outside to kick against the friable brick, which came away in dull reddish flakes.

Soon the bigger boys returned to eat thin porridge, then left for work with the long and confident strides of those who had not yet discovered that employment would cause them little in the way of prosperity.

The other children arrived in dribs and drabs, Esme emerging last, as was her way. Martha knew she mothered her youngest daughter but she could not help herself, because the girl was so bright, yet so fragile and queer, too.

The pot of watery porridge emptied and the children straggled off to school. Esme looked pale but Martha pushed her out with the others, saying school would do her good. "All that learning will fill your head with something useful." The girl peered up, wan and helpless, but Martha decided she had that expression off all too nicely.

Left alone, she tidied up as best she could, not easy in this damp and mouldering place. Another woman might have wished for more, for better surroundings in which to raise her children; and for a more constant husband. Martha tried to find comfort in what she had, even if it did not amount to much. Such unnatural satisfaction was in reaction to the hopeless dreams of her husband, who was always scheming about something or other, always ready with another piece of idle work that would see him right and make his riches. She spurned his foolish optimism, having long ago resigned to making do.

The man was a fool to himself and to her, but she kept her own counsel. Antagonising him would lead nowhere healthy. Such were her thoughts when the knock came at her door.

"That man will be the death of me – the death of all of us," she mumbled as she eased open the door, which no longer swung so handsomely after its misadventure.

A police officer stood filling the doorway, a young man by the look of him, not much older than our Joshua and Joseph, and how fine the boys would look in a uniform like that, with the blue material, the brass buttons and the polished boots. So distracted by this fantasy was she that the words the boy policeman spoke made no impression and she had to ask him to speak again. This made him uncomfortable and his shiny feet shuffled on the doorstep while his eyes sought somewhere else to look. Martha saw that there were rashes under his chin and spots of dried blood from inexpert shaving.

"I have come about your husband. Thomas Percy."

"What has that foolish man done now?"

The young officer gulped down his nerves. "There has been a dreadful occurrence, Mrs Percy. Thomas Percy, has been –" He stopped for a moment, unsure of what to say next, grasping after what he hoped would be the right words. "He is lying dead on the cold slab at the mortuary, missus. The life has quite gone from him."

Martha staggered into the pantry. She sat in the chair by the range and her heart ran away with itself, while her head buzzed with a strange heightened sense of nothingness. It felt as if the very air in this familiar room was trying to squeeze inside her head.

"Thomas dead, Thomas dead."

"That is what I have been trying to impart I am afraid, Mrs Percy." The young policeman had stepped into the pantry while wondering what else he could do or say.

"So where – how – who?"

"Fulford. Down an alley at the side of a grand house, belonging to…" The officer stopped and took out his notebook. "Belonging to a Mr Houseman, a gentleman of some wealth and property, or so I am given to understand."

"Given to understand"…the young man wondered why he was picking on such strange words, the sort of expressions his superiors would employ as they tried to appear impressive and make each other seem small.

"Mr Percy was discovered there early this morning by…" He glanced down again. "Frederick Hamilton, head gardener in the household. With regards to the how and the why in your question, it is a little to soon for us to reveal such matters, although it is fair to say we believe a sharp object to have been involved."

He paused, waiting for Martha to speak further, but she said nothing.

"We will need you to come with us, to confirm that the man we have in our mortuary is indeed Thomas Percy. We are certain this is indeed the case but we would still ask that you carry out this painful task."

THERE are times to act and times to speak. Action would be a good move now, Rick Rounder told himself. Yet here he was, dazed, injured and exhausted, trapped in a wheelchair while a homicidal nurse held a blade to his throat. He didn't know what to do and tried to encourage cogent thought to push through the cotton-wool mush of his mind. He tensed his muscles, easing his back into the wheelchair and stiffening his cramped legs. His breath snaked into the night air, twining with that of his assailant.

It was quiet in Bootham Park, far too bloody quiet. In the distance cars passed along the street but here it was just him, this maniac nurse and the long moon shadows cast by the old trees.

"What the…?"

"You don't remember me, do you, Rounder?"

The "mister" had gone, along with the fake cheerfulness, to be replaced by a blade whose keen edge he could feel against the thin flesh of his throat.

"Can't say that I do."

"Let's have a little history lesson, shall we?"

Rick couldn't see her face as she spoke and her voice was coming through his left ear, almost as if she were whispering sweet nothings; only these were horrible somethings.

"It was all very well for you to go off on your travels, seeing the world and getting yourself a nice looking nigger girlfriend…"

Every bruised and battered muscle in his body tensed. He had never heard anyone use that vile word about Naomi. The logical, fact-sticking part of his brain wanted to point out that Naomi was half-American and half-Australian. But he didn't speak for fear of the blade at his throat. The non-thinking, instinctive side of his brain wanted to kick the shit out of this vile woman.

"You don't like me saying that, do you? Well, the thing is, I couldn't care less about your likes and dislikes, Mr Policeman."

"I'm not a policeman, at least not any more. Are you sure you're not confusing me with someone else, quite possibly my brother?"

Rick breathed deeply and tried to work out what to do. He was bigger and stronger – all she had on him was that blade and the moment of surprise. So he let her talk.

"It was all right for you, wasn't it? I'd lost the most precious thing in my life and you just left your job and swanned off round the world. Someone died and you went on a big fucking holiday."

The profanity surprised him. He had heard the word plenty of times, used it himself a fair few. Yet here it was spoken so closely, so intimately, its full aggression echoed round his skull.

Shards of history filled his mind. He saw bits of the past, then nothing. This couldn't be happening again. One insane seeker after revenge had already sought him out and now this mad nurse was after his blood too.

"So you must be…?"

"Still trying to work it out, are you? That doesn't say much for your memory. How many other lives did you fuck up, how many other little girls did you let get murdered?"

"So you are Tanya's mother?"

"Sonia Smitten, as was. After it happened I decided to turn back to Smith. It was more anonymous and didn't leave me forever associated with my lovely girl.

"People knew, of course they knew. Especially in York. Everyone knows everything in this place – no chance of keeping yourself to yourself. So I got by, trained as a nurse. I enjoy the work most of the time, although there is so much death around. But when Tanya died, I went dead inside, so all the other deaths don't touch me.

"Will Wistow didn't manage to finish you off, did he? Other way round, in fact. The poor old queen ended up dead because of you. So that's two people dead. One I loved beyond life itself, the other a dear, confused man who always was good to me, in his own strange way."

"I tried to save Tanya, you know I did. I tried to talk Smitten out of it. But I failed and that was the greatest failure of my life. I didn't run off on some holiday. I was full of remorse and didn't feel I could carry on being a policeman any more. So I tore up my career and disappeared."

"So why did you have to spoil it all by coming back?"

Rick ignored the question, answering a different one instead.

"I thought that Tanya wouldn't haunt me any more."

"The poor girl's going to haunt me for ever."

"I was doing a job and I messed up. But I didn't kill your girl. Your husband did that."

"He went and killed himself, didn't he? I can't get back at him. But I can get back at you."

"So what are you going to do to me?"

What a stupid question; why had he asked that? Rick's thoughts blurred. Do something, he had to do something. Grab the mad woman, shove her, make a run for it. The inadequacy of it all appalled him; couldn't he think of anything?

The blade was still at his throat, but something had changed. Sonia Smith had moved to face him. She was crying, tears leaking from dead-seeming eyes.

"I thought about killing you – that was my plan," she said. "That way you would get what's coming to you. But I have another idea now."

Sonia Smith eased herself on to Rick's lap so she was straddling him, her breath stroking the narrow space between them. The position was strongly sexual as Rick stared into her tear-smudged face as she settled her weight on his body. Her uniform rose up, exposing sturdy thighs, and she pushed further into him, her breasts resting against his chest. Her mouth was kissing close and under the moonlight he could make out the pores in her skin. Rick's heart pounded in confusion: the combination of hostility and intimacy was terrible. They could almost have been lovers, only she hated him with a cold passion.

Sonia Smitten leaned back a little. Then, locking her eyes with Rick's, she pulled the blade away from his neck and swiftly, expertly cut her own throat. She stayed still for a moment, eyes open, swaying as blood spurted from the gash. Then she slumped forward, letting her full weight fall into Rick, pinning him into the wheelchair. A gurgling, spitting sound escaped the cut. Rick gasped in shock and tried not to breathe, the air warm with blood. He managed to fish out a hankie and held it against the punctured throat, but blood pulsed through the thin cotton. With his other hand, he sought his mobile phone, nearly dropping it at first because it was slippery with blood, but eventually he managed to summon help.

MARTHA had no idea what he would look like dead, yet for a moment had trouble picturing him alive. She could not see him so much as sense him, the sandpaper stubble and sour beer, poking fingers and the sting of his slap. Fleetingly she saw him when they met. She tried to hold this image, but the lodestone of her mind turned back to how things ended up.

"He was a fine looking fellow when young," Martha Percy said, wondering at the strangeness of her voice. She did not know why she was telling this to the young policeman or why she had used "fellow" to describe Thomas. From where had this alien word sprung?

The last time, he had been setting out with her Esme. That was the last time she saw Thomas Percy. He had been wearing the coat, the one that made him so proud, even though it was old and bore the shape of another man. The coat made him swagger; this coat, he had told her, was the cloth of their future. She could not recall his exact words but they amounted to the same foolishness. He had been a foolish man when alive and now he was dead.

Maybe the police had made a terrible mistake and the body was that of another errant husband. That must be it.

The room was like a public bathhouse, only there were no people around washing or waiting to carry out their ablutions. Marble tops and white tiles made this a hard unflinching place. It was sensible what with the cleaning of it she could see that, because everywhere could be washed down so easily. Channels had been cut into the marble to ease the sluicing. She wondered what would need to be washed away in a room like this and then shuddered with half-knowledge.

The young policeman was at her side and a large, florid man was talking to her, a gentleman with a walrus moustache and eyes bright blue behind round spectacles. She did not understand what he was saying; his words floated past her. His hair was grey and swept from his full face. He was a tall fleshy man, fully upholstered from a life of generous feeding. She supposed he must be some sort of medical gentleman, a doctor for the dead rather than the living.

The medical man swayed above her, his words boomed inside her skull. He seemed to be seeking her approval so she nodded her assent. She had not associated the covered mound on the hard surface with her husband. Now she could sense the shape of a person. She continued to nod and the doctor pulled at a corner of the sheet. She was not sure what she had been expecting. She had seen a dead body before and more than once at that. She thought of her mother, laid out cold on the big old table in the kitchen.

She cast her eyes down. There was no doubt. It was her Thomas. His thin pale face was waxy, as if modelled from a dozen mean candles. His chin was dotted with stubble. Sometimes the dead are said to look peaceful, to be accepting in their final repose, but not Thomas. A snarl of surprise captured his face.

"Yes, that is my husband, Thomas Percy of Hungate in York, husband of mine and father to my eight children."

"I am most sincerely sorry."

Martha said she was too and mumbled as much for the benefit of the medical gentleman.

CHAPTER TWENTY FOUR

PAULINE Markham went as far from the house as she could and slumped against an old apple tree. Fallen fruit lay at her feet like bruises. A good view of the house from here. Yet the usual pride had gone. A numbing blankness absorbed everything as her mind wound over and over, straining ever tighter as she thought of Polly. Ordinary life stopped with Polly's abduction, yet it ground on too. She cooked meals in a daze; she filled the washing machine; she cleaned the house; she stood under the shower in the morning, hoping the gushing water might wash away something other than dirt. She still had Samantha to look after, to take to school, to get round to kind friends. She looked at these friends, other parents, neighbours, people she talked to in the street, and she wanted to scream.

Graham would have carried on working if he could. It was not that he didn't care, but he wasn't whole without work. Perhaps he would have been better off at work, out of her face. They should have been a comfort to each other, but his presence irritated her. He was not good at home and did so little around the house. Her mother said early on, just before the wedding, that Graham was "not the most domesticated of males." She specialised in such acid droplets, but she had been right. Pauline never admitted as much, praising what minuscule help Graham gave when her mother was around, building him up as useful. Her mother hadn't been fooled.

They skirted each other like polite strangers rather than parents whose daughter had disappeared. She thought back to earlier that morning when the fat policeman had come into the house with the sweat settling on him. Chief Inspector Sam Rounder was not a healthy man.

Pauline stood as she listened, her restless hands tying and untying invisible knots, while Graham paced circles of agitation. He was suffering, just as she was; but why did he have to look like a man trapped in a meeting that wasn't going his way? He paced and frowned, and made pointless interruptions, as if he were confronting an awkward colleague.

"So what are you lot doing about our daughter?"

"The policeman, the chief inspector, just told us that," Pauline said. "Weren't you listening?"

"We are searching, sir, in the Hungate area of the city. We have reason to believe the person who could have taken Polly may have kept her somewhere in the vicinity."

"So why haven't you asked the old pervert?"

"Because, sir, he is dead."

"What?"

"The man we believe may have kidnapped your daughter was taken to York District Hospital from a history evening class, during which he had been taken ill. A heart attack, from which he did not recover."

"So how the hell did you link him to Polly?"

"The suspect made a garbled admission before he died. His last words were spoken to the teacher. The suspect did not say exactly what he had done, or indeed if he had done anything at all to Polly. But what he said indicated he had kidnapped your daughter."

"And why, exactly?"

"The why of it is a little difficult. We can't say for sure, what with the unpleasant gentleman being dead, but it appears he had become obsessed with a girl who lived a century ago and died in unhappy circumstances. He appeared to believe, and I know this will be difficult for you to absorb, but he felt he could make amends by taking a girl of a similar age to the girl who lived all that time ago."

"But that's fucking bonkers."

"Well, yes, I would have to agree with you on that one, sir."

Sam fell silent for a moment, wondering if he had said enough. People always wanted to hear something and knowing what to say was never easy. Too much could get complicated, too little could be interpreted as indifference.

"We are scouring every inch of Hungate. I've got officers tramping all over the area, but these operations take time and..."

He stopped himself from saying "we only have so much time" or something equally tactless. He had to watch his mouth in this sort of case.

"Can I join in the hunt?"

"Pardon?"

"A simple enough question, Inspector. Can I help to look for Polly?"

"Don't see why not, so long as you are careful and stick with my officers. And do as you are told."

The muscles in Graham's jaw tightened and Pauline knew this was a bad sign. He clamped his jaw when things were not to his advantage. His jaw relaxed a little as the grinding teeth disengaged.

"Yes, I can manage that. Anything to…"

Pauline watched the men go, her husband and the weighty Chief Inspector. She shut the door and looked for distraction, starting first in the kitchen, which always needed cleaning. Today the kitchen did not look dirty or if it was she did not notice. The washing machine had already sloshed and spun through everything that needed washing, and a few items that strictly did not, including towels put aside for holidays and guest bedding.

A coffee would help, the grinding, brewing and drinking of it. She filled the trendy chrome kettle, lit the gas ring on the range cooker and sat by the French windows. It was a chair she loved, bought from a shop she loved, covered in a material she had spent a happy hour choosing. She remembered none of this while she stared at the garden with sightless eyes. When the steam ran off the window, she switched off the kettle. She didn't make coffee. There wasn't the water left.

SAM Rounder was on his way to the hospital. His car was unmarked but it had a siren and he used it now. He needed that siren to dodge the York traffic. At the hospital, he drove round the car park three times, gave up and parked on a yellow line, leaving the note he kept for such occasions: "On police business, don't even think about it."

He was nervous as he walked along corridors which acted as

roads. His apprehension had nothing much to do with Rick. He would be all right, Rick would. He always was in the end. No lasting harm had been done by this latest incident. The anxiety was all for himself. Hospitals gave him the creeps. People arrived in one piece and departed in the tender care of the undertakers. Reason told him some left in a healthier state, but he didn't think of those; it was more natural to imagine the worst. He did not like to linger in case he picked something up, acquired a malicious germ. He was unhealthy enough as it was, without having to play Russian roulette with whatever super-bugs were zipping about the place, waiting to invade the body of a fat middle-aged man.

Another corridor opened before him, the floor shiny and scuffed. Wards off to either side contained people sidelined from life by illness and injury, he gloomily supposed. Poor buggers probably only came in here to visit a member of their family and ended up attached to tubes pumping and sucking vital fluids in and out, hanging to life by a thread.

He found the ward. His brother was in the first bed by the door, tucked against the wall; he was propped up and asleep. Sam eased himself into the chair beside the bed, glad of a moment's rest. Soon his snores were rumbling round the ward. He woke suddenly, cruelly snatched from sleep.

"What?"

"You woke me with your snoring. Probably woke up the whole ward, maybe the whole hospital. In fact I think a bird just fell out of a tree over there, over by the railway line."

"So you're feeling better then."

"Not really, but taking the piss out of you is doing me the world of good."

Sam eased forward and glowered. "Not sure you're made of the right stuff for this private eye lark. First of all you get yourself almost killed by a notable old fruit who posed as a married man, then you willingly go out for a midnight wander with a psychopathic nurse."

"Well, how was I to know she had it in for me?"

197

"Anyone else wanting to finish you off, so far as you know?"

"Who knows? Perhaps I should ask a policeman."

"So this nurse, Sonia Smith…"

"Smitten, as was…"

"Sonia Smitten wanted to harm you because of the girl who died all that time ago, when you left us."

"Tanya, yes, you know the girl, the…"

"The reason you stopped being a policeman and went off on your travels, from which you recently returned to start your glittering career as a private dick."

"Yeah, something like that."

"How is she?"

"Who?"

"The nutty nurse who did a spot of DIY surgery on her own throat."

"She died after they got her back here. It's no surprise, there was so much blood, most of it all over me. They've all been looking at me, some of the nurses and the doctors. Like I was responsible."

Sam tried to think of something soothing to say. Instead, looking around the ward, he said: "I knew you should have gone private."

Rick closed his eyes. He opened them again straight away, because he'd seen again the knife going into the throat and felt again the splash and gush of blood. Sam settled into his chair and rearranged his fleshy personal upholstery. Rick saw his brother's young ghost, slim, handsome, a bit cocky, full of lust and life. How had that lovely, infuriating boy ended up as this middle-aged man with a double chin and buried eyes that darted about, as if seeking something important but out of reach; or maybe someone or something more interesting?

"You look like you're getting ready to say something, Sam."

"Well, yes. There seem to be all sorts of connections with dead girls round here. Two people have tried to finish you off, thanks to Tanya Smitten, killed by her pathetic father…and now both are dead. God, he was a dick-head at school. But who would have thought he would end up doing something like that? So there's one connection. And now we're desperately looking for a lost girl whose fate is somehow tied up with a girl who died a century ago."

"What's the latest on the girl?"

"We're searching Hungate."

"Hungate? Why Hungate?"

"It's this bloody historian's theory, the chap you followed round for the last few weeks. It's the only lead we have. That this girl, Esme Percy, dead a hundred years ago, has something to do with this girl today. Her father, irritating sod that he is, has joined in the search."

"Understandable enough."

"Yeah, of course. It was just that…you know how you notice things? Well, I sensed that his wife was glad to get rid of him."

"Perhaps she was. You know, you have a routine, only seeing each other so often, morning and night perhaps. Then suddenly you are thrown together all the time, and for such an awful reason. Not going to be easy, is it?"

"Too true, little brother."

Sam eased himself out of the chair. "I need to get on. You get yourself better so that you're well enough to get yourself half-killed again in the name of being a private detective."

"Yeah, well, that Philip Marlowe, he used to get knocked around a bit, but he got things sorted."

"Marlowe? Don't remember him at Fulford Road. Perhaps we never worked the same shift."

"Very amusing, Sam. Why don't you make yourself useful? Piss off and find that girl."

"Just what I'm about to do."

CHAPTER TWENTY FIVE

Martha Percy knew he was dead, had seen him laid out cold, but she had no grasp of circumstance or reason. How Thomas had met his death remained a mystery. She had left the mortuary without gleaning any further wisdom.

Martha returned home, lost in apparent purpose. She knew where she was headed and made her way with automatic intent. The children would have to be told, she said to herself, the thought going round and round. He had not lavished much in the way of love, but Thomas Percy had been their father and a duty of respect was required. Martha scuttled into the mossy yard and let herself in through the ill-weighted door. Placing a kettle on the range, she set about preparing tea, working with what she had to hand: there was bread, gone stale; dripping; half a jar of strawberry jam, a paucity of marmalade, damaged biscuits, and not quite sour milk for the tea.

Henry, Peter, Rebecca, Mary, Hetty and young Esme would be home soon, hot and dirty from school, and Joshua and Joseph would return a little later from the factory. Her big lads would be tired from the shifting and the packing, a little of the life gone out of them, until restoration came with whatever food she could provide. Then they would be joking and fighting before going out in search of entertainment. Such was their pattern.

The schooled six came in first, filling all the available space. She hugged them one by one. She was not usually so demonstrative and her open affection caused different reactions. Henry and Peter squirmed, Rebecca and Mary stood still for a dutiful moment, Hetty reciprocated with a hug, and Esme smiled but kept her distance. She is looking pale, that girl, Martha thought. She is not a hale child. Esme stepped further away, as if she could read what her mother was thinking. Martha could have spent a deal longer worrying about the dear scrap of a girl; but there was so much to be done, and besides, Joshua and Joseph had just come in.

She arranged her offspring round the table, telling them to eat and to stay in place when they had finished, instead of crashing off in all directions, as they would have preferred. This unusual request set off a chorus of questions.

"Why, Ma?"

"What for?"

"But me and Joe have made an arrangement…"

She silenced them with a wave of her hand, surprising herself with such authority. The children sensed something was not as it should be.

So they ate the food and slurped the sweetened tea; then, scraping the wooden stools away from the table, they looked at their mother.

Martha stood by the door and regarded her children, their faces tilted towards her like flowers to the sun, she thought, drawn again to long-ago childhood. Fidgety energy came off them. Joe and Josh were exchanging glances, Henry had his finger up his nose, Rebecca and Mary sat with their hands in their laps, Esme waxed paler by the minute.

"There is some news I have to tell you."

She sought the proper words, having turned many variations over in her mind. None of the children had asked about their father, being all too accustomed to his absences. He was missing before his death and now he would be gone for good.

She took a deep breath and exhaled what she had to say using words different to those she had rehearsed, speaking in a broken rush where the mental sentences had been calm and weighted.

"I have news, ill news, about your father. Thomas Percy, is dead. Murdered, or so it seems. Killed in Fulford for God knows what cause or reason. But there you have it."

Before her words had time to settle, a commotion broke out whose cause Martha at first did not understand. Her children pulled away from the table. She could not make out who was who in the human jumble, all arms and legs, the back of heads and curved spines.

"What is it? What is going on?"

"Our Esme has slid under. In a heap under the table."

"She looks to be in a fever or a faint."

"Shall we pull her out?"

"Mind out, mind out."

Esme was limp and lost, but she knew what she had to do. Her fingers sought her favourite, the sharp and wicked talisman. She had to lose this thing, even though she loved it so, and she slipped it from her neck and felt for the crack in the floor. She knew it was there, a secret place where things could be dropped. As she let slip the talisman, the tired and worried face of her mother loomed, and she fainted fully away.

They carried Esme to bed, where she quietened and her breathing fell into a regular pattern. Martha kissed her clammy forehead and went to tidy the parlour, discovering the job had been completed. Rebecca and Mary had done the work, or so they told her. Now they sat at the table, silent.

"Well, thank you for that, girls – and whoever else helped. Now is there anything you would like to ask? Where are the big lads?"

"Out chasing and romancing again. We said we did not know if they should, on a day like this."

Martha sighed out her words: "Maybe it is, maybe it is not, no matter."

"Was Pa killed for being a bad man?"

Martha turned to Rebecca. "You must try not to think of your father like that. He had his faults, but he was a father to you all, this brood for which I now must care by myself. We have his funeral to arrange and the Good Lord alone knows how we will pull that off. There is no money for it. He was a trouble to me in life and so he will prove in death too."

She sat heavily in the chair by the range, the chair he had always owned. She could rest here without fear of reproach, enjoying the only comfort in this damp basement. Blackened white walls, mushrooming damp and a scrap of dirty carpet lost to colour did not offer much in the way of physical pleasure. The range was at the heart of everything, yet it was a leaky, smoke-filled creature that burped and spat. Bugs would scuttle through the shadows;

mice too; rats on a bad day. Thomas had killed a rat once; in a sudden display of manliness he had thrown a boot and cracked its back. In victory he had held the horrible broken thing by its tail and mocked its demise. The rat was old and had had no chance. A more fleet rat would have escaped.

Martha looked at her children, smiling faintly. They talked, there were tears from the older girls, a sob from her own dry throat. One by one, the children braved the midden-privy stink before going to bed. Martha waited up for the lads. She needed to tell them they were the men of the house now. This was what she had decided when she heard a cry from upstairs.

"Ma, come here. Esme has gone queer again. Hot and cold all at once and there is blood on her sheets."

I AM in this place and I know not where. It is a hot place, fierce and slippery wet. My forehead burns dry yet my sweat bathes the sheets. I did not know there was so much to come out. The hot red spittle comes more often now. When I cough my insides want to tear themselves out; the rough sound hurts and I feel something has been ripped away. People crowd into this hot place, some I want to see; some make me angry. Ma is here and I see her now, her face large and then small and far away. Pa too, all bristles and sour ale. But Pa cannot be here because of what I did.

I do not want to see my Pa. I sent him away. He will not bother me with the man in the big house. They cannot touch me. But I can see the crimson-faced man and I want Ma to come back and chase him away. My brothers too, they could give him a hiding and tell him off. The man will not go away, his face looms fat and pink, like the arse of a pig. Pig bottom face. His chin swells like it swallowed another chin. The mouth is open and something horrible is sliding out, a snake from his mouth, all black with a flicking tongue. The man has his trousers open and his thing is out, all pink and hard, a flesh stick with a nasty smell. He wants me to touch the stick, to do things to it, and his breath goes funny, in and out more quickly, as if he was going up the stairs. His trouser buttons are undone, his thing juts out. The room starts to spin like a roundabout. Soon it is moving so fast everything blends into one, the nasty man, Pa with his eyes upraised. His eyes should have that look, the look that says he wants something so much. He does things when he has that look. A mood takes over and nothing can get in the way.

So I sent him away, put him where he cannot ask me to do those things any more. I am safe in this hot place. The room is spinning so fast I cannot make anything out. Nothing is what it should be. Everything speeds so quickly. The whirligig goes faster and faster, then it slows and wobbles. Now I can make out the colours, see the details. When it stops my mother is there, Ma with her anxious face that has lines like furrows in a field. I saw that outside York, the grooves in the earth stretching to meet the sky. Ma grew up on a farm, she is always telling us that. Now she is here in the city with all of us, alone. Not Pa because I sent him away, so that he would not ask me any more. No more. I do not like it. That thing is horrible. So if you make me. You cannot ask me to do it again or I shall jump and scream. And I shall do worse than that.

The turning slows, then stops. Will I be able to stand when I get off? Sometimes the ground carries on moving, as if it caught the habit from the roundabout. When the spinning ceases, Ma is still waiting for me, her mouth tight, her face creased.

MARTHA was liquid with worry as she looked at her lovely scrap of a girl, all delirious and deathly white from spitting the blood.

"Keep hold of your blood," she said. "Your blood is doing you no good on the sheets. It needs to be inside you, keeping you alive, my child."

Esme was a rag, a limp thing, inert and without life. Her spirit was half way gone, packed for the journey. Then she sat bolt upright, as if life had hold of her again and pulled her up in one swift movement.

"Thank the Lord – there is life in you yet."

She quivered in the grip of a greater force.

"What is it, my girl?"

"I know what happened to Pa and I have to tell you or God will be angry and I will go to hell."

"What is this you talk of, lass? You babble when you should rest and…"

"There is a time to rest and it is not now, soon, but not yet."

"What words you do say, child. This does not sound like you."

"What I did was not like me; what Pa made me do with the red-faced man; what he wanted me to do; and what I did to Pa to save myself from the crimson man."

"You do babble so, child. What are you talking about?"

I TRY to answer but cannot say what words are coming out. How can I tell what is said and what remains inside my skull? I am so hot and cold at once; my skin is dry with goosebumps yet runs with sweat; it is November yet I am so hot I could melt.

The words Ma says meet other words, spoken by my father. He is telling me to be a good girl, to play the game with the important man, because he is rich and he can help. The rich have things we do not have, they can make our life better. His eyes are hard and shiny like wet pebbles. I do not understand what he asks. Does he know what the pink man will want? I tell him what the man will ask me to do, putting my hands on his pink spurting stick. Pa says I am a liar; a grand gentleman would never do such a thing. I am to go with the butler man when the gate opens and Pa will wait for me here afterwards, when he will take me home, buying me an ice on the way.

Pa steps towards the door with his fist open, ready to strike the shiny painted wood. Then he sees something at his feet. "That will not do," he says. "It will not do at all." As he bends and fiddles, the rotten bootlace comes away in his hand. He says "fuck" which is a word nobody is meant to say. God could swipe you off the earth just for using that word.

"How can I look right and proper for the butler now?"

He fiddles with the perished lace and then tucks the ragged end into the scuffed black boot. He expels air in a weary puff, putting a hand on the cobbles, ready to push himself up. But he never stands again. I have my special thing. With its tiny sharpness in my hand, no harm can befall me. I run at his bent back. It is as if we are playing leapfrog. There he is, formed into an arch for the jumping. He is surprised when I land on his back, grunts and stumbles. He says that word again, the word God hates, and his free hand scrabbles around, trying to find me, while his other hand holds his weight, the fingers splayed against the stones of the alleyway. He has no luck. Before he can grasp me, the point I have made so sharp is stuck in his neck.

It goes in quickly and stops, having hit something hard. Pa makes a funny sound and his arms buckle. He falls into the alley, with his face kissing the ground. His mouth moves on the mossy stones and blood comes from his nose. I pick myself up to look at Pa, who twitches and then goes still. I pull out my lucky thing, tugging hard to retrieve it from his neck. It does not shift and it takes so much time and effort, but eventually it comes away.

The blade is bloody and I wipe it on the moss. The time between then and now is gone. Somehow I arrive home and now I am lying in this bed, with my mother looming above. She is close to at first, then farther away.

MARTHA let the fevered fragments settle. The dress Esme had been wearing had blood on it, but the girl coughed blood sometimes so that was not surprising; and she was prone to scrapes and cuts. That would explain the blood; it all made sense when she thought about it, with a fall or a tumble leading to a cut; and if she could not see such a cut that would be because she had not looked hard enough. Esme had fallen and she had hurt herself, that was all.

Esme swam in and out of delirium and gradually Martha felt calm. "The frenzy is departing," she said. Here was an interlude in her fever, a cooling of the heat. For an hour or so, this seemed more than maternal optimism, because Esme became temperate, as if the fever were abating.

Martha let her heart hope. Esme would grow to a woman and have children of her own. Martha thought of the children yet to come. With the blessing of the Lord she would greet her grandchildren. That much she deserved after the life she had led. This happy distraction drifted like a sail on a calm sea.

Esme sat upright in a jolt so sudden Martha let out a cry of surprise.

"My God, my girl – what is the matter?"

The girl spoke through her vapours…

MA, I see the lines wriggling across your face but do not worry. Everything is as it should be now. Pa cannot ask me any more. I shall not do that thing he wants, that foul thing with the pink pig man. He is not here any more; not the pink pig man, but Pa; for making me do that horrible thing, I did attack my father, jumped upon his back and stuck my special sharp thing into his neck; stuck it in hard and fast. He did some bloody spitting and fell to kissing the ground. The sharp thing stopped him breathing, but I cannot be sorry for I wanted to stop the terrible thing happening again.

ESME did not last the night, did not last the hour, and the fancy Martha Percy had entertained shattered. Instead she had to busy herself with the practicalities of death because now she had two funerals to organise. She wanted the ceremonies to fall on different days. It was accounted an odd request but Martha won the argument through persistence. Her daughter was placed in the ground one day, her husband two days later. Each funeral was small and unnoticed by many, with only immediate family present. A clutch of drinking friends had wanted to pay their last respects to Thomas Percy, but Martha had sent them on their way, under the suspicion they desired a free drink.

Many tears were shed as the family circled the small grave allocated to Esme. Her place would have gone unmarked if Martha had not found the money, having at first had an idea about how such a sum might be obtained. She took Joseph and Joshua, who were taller and stronger than their father had ever been. Joe and Josh would help her extract what was required.

It had not been easy, not least because she had to be sure of the location. It was fortunate Thomas had been so full of his visits to the grand house in Fulford, for he had described the dwelling in detail and the picture he had painted proved to be sufficient, allied to what Esme had said and the young policeman had told her.

They found the house and walked through a garden longer than any Martha had seen. A butler opened the front door, which was large, shiny and painted green, with panels of stained glass. He made no attempt to hide the distaste he felt at being confronted by such a delegation.

"Any business your sort could possibly have at this house can only be dealt with via the entrance for servants, which you will find down the alley…"

"Down the alley where my beloved late husband was found, stabbed to death after some funny business within this house."

"Your loss is, I am sure a great one, but I do not see how that man could have been involved in this fine family, so…"

"So nothing," said Martha.

Before the door could be closed in their faces, Joseph and Joshua stepped into the gap.

"And so," said Martha, her very soul fluttering with what she was about to say, "I think your Master should help a poor widow woman, especially one who has certain evidence about her person. My evidence suggests your Master likes to amuse himself with poor little girls who have no understanding of the way of the world.

"A little recompense would help for…" Here she started to cry tears she did not have to draw from a false well. "For a poor widow woman who has a husband and a child to bury and no money to pay."

"You have the cheek of the devil himself, if you think a fine upstanding man such as my Master would…"

"Would what? Ask a poor girl to…" Here Martha leaned forward and whispered what foul thing she had to say. Delivered of her speech, and stepping back, she said: "That is what he did, and has no doubt done to other poor girls."

As Martha walked away from the grand house with her boys, she waxed paler than usual and vomited into the beautiful garden, spattering her meagre breakfast over a late rose. Her whispered words had had the designed effect: she left the grand house having settled on an agreeable sum, which was delivered the following day. The money was more than sufficient to pay for two plots in York Cemetery, where a tender and tearful funeral was held one day; and a brisker affair two days later. The graves are still there today. They are difficult to find, hidden away in a far corner of the cemetery, close to a boundary wall, beyond which lies an allotment and a distant view of the University of York.

A FEW days after the two funerals, Martha Percy used some of the remaining money to pay for the services of "a man what knew about the law," as she put it. She dictated a statement, or as much of one as she could muster. Mr Woodthorpe was an imposing man and although Martha was too overawed to take in all of his physical details, she retained the memory of a well-filled waistcoat and a bushy moustache, the ends twirled into question marks. The office where he worked was a cavern of polished mahogany and the tiles on the floor were arranged like herringbone.

The words she spoke to this impressive man in his office on Coney Street were to provide a history lesson, long after Martha had died and been reacquainted with her Esme in York Cemetery, a certain amount of her cleverly-gotten gains having been set aside for the purpose.

CHAPTER TWENTY SIX

JOSHUA Woodthorpe resented paying a cleaner to polish his name. He wanted to buff and caress the carved letters himself. The wretched woman did little more than swipe.

"I could do a better job," he would say to his wife, sometimes more than once in the same day; but Anthea was adamant.

"It would not be fitting for a man of your standing to be seen polishing his own sign," she would reply. So there the matter rested, although on the sly Joshua would extract a spotty handkerchief from his pocket and give the plaque a furtive buff.

Joshua liked to polish. At home the marble in the kitchen was his favourite surface. No polish was required, merely hot soapy water and two cloths: the first to soak up the suds before they dried and spoilt the surface with chalky marks, the second for the final sheen. After that he could see his face in the mottled black glass. He shone his Jaguar to dazzling perfection every Sunday morning, only for dirt, mud and birds to undo his hard work. The shoes he wore to work gleamed like black glass. Even his hairless head shone, an effect achieved without polish or effort.

Joshua was known to some as the shiny solicitor. He reflected light from almost every available surface. So it was that Rick Rounder was visited in hospital by this human gleam. The fluorescent strips reflected on his shiny pate, and in his black leather shoes, which squeaked into the ward; and when he extended his hand, cufflinks twinkled. His teeth, when he smiled, while not perfectly shiny, were impressively white, thanks to a present he had received on his last birthday.

"Yellow teeth just won't do," Anthea had said, when explaining the gift of a whitening session at the private dentist she had signed them up to. Joshua had thought it a little unkind of her to say that, especially on his fiftieth; but he had said nothing, adhering to long-developed habit. It was best not to, easier all round.

"Well, Mr Rounder, you may wonder why I am here. It started with a pint of beer, a very nice one as it happens. At a public house on Monkgate. Lovely, light golden stuff; can't remember the name of it for the life of me, but never mind."

"Golden straw colour, lovely, light and hoppy...slips down a treat?" said Rick, naming a favourite beer.

"You know, I think it jolly well was. Damn fine liquid."

"So how did that pint lead you to me?"

"Ha! Yes, good question. Not explaining myself, am I?"

"As you can see, I have plenty of time to listen."

"Found this, that's what started me off."

Joshua extended clean, manicured fingers into the pocket of his suit and withdrew a black wallet, from which he produced a card.

"Bit dog-eared, I'm afraid to say. Had beer spilt on it as well, by the look of it."

It was one of Rick's business cards.

"Ah, scattered them all over the place when I set up."

"Is it going well?"

"Are you taking the piss?"

"Heavens, no. Never occurred to me. It was just a polite inquiry about how your work was progressing."

"It's not going anywhere much at the moment, thanks to me being in here. Other than that, it's all right. Getting settled in, re-acquainted and all that."

"With who?"

"With York." Rick offered a brief summary of his near four decades. "Born and brought up in this city, had my first pint here, first sexual experience too, smoked one or two substances I shouldn't have, joined the police, buggered off after a few years, travelled the world, came back and set up as a private detective."

"Eloquently put, I'm sure. And that's why I am here. The card directed me to you."

"You have a job for me?"

"Well, I think I do. I rang the police, but they professed to being too busy with 'real cases' to worry about this. Besides, something about your card excited me. One couldn't help but suppress a tremor at the thought of a private detective."

"So spill the Heinz then."

"Spill the what? Oh, I get your drift. Beanz meanz and all that. Yes, I see now. Spill the Heinz – that's genuine private detective talk, I imagine."

"Don't know about that. I just made it up."

"Anyway, that is sufficient badinage. Here is the reason I tracked you down to the hospital. I spoke to your assistant, by the way. She thought you wouldn't mind."

Joshua Woodthorpe, family solicitor, latest in an orderly queue of family solicitors stretching down the decades, pulled two photocopied sheets from a briefcase, which was, unsurprisingly, black and shiny. The original document had been in the vault at the firm's bank for a century, where it had lain unread for all those years. Multitudinous cases had arisen and been resolved, while the envelope with the copperplate writing had waited to divulge its contents.

How exciting it had been to open the envelope, which Joshua had come across a few years ago while sifting unfinished business. The temptation had been to open it immediately, but he had waited, reasoning that the writer deserved such a courtesy. So the concealment continued until a few days ago, when he retrieved the envelope from the bank vault and, once back in the office, gutted its belly with a well-polished paper knife.

Joshua explained all as Rick shifted his bruised flesh under the much-washed institutional sheet. When the solicitor had finished what he had to say, which took longer than for many other people, he offered the photocopies to Rick.

"Here, read these and you will understand what I am talking about."

SAM Rounder was speaking to the father of the missing girl and he felt…what exactly? Sympathy, empathy, whatever you wanted to call it. The man's child had gone missing, after all. Even when his own daughters irritated him with their chatter and demands, or treated him with lofty disdain, he feared for their safety. If Sam sometimes feared the worst, it was because he had seen it happen all too often. Now Graham Markham was facing such a scenario. In other circumstances, Sam might not care. Markham was a flashy, big-mouthed sod who surely earned twice what a hard-working Chief Inspector managed. Irritation prickled over his skin. Sam had to take a deep breath and tell himself that Markham was facing the possibility that his daughter was dead; and no-one, idiot or otherwise, should have to take that on board.

"What are we doing? Look about you, sir. We are scouring all the buildings, looking in cellars. I've even sent a helicopter over with heat-seeking equipment. That should be able to trace a…person."

Had he been about to say body?

"And?"

"And we are still analysing the information received."

He knew the paucity of the words but could summon nothing better. He did not want to raise false hopes or to hint at gloomy conclusions. The girl could still be alive; stranger things had happened.

They were standing in what had once been the Hungate part of the city. A massive development was due, once the arguments and enquiries had blown themselves out, after which another stretch of the past would be gone.

From what Sam remembered of his local history, Hungate had been a slum, so perhaps there wasn't much to regret.

"Can you imagine, Inspector, what all this is like for me – what it is doing to me?"

"I can imagine, sir, yes. I have two daughters. And I am genuinely sorry about what you are going through. This is a difficult time, I know that."

"Difficult doesn't come close."

Police officers walked in a diligent line towards an old warehouse, checking and looking again for clues to the disappearance of Polly Markham. The most unexpected clue could show the way. So the sweep went on, over and over the same ground, like a group obsessive compulsion.

Graham Markham turned away from Sam Rounder and kicked a stone in frustration. The stone hit something, span into the air and then fell to strike an officer in the back. Surprised, the constable stumbled and tripped, putting his arms in front as he went. A reflex action: fingers splayed, thumbs extended.

As the constable hit the ground, a splinter tore into the fleshy mound beneath the right thumb. The constable had a split second in which to acknowledge the pain caused by the needle of wood inserted into his hand, and then he fell headlong into a dank hole. Old sacking took the impact and saved his bones.

The constable, PC Shelby, three years in the force and still young enough to believe in his bright future, sat up and patted himself, then explored his injured palm. He could feel the tip of the splinter and the submerged blade of old wood running under his skin.

"Fuck!"

"So you must be all right then, Shelby, if you've got it in you to swear."

Shelby looked up and saw an angel. Either that, or the late November sun had thrown a gold fringe around his overweight boss. He squinted and shielded his eyes. The sun withdrew and the angel turned back into Chief Inspector Rounder.

"Sir, I seem to have fallen into a hole."

"I worked that one out for myself, lad."

"Yes, sir. Fairly obvious, I suppose."

"Are you hurt?"

"Bit of a gash on my head."

"So nowhere important then."

"And a bitch of a splinter in my hand."

"I'll have the hot needle waiting for you when you get out."

"What?"

"It's what my old mother used to do. With splinters. Insert a hot needle underneath, then ease the bugger out. The good old-fashioned ways of doing things. Hurt like fuck though."

Sam wondered why he had just said all that. He couldn't be sure why he said a lot of things nowadays. Words came out, actions happened, and increasingly he felt like a robot impersonator in his own life.

"Can you see anything down there, Shelby? It looks as though you've fallen into a small loading chute or something."

"Hang on, sir, I'll get my torch."

The fall had dislodged the torch, which could not be found, so a replacement was thrown to Shelby, who caught it with his bad hand and swore again.

He switched it on and shuffled in the hole, illuminating the decayed sacking that had broken his fall. As the beam shone, the matting was animated in horrid waves. A sleek rat emerged, sniffed the fetid air and bolted, scampering over Shelby's right foot as it disappeared into the darkness.

"Oh, shit."

"What is it now, Shelby?"

"A rat, sir. A big, stinking rat."

"Glad I'm up here then. Can't stand the buggers. What else is down there?"

Shelby sliced the darkness with his torch. First, in the direction taken by the rat, he saw a collapsed wall leading to further darkness.

"Some sort of a tunnel, sir. And…" He turned again and shone his light into the corner of another opening, which sloped away from him. At first he could see nothing much. Then the beam picked out the huddled remains of someone or something. His heart jolted and blood thundered across his eardrums. He concentrated on what was in front of him, and the harder he looked, the more certain he became: he was looking at the remains of someone, not something.

RICK Rounder looked at the legal document, which was dated November 25, 1901.

"Almost exactly a hundred years ago," Woodthorpe said.

"Yeah, I worked that much out."

"I'll shut up then."

"Good idea."

Rick started to read what Joshua Woodthorpe, esquire, solicitor of York, had written a century ago...

"I was named after him, you know, and..."

"I thought you were shutting up."

HEREWITH are facts of a certain nature which should not be communicated to any person until the year 2001, by which time the individuals involved will have long departed this world, which can sometimes be a place of darkness...

THE phraseology had been pleasing to Joshua Woodthorpe, although he would have preferred greater poetic weight. He had considered describing the world as "a place of tenebrous gloom" for he had a fondness for the adjective, which he thought had religious connotations; candles were involved somewhere, he believed. However, looking at the scrap of womanhood in front of him, he sighed and admitted that lofty words would be wasted on someone of her standing. Her story had taken a deal of extraction, so it would be best to keep matters simple and to discard the flowery language.

At first she had spoken in such a rush that he had not gained the faintest comprehension. By the third telling, he had begun to understand.

He looked again at this lined, worrisome woman and thought she had had too many children. Those who could least afford to bring young ones into this world often had too many. Such was the habit of the disadvantaged classes. It was not entirely their fault, because they were not educated and they lived in a variety of darknesses. We cannot all be blessed with the fully advantaged life, he thought, finding pleasure at his choice of words.

Joshua Woodthorpe directed his attentions to what the poor woman was saying.

"So you see, the little one, the one what is now dead, killed her

Pa. They are both gone from me now, the man I married, God curse his dirty soul, and the youngest of my little ones, my Esme. She informed me, did our Esme, almost with what was her last bellows-full of air, that she killed her Pa. You do not need to ask the question as to why, because I will inform you straight off. She killed Thomas because he had been selling her to a grand man in Fulford, for services of the sort that a man sometimes needs. But I ask you, how can it be right for a man to want a young girl to do things like that? A man of his riches should be able to find what he wants with someone more like himself. Disgusting, is what I call it. And what sort of a father agrees to sell the services of his own daughter to a rich man with low needs?"

A dead man, that is the sort, thought Joshua Woodthorpe, dead and gone, in keeping with so many of his disappointing type. The solicitor sighed and turned his mind to the matter at hand. This was not easy because he had been having such visions of what he would be sitting down to eat that evening that his mouth had begun to salivate.

"So how do the constabulary think your husband Thomas came to his end?"

Roast duck running with fat, potatoes roasted in goose fat, carrots faintly caramelised, a steamed ginger pudding, with wine, and port afterwards...

"Far as I can see, they do not have a blessed clue. And that suits me just fine. What I am telling you is not for their ears, it is for you and the future."

"But if you told the police about this, relayed to them every detail as you have to me, then perhaps they would do something about this man, this rich gentleman from Fulford."

"Rich but no gentleman. That is all I have to say. Besides, who would the police believe: a man fat with life, or a poor wretch like me; a gentleman in a grand house or a widow woman who lives in Hungate?"

Joshua Woodthorpe had to admit the wretched woman spoke good sense. So, with roast meats and steamed puddings rising in his head, he wrote what Martha Percy had to say, conveying her story with all the elegant care as he could muster. When he had finished, he read the words out loud and inquired of Martha if she had understood. She told him that she did, keeping to herself the observation that she was not a complete idiot, and also leaving unspoken the thought that Mr Joshua Woodthorpe was a good deal too pleased with himself.

"Thank you kindly, good sir," she said. With that, Martha Percy, widow and grieving mother, left the offices of Woodthorpe Solicitors. She walked away and quickly let slip the grander parts of York. Soon enough she found herself back in the gloomy confines of Hungate, a place she was happy to call home, if only because she had known no other since her childhood days on the farm. The past that seemed to watch her was so much more pleasant than the present. She was certain the world was coming to no good and not just because of poor Esme. Perhaps the future would turn out for the better. Maybe she was paying the price for a happy past and a happier future. She had arranged for a letter to be posted into the beginning of the next century, a place so distant she could not imagine what life would be like. It would be better, surely it would be better. Whatever occurred, it would not be her problem; and she felt better for having told the truth about Esme. Everything had been wrapped up in proper fashion. She missed the child so very terribly, and her death had left a bottomless ache, yet she understood that life had to continue. There were other children to love, other cares to worry over.

Martha Percy arrived home with a heaviness inside her chest. This weight would remain on her for as long as she lived, and the great slab of unhappiness would be worn away to a hard pebble of grief. Such longing for what could not be changed would only be released when she let out her last breath. She would again know fleeting joy and laughter in her life, but happiness would dance for a moment while sadness – slow, consolidating sadness – would stay.

PC SHELBY handed the skull to his boss. It was difficult to equate such a hollowed thing with a human being. So many thoughts and desires had once been contained within the empty space now defined by curved and yellowed bone.

"Easy mistake to make," said Sam Rounder, holding the skull. "It could have been the girl, I suppose, but even if she was no longer with us, she wouldn't be that far gone. Not, you know, alas poor what's-his-face. You look like an educated sort. Who am I talking about – Shakespeare or something, isn't it?"

"Yorrick, sir."

"Is that right? Who knows? My brain never was much of a one for all that literature stuff – even when I was young. Now it's a policeman's brain and of fuck all use for anything else."

"So who do you think this is?"

"What?"

"Our friend Yorrick."

"Ah, could be anyone. Some low-life type with any luck. One less of the buggers to deal with. The trouble nowadays, you know Shelby, is that too many people don't know the rules. They go their own way and don't stick to procedure. That's what we're here for. We're good at procedure, at applying the rules."

"And breaking them sometimes, sir."

"That too – but only when the rules require it. Anyway, enough. We've got a little girl to find. She's bound to be round here somewhere. What we need is a bit of luck – before hers runs out."

CHAPTER TWENTY SEVEN

IT FELT like a strange thing to do, but it made some sort of sense to Rick Rounder. Or as much sense as anything was making in his hospital-befuddled brain. He had followed Hunt and the lovely Wendy for ages. Naturally enough, his attention had been drawn to the female half of that coupling, as Wistow had calculated. How he had been hooked by that ruse. The camp old sod, God rest his fluttering soul, had certainly got that one right. Rick had fallen for Wendy and allowed himself to be dragged all over, and eventually almost towards his own death. He was, he had to allow, some kind of idiot. But at least he was a living idiot, not a dead one.

All that time, he had been watching the beguiling Wendy, and now it was time to turn to her partner. He was a historian so he should be able to help.

MALCOLM Hunt picked up the phone, heard the name and sighed. Rounder was such an irritant, so stubborn and sure, yet without the wit to drag a single original thought from inside his fat head. What more could the corpulent copper want from him? The wretched man should be out hunting that poor girl, not bothering academics who had higher matters to occupy their minds. In fact, if truth is the thing, he had been trying to work out when he could next engineer having sex with Wendy.

The thought uncurled in his mind as he sat on the battered leather sofa in his flat, which was small and just off Bootham. He used to love the flat and it had served him well, rising dramatically in value, even though he had done little in the way of enhancement, aside from allowing an accumulation of artistic neglect. Ten years ago, this had seemed an exciting place to live; close enough to the football ground to inhale a whiff of rough populism, yet not far too from the fine houses of Bootham. Oh, those houses with all their storeys, one grandly imposed on another. One day he would live in one of those houses; once he had written his classic history, a popular work about York, yet strictly academic too. This work would be so successful that it would lead to a television series, more books, appearances on Start The Week on BBC Radio Four and, eventually, a hard-won turn at Desert Island Discs.

Diverting his mind from sex, he began to compile his list (not for the first time). A spot of Van Morrison, one from Astral Weeks, just to show his tastes were impeccable but a little bit difficult. Something classical too, a gloomy rumble of Verdi, perhaps the Requiem, and…

"Mr Hunt?"

Malcolm shook the music from his head.

"Ah, yes, sorry Chief Inspector. What can I do for you?"

"You can stop confusing me with my brother for a start. He's the balding wheezy one with a bad marriage and a good pension scheme. I'm the younger brother with a good relationship and no pension scheme. I'm the one who got out…"

"…when the going was good?"

"No, when the going was shitty. Anyway, I'm back working as a private eye. Or I am when I'm not in hospital. This job seems to involve more recuperation than I'd banked on. Anyway, what it is, I've been brought an old document which explains about how a man – one Thomas Percy – died a century ago, and also contains the last confession of his daughter, Esme."

Malcolm Hunt was brought up short by the name.

"Esme Percy? She's the one my student, poor old Frank Helmsley, was obsessing about when he died. Well, I say 'poor old' but he was a funny old sod, bit of a loner and a weirdo."

"I think this document could help trace Polly Markham. Could your history guy, your dead weirdo, have found out where Esme Percy lived and taken Polly to the same place?"

"It sounds like the sort of thing he might have done."

"Do you fancy paying me a visit in hospital then? And no grapes. I'm sick of the bloody things."

AS MALCOLM Hunt walked towards the hospital, he thought himself into another life, a favourite place of retreat. That book, the book, was written. Perhaps it was even about this very girl lost in history, with scholarly detail spent on examining the inescapable grind of poverty, as well as nicely judged emotional observations, included to give his history a novelistic spin, and hopefully a better chance of selling. Yes, he was a celebrated historian, appearing on the radio and in the posh newspapers, feted everywhere. The Malcolm Hunt who taught history to evening classes was a creature of the shabby past, a forgotten relative to his newly successful self. That Malcolm was history – and the new one was Mr History.

Ah, what a life.

So swept up was he in his engaging diversion that Malcolm forgot to feel nervous until he was halfway over the rough concrete bridge spanning the railway line behind the hospital. This could be a lonely spot. His heart raced when he realised where he was, but he took a deep breath. He had a date with history. He couldn't afford to worry about muggers.

The muggers were kind that afternoon, or having a day off, and Malcolm Hunt arrived unscathed at the hospital.

"SO what misfortunes brought you here, then?"

Malcolm Hunt sat in the hospital chair and directed the question at Rick Rounder. Rick thought it best not to mention that he'd been following Malcolm on his intimate moments with his girlfriend.

"A kidnapper first, then an unbalanced nurse. They had a load of grudges between them. People have long memories in this city."

"Lots for them to remember, the place resonates with history. You know, one only has to look around and there is so much of the past here, from the grand history of kings and queens to the social story of people burdened with poverty and…"

"Yeah, my brother said you went on a bit."

"A professional failing."

"That's all right, I've got lots of unprofessional ones, which probably explains how I ended up in this place. Anyway, here it is. This is a copy of a document written a hundred years ago by a York solicitor, Joshua Woodthorpe, whose descendant, another

Joshua Woodthorpe, brought it in for me to look at. He rang my brother's lot but they said they'd get back to him, because they were too busy hunting for a lost girl to worry about a document from the past. So he got in touch with me. If the dead girl helps us find the lost girl, I'll have done some good for once – and be able to indulge in a little fraternal piss taking, which would be nice."

Malcolm accepted the photocopied document and began to read. While he was occupied, Rick looked around the ward and decided it was time to get out of this place; never mind what the doctors said, he was through with hospitals.

"Get me those jeans, will you? And my shoes, please. I need to go home and wash this bloody place off me."

"Are you sure you're meant to do that? And, besides, isn't it a bit of a cliché? You know, the bloody-minded private eye, or cowboy, or rogue policeman stalks out of hospital against medical advice, carrying his wounds close to him in a foolish display of macho bull-headedness?"

"Sounds about right to me."

RICK Rounder felt light-headed as he stepped into the darkening afternoon. The fresh air, or air fresher than the germ-laden gaseous substance he had been breathing at the hospital, rushed about his body with all the gusto of alcohol seeking a bloodstream to pollute.

"We'll go to my office, well, it's more of a garage than an office, but it does the job. On the way, we'll stop off at a pub so that I can remember what a pint of beer tastes like. It's been a while. I'm losing track of time."

"Shouldn't we be working out how to find Polly Markham instead?"

"Don't you just hate that?"

"What?"

"When some bastard goes and ruins a perfectly good plan by talking sense."

Traffic ground past the hospital. Some cars already had their headlights on, while others pushed on without illumination. It was as if the glass-half-full syndrome applied to the approaching dusk: it was either half light or half dark.

"So what do you reckon then, Mr History Teacher?"

"We could try the archives first."

"Went there once when I was at school. Next to the art gallery?"

"Until it gets closed or moved somewhere else. This city doesn't always look after what it should."

After a short walk, and a spot of business at the door, Rick and Malcolm entered a place where York keeps its memory in dusty boxes and filing cabinets.

They had timed their arrival badly, and the archives closed in half an hour. It didn't seem much time to chase through history and save a life. Malcolm glowed with purpose as he told the keepers of the archive what he was after. They scurried off to return carrying boxes and folders, allowing Malcolm to begin a study more frenzied than usual. He sifted through the old maps and documents, trying to find out what had happened to the address where the Percys had lived.

"We have an address here, you see."

He showed one of the archivists the photocopied letter from Joshua Woodthorpe.

"This is where the family lived and what I want to find out is if that building is still around in some form today and if my student, the late and unlamented Frank Helmsley, could have located it and used it to hide the girl he kidnapped."

Ten minutes to go.

More documents were unearthed, smelling of dust and old paper.

"It's funny that the past should smell like that," said Malcolm, raising his head from the mouldering paper. "Old paper, dust and all that. Yet the past was so alive. It's a bit like we think of the more recent past, 30 or 40 years ago, as being black and white, because of old films and television programmes, and old photographs. Yet the past was full of colour, with as much depth and vibrancy as today. It's…"

"All very pretty, but time is ticking," said Rick.

"So it is, so it is."

Five minutes to go.

Malcolm sneezed loudly, then did an encore. "It's the dust, paper mites or something. Always gets to me."

"We will have to close in a few minutes, sir," said one of the archivists.

"This could be a matter of life and death, you know."

"I know, it's just that we have to obey the rules and…"

No minutes to go.

"Take five or something, won't you? I'm sure I must be nearly there."

So the rules were bent, five more minutes passed and nothing was discovered to indicate the possible whereabouts of Polly Markham.

Five more of the archive's minutes were squeezed out, then their time was up, as if they were playing a TV game show and had just lost.

Malcolm rubbed his eyes and sneezed again. Rick yawned and said: "Funny that history should get up your nose."

"What?"

"Make you sneeze like that."

"Are you always so droll?"

"I try my best."

The archivist loomed again. "Look, I'm sorry but we really must close now, and…"

"I know," said Rick. He had started thinking about that pint again and the liquid vision was blurring his concentration, almost as if he'd already drunk the bloody thing; if only. He bent his mind to the girl, incarcerated somewhere in Hungate, trapped in a past not of her own making. He hated himself for wanting that drink, but hating himself didn't switch off the desire. Sometimes you were just stuck with yourself, whether or not you liked what you found.

The documents were gathered, ready to be returned to wherever they had come from; to be tidied away until another, less urgent, inquiry called for their retrieval. Rick sat back, stretched his arms and yawned, tipping his uncovered mouth to the ceiling.

Disappointment seeped through his pores. This had seemed such a good idea, to chase through the past with Mr Bloody History; to find the answer and give his bloody brother a bloody nose.

The last document was being returned when Malcolm shot out his hand. "Hang on a second. There was something about that one, something I glimpsed then forgot. It was there, then it was gone and..."

He trailed off and read the same passage twice.

"It's here look, I'm sure of it."

His finger ran along old roads and traced out a forgotten alleyway. "Here it is and the Percys lived here, I'm sure of it. All we have to do is work out where that is today and we may have the answer."

Rick rang his brother, who sighed, observed that they'd better not be wasting his time, then sent over a patrol car, just in case they weren't. The car screeched up to the fountain as they emerged into the square.

"Hey, this is exciting," said Malcolm as he saw the blue flashing light. "I've never been in a police car before, let alone one with an agitated illumination on top. Historians don't travel at speed very often. A stately progress back through time is more our thing and..."

"Why don't you shut your stately mouth for a moment and get in. Agitated illumination indeed."

The car made thrilling excursions onto the wrong side of the road. Soon enough, they arrived in Hungate with a satisfying skid across loose gravel. Doors opened, shoes hit the dust. It was almost dark now and difficult to make out what was going on. Rick could decipher movement of some kind a little way off as torch beams slashed the dark. The lights worked with a single purpose for a while, pointing in unison; then they became distracted, shooting off in random directions. One beam broke from the others and turned their way. The wavering eye of light came closer. Behind it was a large, slow moving shadow. It might have belonged to a bear, only one that wasn't as fit as it once had been, having been too much at the honey. Chief Inspector Sam Rounder pointed his torch at the two men.

"So, it's that private eye brother of mine and the shagging history teacher. Have you two joined forces to solve York's crimes? God save us...that'll be a good laugh. The history man and a man with a history."

"Are you in one of those moods of yours? He used to be like this sometimes when we were young."

"Oh, I was never young," said Sam. "I had to spend too much time looking after you. I wasn't allowed to be young, but you were. Darling Rick had to be given his space – allowances had to be made. Because you were the young one, the baby of the family."

"God, what's got into you tonight? We're here to help you find that poor girl."

"Yeah, sure you are."

"We have information that could help."

"What, from the history books?"

"Yeah, that's right."

"Spill what you've got."

Sam moved in close, his moon face thrown into eccentric shadows by the torch. His eyes disappeared beyond his large nose and his mouth was set in a hard, unsmiling line.

"The Percy family lived here, you see," said Malcolm, placing the photocopied map under the torch beam. "So we need to find our bearings and work out where that was. It's a little hard in this light."

"I'll get one of my officers to turn on the full moon."

"The what?

"You'll see."

A few moments later, the shudder of a diesel engine heralded a dazzling, blinding light.

"Runs off a generator, you see. We don't run it all the time because if you look into its beam by mistake, you can't see a bloody thing for a week."

They stood to one side of the punishing light, which cut an unnaturally bright swathe across the abandoned land, picking out rubble and shadows.

They studied the photocopied map, which Malcolm turned round, trying to find a rotation that fitted with their position.

"I can't work anything out if you keep doing that. Keep it still."

"I need to get our bearings right. Now we're right you see, with the Minster over there. York Minster always helps you to work out where you are."

Malcolm was silent for a moment. The generator rumbled and the searing light assaulted the darkness. "So I reckon we should be looking over there."

He pointed off to the far right of where the officers were searching.

"I'm sure we've looked there already," said Sam. "We've already combed over every bloody inch of this place without finding a thing."

"Why don't you drag your moon over that way and we'll see."

As the beam bumped over the rough ground, dust rose up. By the time the light was in place, nothing could be seen except dust. Soon enough, it began to settle until only a few motes darted, driven mad in the heat of the beam.

"So what now? It's a patch of waste ground, just like everywhere else," said Sam, his voice a grinding millstone of complaint. "Just more fucking waste ground."

"Ah, that's where you're wrong, Chief Inspector. Look carefully and you can make out the shape of where the building must once have stood. You see the ridges running off to left and right, and then the parallel ridges behind? Well, those mark where the walls would have been.

"Now, as I understand it, the Percys lived in the lower part of the building. Nobody would have lived beneath them, but there would quite possibly have been a cellar of some sort underneath their part of the building. So what we're looking for is evidence of a door, you know, a trap door or something."

The beam burnt across dust and rubble. Malcolm was building a picture in his mind, almost as if he were watching a computer-generated image take shape. The walls rose from the ground, tall walls to accommodate two or three floors. There was a door, and windows too, although the glass would have been grimy and cracked. Outside the door and in the yard, there would have been the toilets, the privies with their vile communal stench. Inside there was a range for cooking. It would probably have been smoky and inefficient, filling the room with fumes. There would not have been much in the way of food. Scraggy bits of meat or gruel, maybe jam and stale bread. The whole family would have lived in a few rooms, all the female members sleeping in one bedroom, the males in the other.

While Malcolm lost himself in this historical reverie, the others looked at the hard, dusty ground and tried to make out a shape.

"Just looks like a bloody waste ground to me," said Sam. "Those ridges you're on about, they could be anything."

"No they couldn't, Inspector, they are evidence, you see. You should know all about evidence in your line of work. Well, these ridges provide archaeological evidence of what was here before and…"

"Never mind that! We need to find that girl and you're wasting my time with a bloody history lesson. You should stick to the classroom and leave the detective work to me."

An old anger swept over Rick and he stepped up to his brother, squaring off, slim chin to fat chin.

"What is it with you, Sam? When did you become so sour and shrivelled up inside? Malcolm is trying to help. It looks like you lot could do with some help. You don't seem to be having much luck finding this girl."

"Don't push your luck. Brother or not, you're getting in the way of a police investigation."

"This hasn't got anything to do with your investigation. You're just pissed off with me because I've come back and set up in your patch. You just don't want me working in York, which you see as your territory. I was born here as well as you, you know. And I've come back so get used to it."

As Sam stared at his brother, for once not saying a word in retaliation, he felt a confusing mixture of emotions. It was true: he didn't want Rick back here, dragging up what was past and getting in the way. A private detective was always a nuisance; a private detective who was also your brother was a double bloody nuisance.

"So get used to it," said Rick, in refrain.

Sam broke his short silence.

"And you get used to the idea that I'm one of York's top policemen and you're a private eye who seems to spend most of his time in hospital."

"It's only been a few weeks. You just envy me my freedom."

"Yeah, right," said Sam, wondering for a moment where the alien expression had come from. It must be down to his daughters and their American viewing habits. "That's right, I envy your ability to get injured and wind up in hospital. And..."

Malcolm had moved away to squat in the dust. He ran his fingers across what he supposed would have been the floor of the kitchen. He imagined all the feet which had walked across this floor. He saw the mother, harassed and worn, because surely she would have been so, turning between the range and the table as she tried to feed her brood, putting to good use whatever scraps of food she could find. He lost himself to this vision. He liked to become submerged in his subject, to try to build a human picture from the historical bones. History to him was more than dusty old facts; it was warm with old lives, real people who had lived real lives. Lost to his imaginings, he did not realise for a moment what his fingers had found. He was too wrapped up in imagining the lives spent on this spot, and picturing the drunken and neglectful husband, who would almost certainly have been of scant use to his family. He tried to build a mental image of the man who had been killed by his own daughter. What sort of a father deserved such an unnatural fate?

Again his fingers played with the hard ring, and again thought did not keep up with touch.

Malcolm Hunt, a historian in search of greatness, yet a man who feared he would never find it, broke off from his reverie and looked towards the Rounder brothers. He glanced away immediately, temporarily blinded by the light. The diesel generator throbbed and vast, elongated shadows were thrown across the ground. His train of thought broken, he looked down at what his fingers had been trying to tell him. He was grasping a rusty metal ring. Flakes of rust stuck to his skin as he relinquished the hoop. He rubbed away the leaf-like flecks. At last, thought translated into action. He stood over the ring, bent his knees and pulled as hard as he could. Despite his effort, nothing happened. He grunted and pulled harder still until the rust-blistered metal ring began to dig into his skin.

"Shit!"

He let go and then grasped the ring again in a burst of renewed fervour. This time he fell on his arse in the dust and rubble. In front of him there was an opening in the ground.

Chapter Twenty Eight

SHE came to and tried to work out where she was. What gloomy place was this? Sleep had let her forget, and how good it had been to escape. She decided not to move, enjoying the lack of motion and the still shadows. She shielded herself from the oblong of light above her head. She wondered where it was coming from. She screwed her eyes until white lines danced uninvited into her private darkness.

Then, propelled upwards by a deep sigh, she stood and rubbed at her eyes. Like almost everything else, this action reminded her of Polly, who would rub her eyes when tired. She told her off so many times, telling her she would damage herself.

Pauline Markham stumbled from the sofa and pulled open the lounge door, drenching herself in light. The switch in the hall had an automatic timer and the bulb was pulsating like a headache made visible. She staggered, then gathered herself. She would have to put that kettle on again. As the water turned towards steam, she wondered why she hadn't heard anything. How long had she been asleep and how long had Graham been away with the police? She doubted he was being much help. It was strange to her, the way she could think like this, ordering her thoughts into tidy queues when all she wanted to do was to retreat to an anguished curl and scream herself silent. Tidy thoughts hid nothing and wondering about Graham, dear bloody infuriating Graham, merely stopped other thoughts intruding. Inside she felt a spiral of despair, as if a corkscrew twist of pain were threaded through her being. Whichever way she turned, the pain turned with her. She was playing games with herself, trying to put into words how she felt. She wondered what language had to do with anything. Here she was, flicking through her own dictionary of emotions, chasing through the pages as words flew off in a blizzard of black dots. There, she was doing it again. Playing.

Enough water escaped being turned into steam for a drink to be made. She sat at the kitchen table, sipping the scalding liquid, and tried to avoid her surroundings, because everything that had made her so proud and so happy now seemed so hateful. Only Polly mattered and she could do nothing to bring her baby back, to put her here again where she belonged, in their house, filling out their lives with her beautiful aggravation, her lovely nuisance.

She sipped again without noticing the heat of the liquid. Had she made tea or coffee? She couldn't tell. So long as it's hot and wet, isn't that what people say? She hadn't eaten for hours or maybe days but the thought of food turned her stomach into a cramping ball. If she ate anything, it would come out again faster than it went in. She wondered if she would ever be able to eat again and did not care. You've got to eat, that's something else people said. People said a lot of stupid things.

THE hatch crashed on to what would once have been the parlour floor, raising a cloud of dust. The sound reverberated around the dead land. Then the throb of the generator could be heard again. Malcolm Hunt, holding a hand to his mouth, coughed. The dust began to settle in the harsh beam.

A family had lived here once. Meals had been taken in this parlour. Bacon, sardines, bread and butter had been eaten; eggs, cold mutton, chicken and tongue, too. Potatoes had filled out a meagre meal, along with bread and butter, although often not the butter.

Children had crowded round the table, which had always had one uneven leg and so tilted a little towards the range. Heat had escaped the inefficient range, a thing blackened with smoke and furred in grease-treacled dust. Some distance away, the family had slept, the female members in one crowded bedroom, the males in the other, all grubbed together for warmth.

Lives started here had put out roots in all directions, leading to the creation of other families down the generations. Some still lived in York, others had scattered, but all were traceable to this spot: the dusty ghost of a building. All those people, washed in the same blood, could be followed to this place and down deeper.

Malcolm had never been much of a one for outdoors action, indoor action being more to his taste. Yet he was enjoying doing something instead of reading about it or talking about it. So often he lived through what had happened before, through the significance of lives lost to the past, to facts and figures, dates and documents. Yet now he was getting his soft historian's hands dirty with the real rusty past, and he liked it.

The trap door had been bloody heavy and he had shifted it by himself, dislodging its weight in one mighty, tendon-stretching effort. He panted unevenly while he stared into the dark hole. With the light of exposure beating down on him, Malcolm crouched and, before he could hear Chief Inspector Rounder's objections, he lowered himself into the darkness, feeling for the first time in his life like Indiana Jones or some-such rashly physical type. He was on a step, the first of a flight. He eased down the others until he reached compacted earth. He steadied himself and gingerly stretched to his full height. This was not a sound idea as he banged the top of his head on the roof. Craning his neck, which creaked in protest, Malcolm looked round the cellar, sniffing its mouldered secrets. His back was starting to hurt, from the effort and not being able to stand straight. This place smelt musty and earthy, yet it was not as damp as he had imagined. Subterranean ferns of some sort slithered up a wet area of brick close to where he had forced open the hatch, but other than that this man-made cavern seemed reasonably dry.

Rubbing his head, Malcolm glanced around. He found it hard to make out what he was looking at, especially because light from the generator confused the task. He was standing in a pool of brilliance, picked out so sharply by the furious beam from above that he felt his skeleton should be exposed, every bone thrown into relief.

"What the fuck are you doing down there, History Man?"

He heard the voice, how could he not have heard it, but he took no notice, turning instead to explore the basement. Two of the corners lay on either side of the steps. Malcolm inched towards the right-hand corner. This contained evidence of recent occupation, with discarded newspapers, chocolate wrappers and empty drink bottles. He edged into the left-hand corner, which was empty except for a soggy urine miasma. Holding his nose and coughing, Malcolm emerged back into the unforgiving pool of light and inched towards the other side. A weighty shadow loomed above him, like a gargoyle on day release.

"I said, what the fuck are you doing down there, History Man?"

Malcolm looked up and regretted doing so immediately, because his neck creaked again. "Yes, I know. Heard you the first time. Why wouldn't I – what with the way you shout so? What I'm doing is exploring this space."

"Never mind exploring, lad. What about the girl?"

"Give me a chance."

Malcolm broke off the conversation, such as it was, and pushed away from the light. He repeated the pattern, looking first in the right-hand corner, where he found nothing except dust and rubble. He paused and took a deep breath, which set him coughing again. When he had regained his breath, he edged along the line between the slab of light and the darkness, finally reaching the only corner he had not yet explored. He thought he saw movement, but dismissed this as an illusion or a trick of the eyes caused by passing between light and dark. It was bound to distort your vision, throwing shadows into the brain. He peered again into the gloom. Something was moving, he was sure.

"Hello, we've come to help and take you home," he said, feeling foolish. You're not speaking to a bloody alien. If there is anything here it is a poor lost girl. Just talk normally, as you would to any child. He realised, as he reasoned to himself, that he didn't really know how to talk to children, rarely having had the need.

Something in the darkness jumped. He sensed what it was, its movement and ephemeral physicality, before he saw it, a wild-eyed creature seemingly made of dirt and dust and foul smells. The creature let out a howling scream echoed by Malcolm as he felt a sharp, jagged pain down the side of his neck.

"Shit! What the hell?"

This slight creature stood electrified with fear as Malcolm's fingers explored the wound in his neck. There was blood but not too much. He removed his fingers and held out his arms. He wasn't sure if he should be welcoming this thing or defending himself against it, but the decision was made as the shabby sprite collapsed into his arms.

Malcolm Hunt, man of history, had found Polly Markham, a girl haunted by someone else's history, and she was alive. He struggled with the poor girl as her limbs dangled.

Up above, Sam rose from his knees in the dirt and shouted for help across the dusty space. An ambulance was summoned and officers ran towards the large Chief Inspector.

Rick, still smarting at their exchange, slipped out of his brother's shadow and stepped into the hole, descending the steps. Malcolm was holding the girl. Her hair hung in a matted mess, her face was porcelain pale beneath the dirt and her fogged lungs took breaths so slight they hardly seemed to be breaths at all.

"Here, let me help you."

"I thought you were injured."

"Well, yes."

"And didn't you just discharge yourself from hospital?"

"That too – but I want to help."

The two men eased up the steps with the limp girl, emerging into the false daylight. Rick removed his coat and lay it on the dust, and Malcolm, rolling up the hood, lay Polly down with her head on the makeshift pillow.

Officers scurried across the urban wasteland to crowd round. Then the girl's father broke through and knelt by his daughter. He had feared the worst, feared it still. He had thought her dead, known for sure she was dead, and even now, as he knelt in the dust, he did not trust she could be alive.

"Polly girl! My Polly…"

She did not respond to his words, did not even hear them. She was still locked in the nightmare, sectioned off somewhere. Graham Markham lay in the dust and put his arms round his daughter. For a man not much given to gentle reflection, he was surprised by so many thoughts and memories: Polly just born, her first tottering steps, her first words; he saw holiday snaps and camcorder images; Christmases and birthdays. He saw this girl, his girl, and felt the trap of parenthood, the fear of loss and misfortune waiting to happen. He mostly left the worrying, the imagining of the worst, to his wife. She did plenty for the pair of them.

The wider world receded and he and Polly were alone, thrown among strangers. Soon other strangers arrived, heralded by a frantic blue light. Graham detached himself and stood in the on-off blue aura while the ambulance team attended to his daughter. Soon she was laid out on a trolley. There was room in the back of the ambulance so Graham squeezed in and sat opposite Polly as the vehicle inched across the bumpy ground, jolting this way and that, until the firm road allowed a build up of speed. He listened as the siren changed its note, becoming more urgent and agitated, and reckoned that they must have been crossing the junction close to Sainsbury's.

POLLY Markham was the quick centre of attention as doctors and nurses examined her. She lay pale and unaware as her condition was assessed. Cuts, abrasions and bruises decorated her body, alongside splinters of rust inserted beneath the fingernails of her left hand.

"She must have tried to beat her way out," said one of the doctors. He held Polly's grubby, bloodied hand as he spoke, then gently put it down, turning his attention to her right hand, which was bunched tight. The doctor inserted his own finger into the locked fist and tried to prise it open, but it closed tighter still, trapping his finger for a moment. Polly then relaxed her grip, letting the doctor remove his finger; but as he did so, her freed hand shot out and the doctor felt a small, sharp pain across his left cheek. Polly had sat up with alarming suddenness and was shaking

237

uncontrollably while she stared out of eyes drilled from blue nothing.

"Shit! What's that?" Blood wetted the doctor's fingers.

"I'd get one of the nurses to have a look at that," said another doctor. Whatever had animated Polly relaxed its grip and she slumped, panting from the exertion. She began to breathe more deeply and her body relaxed.

"What did she scratch Steve with?" asked one of the nurses.

"I don't know. Something sharp she's got in her hand, I think. Never mind that for now. Let's get some liquid into this poor girl. Hook her up to a drip and keep an eye on her, in case she becomes restless again. Poor little sod has been through hell by the look of it. I need to talk to the parents."

PAULINE had raced to the hospital as soon as Graham had rung. She was in the waiting room, sitting next to Graham, the man she loved. Did she really love him or had affection dwindled into a half-hearted habit? She could not have said before Polly disappeared and was even less certain now. She banished such thoughts and stretched out her hand. They held tight, squeezing until it hurt, each unwilling to relinquish, united by a unifying blankness, as if the unthinkable had taken physical shape during the days of their daughter's disappearance. They had bonded so strongly in wanting Polly back, unharmed and well, and now that cause of unity was about to be removed.

"How did she seem to you?"

"Like a poor, pale thing. A shadow of herself, but still alive. She'll be…"

Time can be elongated or snatched away; a minute can pass for an hour and an hour can surrender to a minute. They couldn't say how long they waited before the doctor arrived, although an observer with a calm eye and a watch would have put it at forty minutes

"Right, Mr and Mrs Markham? Yes, good, thought so. I'm Dr Whittle and I have been looking after Polly."

"How is she?"

"Can we…?"

"If you would just give me a moment to explain. Polly is very dehydrated and in shock, understandable when you consider what she has been through. She doesn't appear to have drunk anything at all for two or three days and has probably eaten nothing other than snacks since she was put in that place.

"We need to rehydrate her, get some liquid and some nutrients back into her. After that, she should be fine, so far as we can tell. The man who kidnapped her does not seem to have done her any direct physical harm. Certainly, she doesn't seem to have been interfered with in a sexual sense. But an experience like that is bound to leave its mark, on the mind if not the body. She will need careful handling from the two of you, as well as professional counselling."

Pauline gazed through the young doctor into a distant place. "She only went out to play with her friend, you see. In our road. It's a nice place, where we live. The houses cost a lot of money to buy, especially these days, a real fortune. Everyone has good cars and takes holidays abroad. How could we have expected something like that? She was only out playing when it happened. And the man who did this to her, he killed her poor dog, you know. Left him to hang on the gate, throttled by his own lead. Do you know why this man did this to our girl? Our Polly's a good girl, a bit too lively sometimes, but a good girl."

"Well, you need to talk to the police about all these things. They should have some answers. I can't do much more than talk about how Polly is and what to expect. We need to keep her in here for a day or two, just to carry out a few tests and to ease her back towards her old self. Right, follow me and I'll take you to Polly."

They walked in a daze along the shiny, scuffed corridor and emerged into an area with a large central desk, surrounded by curtained-off beds. Dr Whittle pulled back the curtains that partitioned one of the beds. A nurse was touching a doctor on the cheek. Pauline, thinking they had interrupted a private moment, began to glow with anger and embarrassment. What were they doing, touching each other when they should have been looking after her Polly?

"That's got that cleaned up," the nurse was saying. "You should be all right without any stitches, and that's a relief because I know you doctors can be such cry babies."

Dr Murton, who was just as impossibly young as Dr Whittle, smiled while his fingers traced the scratch on his face.

"So here she is then," he said, turning to reveal Polly, who lay pale and still, eyes glued shut. Pauline, gulping with shock and joy, sat on the edge of the bed, holding her daughter's hand in a loving vice. With her free hand, she stroked Polly's damp forehead.

"My girl, my Polly."

She had feared the worst and this was so much better than that. She had Polly back, a pale, eyes-shut, faded away Polly, but her Polly. Her girl, her baby.

Graham stepped up too, suppressing the thought that Polly barely looked alive. Her face was lifeless and grey; if it were not for the puny undulation of her chest, she would hardly be there at all. He perched on the other side of the metal bed and stared at his daughter, watching the inflation and deflation, aware that his own breathing was racing ahead of her slow, slight process. She was such a lively girl, always talking, with so much to say she drove him mad; so bright and energetic, so full of everything. Now she looked empty, as if someone had stolen her spirit or whatever it was that had animated her. He didn't even believe in spirits, so why was he thinking like this? He wondered if he could ever go back to being the way he was, off working and leading his own parallel life while Pauline and the girls filled out his house. Perhaps he should give it all up, do something closer to home. The trouble was, he liked what he did and was good at it. He reached for the hand of his rescued daughter, but found instead her clenched fist. He tried to imagine an alternative life, one where he stayed closer to home, but could not see its shape.

CHAPTER TWENTY NINE

CHIEF Inspector Sam Rounder put his feet on the desk and sipped cooling coffee; hot or cold, it tasted foul. What he wanted was resolution – or resolution and a few pints of Yorkshire ale. Instead, he was stuck in the office with fake coffee from the machine. There had been a result, he supposed. The girl had been saved and the pervy old bastard who kidnapped her had died, so nature had meted out its own justice. What high pleasure he took in the thought of Frank Helmsley's heart seizing up and dispatching him: that had been a fitting retribution.

To think about Helmsley's treacherous heart was comforting, but the consolation lasted only until he began to consider the likely state of his own furred arteries. He took another foul sip and tried to remember if coffee was good or bad for the heart. Bad, probably: everything was bad for you these days.

What had Helmsley set out to prove? Sam was still not certain why Helmsley had kidnapped the girl and hidden her in that basement. He could ask Malcolm Hunt, but he couldn't face another conversation with the bloody History Man. Too much like chewing through a dictionary, listening to that bugger.

The History Man and the Private Detective – damn the pair of them. With luck, he would never again have to speak to Hunt, but he would have to talk to his brother. He hadn't been happy to have Rick back in York, poking his nose in where it no longer belonged. Why hadn't he stayed in Australia or wherever it bloody was?

He had become accustomed to Rick not being around. Brothers were all very well but they came with baggage, a shared history, old sibling hurts and rivalries, ancient resentments. Some good things too, he supposed, but he couldn't summon up anything much as he sat with his feet elevated, but his mood low.

The end of a case always left him sterile and disappointed. The outcome had been good: one girl rescued, one old pervert dead – yet he still felt incomplete.

It hadn't helped that his brother had got in on the final act. Rick and the History Man had guessed at the girl's whereabouts, rescued her from that hole in the ground, while he had stayed up on top. Other people should do all that physical stuff, he was above grubbing round a smelly basement looking for a lost girl. He had told himself this and he had tried to believe it – but had he avoided the basement because he might not have got out again? He was too fat for physical heroics. How galling it was that his brother could still manage the bravery stuff.

He thought back to yesterday and his interview with the girl's parents. They had been happy, relieved – all of that. They had feared the worst and something good had come along instead, which did not always happen, as he knew from years of having to pass on the gloomiest sorts of news. He sometimes wondered if being a messenger of doom had damaged him, pock-marked his soul in some way.

Compared to all the bad days, yesterday had been good, a result. The Markhams had been pale and lost for days, and then resolution had come their way. He thought back to what he had said.

"Mr and Mrs Markham, everything is as good as it could be. There have been times when you must have thought the worst, I know I did. But you always have to have hope. And this time hope won through, with a bit of help from North Yorkshire Police."

"And that private detective, the one with the same name as you."

Sam knew what Graham Markham was going to say next, and he did not disappoint.

"So, is he some sort of a relation?"

"Yes, he is my brother."

"Well, you must be proud of him – I know we are."

"Yes, my brother is a constant source of pride to me. Anyway, this interview is just to wrap things up officially. A trained counsellor will speak to Polly in a few days, once she is ready. This is mainly to help with her recovery, although some information may be useful to us, in case a similar case ever arises."

"Do you think that's likely, Inspector?" It was Pauline Markham speaking this time.

"Good God, I certainly hope not. Anyway, this wraps things up. We've done our bit and now we have to hope Polly gets well again as quickly as possible. Anything else you would like to say?"

Graham and Pauline looked at each other, then Graham spoke. "Not really, except to thank that brother of yours."

"Of course I will. I can't wait to pass on your best wishes."

Sam shifted his feet on the desk, trying to find a more comfortable position. How would the girl grow up? She will probably be right as rain, then a few years down the line turn into a sulky madam who barely exchanges two civil words with her father.

He dropped the half-full plastic cup into the bin. Cheap machine coffee spurted up out of the bin before subsiding to dampen the half-eaten sandwiches and a copy of that night's Evening Press. The discarded coffee seeped into the newsprint and obscured the main story on the front page. Sam didn't need to look at the newspaper to be reminded of what it said: he knew too well what it bloody well said, having read the story three times before depositing the newspaper in the bin.

"POLLY'S SAFE," it said in large type, but it wasn't those two words that bothered him. No, it was the smaller headline below: *"History teacher and private eye find kidnapped girl."*

His own role in the rescue had not merited a single line. Rick and Hunt were splashed all over the front page, pictured in Hungate, where Polly had been found. The photographer must have been one of the more artistically inclined snappers, because he had aimed his lens from low on the ground. Rick and Hunt reared up impressively in the photograph. They seemed unnaturally long and the angle tapered so that while their firmly-planted feet were quite far apart, their heads were close together. Arms folded resolutely and shadows slanting across the wasteland behind, they appeared taller still.

The story under the picture began: *"YORK kidnap girl Polly Markham has been found alive and well – thanks to the efforts of a private eye and a teacher..."*

A private eye and a teacher – and not a bloody mention of the policeman in charge of the case.

"Private investigator Rick Rounder and adult education lecturer Malcolm Hunt worked out where Polly was being confined – and heroically rushed to her rescue."

Oh, yeah…all by themselves and not a mention of me and my officers, of the endless inquiries and the fingertip searches. Not a single bloody mention.

"They discovered Polly had been kept in the basement of what had once been a tenement block in Hungate in the city. It is thought Polly had been kidnapped by an amateur history enthusiast who had become obsessed with another girl who had lived and died a century previously.

"Polly is thought to have been incarcerated in the basement by Frank Helmsley, the history enthusiast, who then died of a heart attack, leaving no immediate clue as to the whereabouts of the girl he had kidnapped."

There had been more. Readers were directed to pages eight and nine for the full story, and to page ten for the editorial comment. Well, it was the most interesting thing to happen in York for years, Sam knew the paper would milk it for all its worth. Rick would be insufferable.

The leader column had been enough to send Sam's blood bursting out the top of his head, like a geyser…

"YORK'S newest private eye deserves the city's fullest gratitude for helping to locate and save kidnap victim Polly Markham.

The success of Rick Rounder in helping to save the life of Polly, who had been incarcerated in a Hungate basement, is all the more remarkable because he had only recently returned to York after spending years living and working abroad. What's more, he was on his first case.

With a clear up rate like that, York's official police force had better look to its laurels…"

Not a bloody word about how he had to be rescued from that old queer who had duped him into believing he was a wronged husband; not a bloody word about the homicidal nurse who took him for a midnight walk and nearly finished him off. It was one cock-up after another, yet he is proclaimed a hero.

It was just as well Sam never got as far as the diary column on the page opposite the leader. Here, the diarist had made the connection between the two brothers and had poked fun at the leading policeman being shown up by his younger private eye brother.

"It looks like York's own Philip Marlowe has pulled one over on his big brother. Enterprising private dick Rick Rounder managed to find missing York girl Polly Markham before his policeman brother. What's more, it was almost his first day on the job. To dip into a few Raymond Chandler titles, it was a case of: Farewell My Not So Lovely Brother, it looks like while you were having The Big Sleep, I found the Little Sister in the basement. So maybe now it's time for the Long Goodbye."

The diary item ended with a small competition. *"The first reader who can translate the following piece of Chandleresque dialogue will win a set of Philip Marlowe novels. The line for you to unpick is: 'The flim-flammer jumped in the flivver and faded.'*

We don't mind how accurate your translation is, as we don't much bother with accuracy round here (but don't tell the editor.) All contributions welcome, with the prize going to the wittiest.

And if a certain senior York policeman is trying to work out his flims from his flams, we wish you the best of luck, Sam. You're going to need it."

CHAPTER THIRTY

POLLY Markham resumed her childhood. There were differences, unseen snags to her soul, but youthful resilience saw her through. So Pauline told herself while reiterating the same phrases in circular conversations with family and friends. She took particular pride in "unseen snags to her soul," repeating the phrase often, until its imprint wore to nothing, without ever capturing what she felt when gazing into her daughter's newly distant eyes. Pauline was finding something to say, dropping words into the vacuum. Quite quickly the words began to lack meaning, yet still she spoke her lines, without ever fully understanding the role she had to play as the happy but almost tragic mother.

Graham adopted a similar tactic, but he never tired of saying his lines, reprising "She's a tough one, our Polly. She'll be all right," whenever duty called, and sometimes when it did not.

She couldn't deny it had been a trauma for Graham too, and to borrow the hackneyed words the newspaper had used about them, they had both "been to hell and back." Now, they felt like they were made whole with the return of Polly.

Graham appeared to have changed, becoming more caring and less aggressive. He had withdrawn a little from work and concentrated more on his family. It had been strange to have him around more, unsettling in a way. He kept buying presents for Polly, so many presents, none of which she needed.

With Graham at home so much, almost as if he had retired twenty-five years too soon, Pauline recalled all the high-powered meetings he used to attend so vigilantly; then she began to wonder if such meetings had ever existed.

Given time, little more than a few weeks, the slippage began. There had been no late meetings for ages, then one in a week. The week after, two. Now, another week on, Graham was out for a third night.

So it was all girls together again, Pauline, Polly and Sally. Sally had been distraught when Polly "went away" and had not understood anything after she returned. At first sight of her sister, she had obliterated her with affection, covering her with kisses, hugs and friendly thumps. Yet now Sally had started playing up and behaving badly. There had been fights with Polly, fights with friends in the road, fights at school. Previously Sally had such good reports, but lately her behaviour had changed.

"Of course, Sally is still a lovely, bright girl," as her teacher had put it, offering a routine hymn of praise before turning to her truer purpose. "It is just that – how shall I put this? – she has become a disruptive influence in the class. She seems to look for confrontation, and is always at the heart of some squabble or other. Whereas before she was a happy member of the team, now she seems to shout 'look at me' all the time, as it were."

Pauline had bitten her lip and resisted the urge to slap the teacher across her too-pretty young face. Instead, she had reiterated the extreme difficulties her family had been through, and how such an experience was bound to have had an effect on Sally.

The teacher had said "of course" again, which was how she prefaced most of what she had to say. She used "of course" as the verbal equivalent of a pat on the head.

Pauline set about her tasks. There was the tea to make, washing to get out of the machine, rooms to tidy, surfaces to dust, floors to vacuum, now that life was normal again. She went into lasagne auto-pilot, sweating the onions, adding the mince until it browned, then the tinned tomatoes, and a splash of red wine from the bottle she had just opened. She made the white sauce, with a grating of nutmeg, a small act of rebellion against the fussy ways of children. She layered the meat and tomatoes with the sheets of pasta, then the white sauce, repeating this pattern until the large dish was full. Grated cheese decorated the top and the lasagne went in the oven.

All this cooking was an endless cause of worry and irritation. It made her so bad tempered, yet she had brought it on herself by spurning convenience food. She wanted her girls to eat proper food. Such good intentions wore her down, but she persisted because that was what you did. Keeping on was part of the deal you never realised you had signed. She thought about making tea or coffee but, after glancing at the kitchen clock, pulled the cork back out of the wine. She half-filled a small glass stopped the bottle with the cork, and sat in the chair by the window, looking down the garden.

She slurped the wine until it was gone, rose to free the cork and half filled the glass once more. Back by the window, she drank a little too quickly and then closed her eyes. She slept for a few minutes, perhaps five, until a noise jolted her awake, leaving her to struggle for a sleep-smudged moment. Dream contours mapped a memory she couldn't recall. She rubbed her eyes. George from next door, who had been playing with Polly in the house, was crying and her tears mixed with blood from a gash in her cheek. Polly was standing at a sulky remove, arms crossed tightly. Her eyes blazed with defiance, shame coloured her cheeks.

"She cut me with that thing she's got."

Pauline stumbled from the chair, rustled a crumpled tissue from somewhere, and touched the paper to the girl's bloodied cheek.

"What thing, George?"

"That wicked necklace she got since she came back."

"I'm not sure I know what you mean."

"Round her neck, that sharp thing, like a big tooth or something. She cut my face with it."

"Why?"

"We had an argument?"

"What about?"

"Something stupid."

Pauline looked over at Polly. "What's all this?"

Polly glowered: "Like she said, we argued. Had a row – you know, like you and Daddy do sometimes. We were having 'a robust exchange of opinions' just like you and Dad."

"What are you talking about?"

"That's what you said to me once, after you'd been shouting at each other. 'Mummy and Daddy were having a robust exchange of…'"

"All right, I heard."

Pauline tried to remember those words. Had she really spoken them? She relinquished the hurt girl and turned to her daughter.

"Show me what you used to scratch George's face."

She held out her hands, palms upright in supplication.

"Let me see, Polly. Let me see how you hurt George."

Pauline could not say how the cut had appeared in her right hand or what had caused it. She felt nothing as blood beaded through the skin, and only recognised the injury with the stinging that followed.

Polly ran into the hall and out of the front door. Pauline chased after on to the gravelled drive, skidding across the loose surface as she grasped her daughter.

"Show me, Polly. Show me what it is."

Anger resonated through Pauline yet she wanted to stay calm, to understand; so she put out her hands again, placing her palms on Polly's cheeks. Polly pulled away, blood smeared on her face.

"Tell me, Polly. And show me. Show and tell, like at school when you were younger. Show and tell."

The girl stared at the mother with diamond indifference. She was hard, uncaring, not connected. When that man had put her in the ground, something had sprung up round her, a defence she could hide behind.

The girl and the woman locked stares, testing each other. Drops of blood decorated the gravel in the drive, crimson pinpricks in the grey.

Polly cracked first. Her face softened and a single sob escaped from somewhere deep inside.

"Show me, Polly. Show me what it is."

Polly slipped her hand inside the neck of her T-shirt and pulled out a chain, closing her fist round what it supported.

"What's on the chain, Polly?"

"It came from where I was kept."

"What do you mean, love?"

"I found it at the dead girl's house. It used to belong to the dead girl who lived in the house that isn't there any more. You know, the dead girl the nasty dead man told me about."

"What do you mean, you found it?"

"I found it – in the dust on the floor. It must have dropped from above."

"So how do you know it used to belong to the dead girl?"

"Dunno, I just do. Makes sense, doesn't it?"

"None of this is making much sense, Polly. So why do you think what you've got on your neck used to belong to the girl?"

"Like I said, I dunno. But it's obvious, isn't it? Must have been hers. Anyway, I'm bored with what you're saying."

"Polly, show me what's in your hand."

"This is so boring, Mum."

"Show me what's in your bloody hand, girl."

ESME Percy fashions the small sharp curve from a discarded blade she finds in the alley. She thinks it has come from the place where they kill the cows. She rescues this shard of sharpness and turns it into a talisman, without knowing the word or what it means. She winds fine wire round the root of the blade, at the point where it had broken off from its original handle, and fashions a tiny, thin scimitar by working it against an improvised whetstone. The blade is barely more than two inches long, sharp at the end and equally keen along its curve, and she attaches it to a fine chain.

This makeshift weapon comforts Esme. She clutches it to herself, taking her cruel comforter everywhere. She has it with her when the fever begins to take hold. As unstoppable shakes and violent shivers possess her frail body, Esme lies beneath the parlour table. Before her brothers reach under the splintered wood to convey her upstairs, she relinquishes the blade with which she had murdered her own father and lets it fall through a gap in the floorboards to land in the damp dust below. A century later another girl finds the fashioned implement. She rubs at the rusty dirt, cleaning the blade on her clothes. Then, groping about in the darkness, a long time after the nasty man has left her, she finds a piece of stone. She uses this, just as Esme Percy had done, to whet the blade, running it up and down until it glints in the darkness.

PAULINE looked at what had been concealed in her daughter's hand and shuddered. Her voice became high and agitated and her words sounded alien to her.

"What are you doing with this thing? You could really hurt someone...you could really hurt yourself. It's dangerous, that's what it is. Dangerous, lethal. Give it to me. You've cut George and you've hurt me. This has got to stop, Polly. Do you hear what I am saying? This has got to stop, right now."

"This blade was there for me when you weren't..."

"Polly, that's an awful thing to say. You give me that horrible thing right now, or I swear I'll hit you."

Polly hesitated for a moment. She had the dead girl's blade and her mother had nothing. She was the one with a weapon. She was the one who had had to survive in that stinking hole. Sighing, she handed it over.

"Oh, Polly. You really could have hurt yourself, you know. That thing's so sharp and you had it hanging round your neck. God, you didn't ever use this round Sally, did you?"

Polly scowled. "Why would I let her see it? It doesn't have anything to do with Sally. It's mine."

"And did you hurt yourself? You know, with this blade hanging round your neck?"

"I tied material round it, so mostly it was all right."

"What do you mean, mostly?"

"I got cut once, down here." She indicated where her breasts will one day be.

"Show me."

"Mum...no! We're outside, in the drive. Anyone could see. And..."

There had been blood, a scab, then a small white scar. This blemish would stay with Polly, changing as her body altered to eventually settle under her right breast, the ghost of an almost imperceptible incision. She would be conscious of the scar, but never embarrassed about it. Sometimes her fingers would seek out the slight thickening of tissue under her breast and she would think of what had happened. She would show the blemish to lovers, although only the ones she truly loved, or thought she did. She would say they were lucky to have her, she should have been dead, she could have died, like the other girl. When her lovers, or the curious ones, asked about this "other girl," Polly would sigh and say, "Oh, it all happened a long time ago."

Polly's mother kept her own memento, an inch-long scratch of a scar on her right palm. It joined the other cuts and blemishes, the burns on her wrists from the oven trays, the accidents with knives while cooking in a hurry. Mostly she could not recall how the tracery of injuries had been caused; but she never forgot the provenance of the scar on her right palm. As to the handed-down blade, Pauline placed this in a box, which she hid in the loft, where she hoped it would remain hidden for another hundred years.

EPILOGUE

SUNDAY morning found Rick Rounder enveloped in post-coital warmth. They had been summoned from sleep by the Minster bells and had made mouth-sour love to the loud peels. Naomi had fallen asleep afterwards and Rick had admired the patterns the morning light cut on her skin. She was breathing deeply with her strong, sculpted back towards him. She was almost athletic in build, with powerful, slim legs, long arms and wide shoulders tapering to a trim waist; but she had curves too.

He tore himself away from the view. Sam and Michelle were coming for lunch. Rick had been surprised they accepted the invitation. Maybe they were "making a go of it" as people said, usually when they were stepping up to the ledge and about to jump.

Rick had made a stew and left it overnight. Two nights would have been better, but one would do. Beef in beer, one of Delia's, served with cheesy croutons. It was a favourite recipe, as he would tell kitchen-useless Sam, one he always liked to make. In truth, it was the only recipe he ever made, apart from beans on toast. Naomi was doing roast potatoes and salad. Pudding was down to posh ice cream from the supermarket.

Rick showered in the main bathroom, sluicing away the sex. Then he dressed and went downstairs to the garage and his tiny office. He had something to do before Sam arrived. He found the tools he needed without having to shout up to Naomi. Job done, he attended to his stew, which was solid and congealed. Heat would loosen the gelatinous mass and turn it into a delicious, meaty slop. He opened the wine to let it breathe – Australian, Naomi wouldn't have anything else – and poured a glass, telling himself the rest of the bottle could happily oxygenate. That first glass tasted so good, as a first glass will, that he poured another, then opened a fresh bottle.

There was white wine in the fridge and beer for Sam. His brother didn't hold with wine. Rick considered that to be his loss, saying that when it came to beer and wine, he was happy to swing both ways, although not on the same night. His head wasn't what it was, although he did not like to admit as much to Sam.

"You on the wine already?"

Naomi's long patterned skirt floated as she moved, showing off a creamy layer of petticoat. There was pink in the skirt, a different sort of pink in the T-shirt, and another shade again in the slim-fitting cardigan.

"Oh, you know, midday on Sunday, the day stretching out ahead."

"And your charming brother coming for lunch."

"That too."

"Perhaps you'd better pass the bottle."

SAM and Michelle were all awkward smiles when Rick opened the door, yet the shadow of a row remained. Cheeks were kissed and backs tentatively patted in the narrow hallway.

"You've not been here before, have you, love?" said Sam.

"No, I haven't." Michelle held back from saying that he bloody well knew she'd never been in Rick's flat.

"It's a really nice place. Much smaller than our house, of course, but very nice," said Sam, navigating his bulky presence along the hall.

"That's my office," said Rick, pointing at the door to the tiny room.

"Where he does all his great detecting from," said Sam. "That's when he's not recovering in hospital."

Sam chuckled a deep gurgle of self-pleasure. It hadn't been much of a remark, but he was happy to have scored a point. Rick did not mind because he knew what was waiting on the way upstairs.

"So we go up here to the kitchen and the main living area," he said, leading the way. Michelle saw it first.

"Oh, you've had it framed, how sweet."

"What's that?" said Sam, peering round his wife. "Another bloody snap from the world trip or summat?"

"No," said Michelle. "That front page from the Evening Press, you know, the one you didn't stop muttering and swearing about for a week. Proper annoyed you, that did."

She spoke brightly and patted Sam on the arm.

The others carried on but Sam was rooted to the spot by a bolt of annoyance. He read again the large-print headline "Polly's safe" and the sub-heading below, the words that had so infuriated him: "*History teacher and private eye find kidnapped girl.*"

Sam glared at the page and the glass caught his anger. He raised his fist and swung it, stopping just short. His ring squeaked into the glass and made a tiny crack. He breathed deeply, trying to calm himself. No one had seen, no one had to know. Rick would wonder about the imperfection later; but there was no reason for him to suppose that he, Sam, had been responsible.

He went upstairs. Rick was pouring wine with one hand and holding an opened bottle of Timothy Taylor's Landlord with the other. "Here, grab this," he said, passing over the frothy bottle. Sam accepted, took a powerful glug and sat down. He rested the bottle on his stomach, propping it on the buckle of his belt. He needed a belt these days. He didn't understand why, having supposed that a stomach would do a good job of holding up his trousers. But nothing worked without a belt. His shirt was tucked into his belt and he wasn't sure if this was a good idea. When he had caught sight of himself in Rick's framed page, the belt had seemed to emphasise his middle, as if pointing out his circumference. Putting down the bottle, he went to loosen his belt.

"Oh, no, not that – we're in mixed company," said Michelle, laughing, and laying a hand on one of Naomi's pink layers.

"I was feeling a bit constrained," said Sam. "So I thought I'd unburden myself."

He smiled broadly and Michelle was taken aback, seeing a handsome ghost.

"There, that's better," said Sam as the shirt fell about him in a crumpled curtain.

"Hides a multitude of sins, a big shirt does," said Rick.

"Some of us have been working for a living, rather than taking a ten-year holiday. Too much pressure in my job to worry about the shape we're in."

"Fair enough. But you should try it some time, travel, relax, see a bit of the world – it would do you the power of good."

"Mebbe. Then again, I don't hold with abroad. No Yorkshire ale, too bloody hot and too full of foreigners."

"That'll be me then." Naomi had a smile that could knock a man over if she chose to use it. She was using it now, directing all her power towards Sam. He reciprocated and again Michelle saw the ghost of a handsome past. Sam had been good looking when younger but now he seemed weighty with resentment. She had been so close to Sam, closer to him than to any other person, yet she hardly knew him any more. You meet a stranger, gradually unpeel this other person and get to know every intimate layer; and then, some years down the line, the stranger starts to re-assemble before your puzzled eyes. She wondered, as she had done before, how what had seemed so exciting, so completely enrapturing, could become so ordinary. She had changed too, since the affair. She had suffered from guilt, but God she had enjoyed the sex. She could feel herself stir now at the thought.

Michelle accepted a refill from Rick. Sipping the wine, she glanced at her husband. He was tipping back a beer bottle, his second, and showing off a chin than had been strong until the slow accumulation of flesh had blurred its outline. When he stopped drinking he stared at Naomi, who was bending over at the oven. A cloud of steam rose from the opened door as she took out the roast potatoes. Soon they were sitting round the kitchen table, eating the beery stew, roast potatoes and salad.

"This is good stew, Naomi," said Sam, in between generous mouthfuls.

"Well, thanks, Sam – but I didn't make it, Rick did."

"Is that true, little brother?"

"Certainly is."

Michelle looked between the brothers and said: "You should give Sam the recipe – along with the Ordnance Survey map showing the way to our kitchen! Sam has difficulty finding his way there, unless it's to pick up another beer."

"Beer like this is a Yorkshireman's birthright," said Sam, taking another glug. "Besides, if God had meant men to cook, he wouldn't have invented frozen pizzas."

"It's very easy, Sam," said Rick. "Even you could manage it. It's one of Delia's."

"Since when did you get so domesticated?"

"Oh, I don't know that I am, but I do know how to make a stew."

"Well, it's good, I'll grant you that. And it goes with this posh cheese on toast too," said Sam, in between mouthfuls.

Rick thought a change of topic was required. "So how are those two nieces of mine?"

Sam let the bottle fall from his lips. "Dunno. Not much point asking me, I'm only their Dad. I'm redundant as far as they're concerned. Good for the occasional lift or to donate notes out of my wallet, other than that they take bugger all notice of me."

"That's not true, they're very fond of you, in their own way," said Michelle. "It's just the way growing girls are."

"They're about as fond of me as you are."

Michelle turned to Rick. "The girls are fine. Sam Too is off to the Sixth Form College and Lotte is a year away from her GCSEs. They're both funny and clever and beautiful. They've got lots of friends and everything to live for."

"Well, that's nice to hear," said Rick. The words felt foolish as soon as they were out of his mouth, but sometimes a foolish word is all that can be found.

"Ice cream, anyone?" said Naomi. "We've got the posh stuff. It was on offer at Sainsbury's. Three for two."

Gravy-grained plates were tidied, wine glasses replenished and another beer opened for Sam – "to drink while the ice cream warms up," Naomi said.

The ice cream came and went, as is the way with easy pleasure.

"You can't beat ice cream," said Naomi. "But it's terrible for the figure." She patted her more or less flat stomach.

"Tell me about it," said Sam, slumping back in his chair and burping. "Pardon me, must be all that good food."

"And all that beer," said Michelle, with a smile that could do frost out of a job.

"A man's got to have his pleasures," said Sam. "Especially when his…"

"Coffee anyone," said Naomi, with a brightness she did not feel. "Ends everything off nicely, doesn't it? Would you like to start blitzing those beans, Rick?"

Rick obliterated the beans, boiled the kettle and returned to the table with a full cafetiére. As he depressed the plunger, Sam said: "Not for me, I'll stick with beer."

"I think you'd be better off with the coffee, dear," said Michelle.

"That's as maybe, but beer it is."

"There are a couple of bottles left," said Rick.

"He's had enough," said Michelle. "He's always had enough."

"I suppose that's code for something or other?" said Sam, slouching back in his chair and looking across the table at his wife. "By 'enough' you mean too much."

"You said it. Too much for your liver, too much for that stomach of yours. You need to learn some self-respect and return to being the sort of man you were before…"

"Before what? Before you started fucking around?"

"That's right, blame it all on me. It's easy, that way isn't it? Everything's my fault and you're the wronged party, the injured one. Well, think of this. Perhaps I 'fucked around', as you so charmingly put it, because you neglected me, hiding behind your job and then drinking too much. And neglecting yourself so much that you end up as this grumpy fat person. What happened to the lovely man I married? He's got lost somewhere, buried under all those layers of flesh and contempt."

Michelle was standing, pointing at Sam, her index finger jabbing. Black mascara leaked from eyes glistening with fury.

"What happened to him? He's here still, just fatter, that's all. The same man is underneath, just with a deposit of life round him. I'm the same man inside, the same old Sam, just with a bigger stomach and a life going to shit."

Rick, standing, held out his arms in a calming gesture, but this had no effect. Michelle departed in tears, followed by Naomi, who tried to find consoling words. Rick looked across at his brother.

"Why did you come here today, Sam?"

Sam sucked on an empty bottle, tipping his head in search of more beer. He put the bottle down and looked at his brother.

"Why did we come here? An attempt at reconciliation, trying to make things better. Doing something pleasant and ordinary together, which is how I recall Michelle describing today. Ordinary and pleasant – you've got to laugh, haven't you?"

Naomi was back upstairs now and standing behind Sam. "I think you should go after her, Sam."

"What, so we can have another one of our arguments – so that she can drone on at me all day and night, listing my failings as a man, husband and a human being?"

Rick's mobile rang before anyone could answer.

"Rounder. Yes, that's me." He was silent for a moment, listening. "Well, yes that sounds like something I could investigate. And yes, I can be discreet. Tomorrow at midday. Small coffee shop in Goodramgate? Yes, I know the one, with the wobbly stairs. Just round the corner from me. I'll see you there, upstairs by the window. Bring a photograph and some details to get me started. Right then, see you at midday."

Rick turned to tell Sam he had a new case, but his brother had gone.

"Did he go after Michelle?"

"Don't ask me. He went after her, in that she went before he did, but I don't know if he was intending to talk to her. Anyway, I don't care. I've had enough of your brother and his wife. Next time we cook a meal, let's invite someone we actually like."

"Good point. Now do you want to forget my bloody brother and his wife by going up to bed and making mad passionate love, or do you want to wash up?"

"Let's wash up first, it's awful to come down to a mess."

Rick loaded the dishwasher and put the remains of the stew into the fridge, while Naomi wiped the table and the shiny kitchen surfaces.

"I'll be up in a minute," said Rick. Naomi was asleep when he joined her a few minutes later, the afternoon wine and good food exhausting her. Rick undressed, climbed into bed and nursed an erection for ten minutes or so until it subsided, when he let himself go and tried to sleep.

He turned the light on and read for an hour or so, then tried to sleep again, still without success. This pattern was repeated for the next few hours. He had no idea when he pulled off the sleep trick, found that elusive moment of forgetfulness, but in the morning the bedside light was shining directly into a headache caused by too much red wine.

Pushing away the lamp, he shifted uncomfortably and found he had slept on the book he had been reading. He dropped the squashed paperback on the floor.

Washed and dressed, he made tea and took a mug to Naomi, who was still asleep, so he left it to cool on the bedside table. He drank half of his tea before noticing the time. When he got to the coffee shop on Goodramgate, he was yawning widely as he negotiated the tortuous stairs.

"I tripped on those stairs too," said the blonde in the window seat. Rick put out his hand and the woman extended thin, pale fingers dipped in red. Her handshake was soft and hesitant. She was attractive, one to snag a passing stare. Rick looked closely and saw fine lines webbing her eyes beneath the heavy make-up.

The waiter arrived and Rick made a feeble comment about the stairs. The waiter smiled pleasantly but said nothing. It was the third time today someone had said that.

The woman ordered peppermint tea, saying she was cutting down on the caffeine. Rick yawned and said he would have a double espresso.

"After the rotten night's sleep I've just had, I need all the caffeine I can pump into my system," he said.

Then he looked again into woman's pale blue eyes and asked

what she wanted. She unfolded a tale of soured love and infidelity, a husband straying with a colleague – "Twenty years younger, the scheming cow."

As Rick listened to the pale-eyed woman's tale of marital woe, he thought: "This is my life now, a world filled with other people's mess and failed relationships. This is what I do, mopping up the spilt milk and snooping on people who are doing what they shouldn't be. It's a funny sort of a job but someone's got to do it and…"

The woman sounded annoyed. There was an edge to her voice and he started to feel for the straying husband.

"So do you think you will be able to help me, Mr Rounder?"

Rick sipped the caffeine-impregnated sludge.

"Well, I am very busy. But I think I could just about take on one more case."

THE END

ACKNOWLEDGEMENTS

This novel was in part inspired by reading *Poverty: A Study Of Town Life*, published in 1901 and reissued a century later, which was when this author read this pioneering work of social policy by Seebohm Rowntree. It was also inspired by a liking for crime novels, and remains a work of fiction, although the present day setting is real enough, as too are the historical privations explored. As far as the author knows, the Percy family never existed, although Hungate in York certainly did, and still does in its modern changing form; the Rounder brothers equally owe their genesis to invention.

Thanks to Gina, Meg, Ken and Jo for reading *The Amateur Historian* at different stages of composition – and thanks to Adam for having faith.